I called  headache w~~ ~~ Japanese and tuba music.

Rory linked his tablet to my office projector as I went heads-down on my forearms at the table. "Now," he said, "Let me show you something. Are you okay?"

"Just don't stop and keep a trash can close."

"That giant man leaning against the Texas School Book Depository—his name is Sampson—Maurice Sampson."

I reexamined the image on the wall. *He's a Sampson if ever I've seen one.* Rory walked around me, stopping at the head of the table near the image. He circled a second area on the picture with a blue laser. "This piece of the other guy's face matches Kelly Lake. So, you got both of your guys in one shot. Good on you."

"Do you have a front view of Kelly Lake?"

"No, but this side shot matches that photograph from the Denver News."

"Then he's not our Kelly Lake. At least, according to Carissa Scaffe. Besides, if Lake was at the depository, she would have told me."

"You're getting too close to her. What can I say?"

"You can say I'll keep looking."

Praise for Lee Wilkins

"I had to find out what happened."

"Fast-moving."

"Great work from a new author."

"Curled up with a glass of wine soaking it in…"

Moscow Down

by

Lee Wilkins

This is a work of fiction. Names, characters, places, and incidents are either the product of the author's imagination or are used fictitiously, and any resemblance to actual persons living or dead, business establishments, events, or locales, is entirely coincidental.

Moscow Down

COPYRIGHT © 2022 by Lee Wilkins
COPYRIGHT © 2021 by Lee Wilkins

All rights reserved. No part of this book may be used or reproduced in any manner whatsoever without written permission of the author or The Wild Rose Press, Inc. except in the case of brief quotations embodied in critical articles or reviews.
Contact Information: info@thewildrosepress.com

Cover Art by *Debbie Taylor*

The Wild Rose Press, Inc.
PO Box 708
Adams Basin, NY 14410-0708
Visit us at www.thewildrosepress.com

Publishing History
First Edition, 2022
Trade Paperback ISBN 978-1-5092-4467-6
Digital ISBN 978-1-5092-4468-3

Published in the United States of America

Dedication

I know most authors say this, but they're wrong. Mine is the best and most supportive wife a man can have, my Rosemarie.

Chapter 1

Dallas, Texas
Rick

I thought I was going to have a restful night's sleep. But a slap on my arm changed that. I started to ease back from my brain void, getting stuck in that layer of not awake, and not asleep.

I curled like a kid, conflicted between forcing a few more hours of welcome-home-honey warmth and the reality of another Saturday of work. Somewhere in my head, Laura's voice, was saying, "Can I blame all of this on you? I could, you know. But…"

I barrel-rolled between the sheets onto my back, leaning toward unconsciousness, my head went deep in the feather-down, where I fought the inevitability of having to get up. Saturday would come too soon; in fact, it already has. I cracked one eye open. "I agree."

Then an evil force connected with my ribs from the heel of a hand, with a power strong enough to make sure I gave her voice proper attention.

"What'd you say?"

"I'm trying to decide if I want to blame my miserable life on you or not. I pick yes."

I bunched the duvet in my fist, swaddling it close around my skin. "Whatever you're talking about," I asnwered, "I changed my mind. Blame yourself."

An early spring morning came through the window painting our North Texas bedroom a Fort Knox gold. Laura scooted herself upright with her back pressed against the headboard. Her knees were against her chest, arms wrapped around her knees, her frigging lit cigarette between two smoldering fingers. It's strange how Saturday mornings somehow permit her to forget our agreement; that she would not smoke in the bedroom—period. Gray puffs fell like London fog over her bottom lip. It rushed toward me — a locust pestilence converging on my pillow. I swatted at it with my free hand, shoving random bits of the cloud back to her.

"In a way," she spoke again, "I do believe it's because of you."

I glared at her. "Laura, would you put that thing out? I'd like to have at least one room in this townhouse safe for me to breathe."

Her fingers extended, pinching the damn hundred-millimeter anti-god, and swept it at obtuse angles toward the ceiling, dodging my hand. "You should never have let me take this job. I'm sure all of this is your fault." She stiffened, appearing to be readying herself for our weekly battle.

I flipped my half of the covers off in a quick move, passing it through the smoke and blowing it back in her direction. "You really don't want me to sleep in," I said. "Am I right? I had a tough week." I stood, straightened my jammy pants so they were facing forward, and made a cow trail to the shower.

Stepping out, dripping, and watching Laura's image in the mirror, I could see her eyes were following me. Were they witnessing my aging process? I spoke louder in a more forceful tone, "What did I tell you this same damn time last Saturday about your freaking job? Quit it. Be free. Beyer can survive without you. God knows we don't need the money."

We stood close to one another in the bathroom as she began undressing in the shower door where I had been standing. "Your scar's bright red," she said. "Are you gonna let the doctor take a look at it or not?"

Checking what remained of the decades-old wound in the mirror, I found it identical to any other morning when I got out of the hot shower. "It's the hot water."

Focusing to my scar was Laura's way of avoiding our weekly argument about what Beyer is doing to her. "It's been years since you got shot," she said. "It shouldn't still be doing that."

The war wound made its way onto my left shoulder long before she came on the scene, compliments of a British S.A.S. Staff Sergeant who either drew aim at the wrong person, '*me being that wrong person*,' or acted totally beyond reckless and should have his pistol bullets taken away. I swear I could see the 9mm muzzle flash and could see the copper dot spinning my way, then sensed a hellfire burn as it split apart in my shoulder below the collarbone. And as quick as that, I was on the road bleeding for the looky-loos.

I said to Laura, like last week and the Saturdays before, "They got all of the bullet out when I was in the hospital. I've been fine for years."

A pleasurable look at my wife's body reminded me what a lucky stiff I've been all these years. Her Japanese kanji nightgown succumbed to gravity and slid down her tan skin to the granite floor tile. She stepped out and raised the silk present I'd given her to a hanger.

"Even so," she rebutted. "You should have the

doctor take a look at it."

"There's never been anything on my x-ray. If there were, Dr. Holden would have fixed it by now."

"Well, it's your arm that's going to fall off, not mine."

"Thanks for not letting the weekend pass without reminding me. Now—why don't you explain why you refuse to quit that god-forsaken job of yours when it galls you so much?"

She stopped the shower from running and showed me her wet body in the doorway, reaching for me to give her a towel. "Believe it or not, my good Mr. Ricky," she declared, "I've moved on from that for this weekend."

I made way for Laura to step from the water. I tried to pull her lovely hips close to mine.

But she whispered in my ear, "Not this morning, babe. It's my time of the month, and you hate it then."

Still, her soft, warm skin against mine validated me. "Well…I wish it wasn't so. But, then, nature doesn't give me votes about that, does it?"

She stepped around me, my towel now wrapped around her hair. I followed. She made her way to her closet, saying, "Let's don't talk about Beyer anymore. There's nothing I can say. I can't talk about my work the same as you can't talk about your work."

"I'm not requesting you tell me any Beyer secrets. I'm only suggesting you tell them to f-off and put sanity back into your life."

A black and orange Picasso spring top over white shorts were her choices. She again changed our banter, "I'm not going to be here for my birthday, Tuesday. I have to go to Pittsburg for a lab conference."

I'm sure the lady next door could hear the

disappointment in my voice. "A lab conference—for real? It's your birthday. Fine. I'll reschedule it for Sunday night. We don't get to do birthdays anymore. We used to like it."

"Not tomorrow either. My flight out is tomorrow afternoon at 2:30. See if you can set it up for tonight if you want to celebrate."

Her hair towel came airborne toward me.

****

It was short notice, but I got two seats at Abacus Jack on Turtle Creek. Jack's had been a private home straddling the creek until its present owners bought and reconfigured her. The lower level is restaurant dining, the second level, their kitchen, with a private culinary institute on top, or so it's rumored. Laura ordered a roasted spatchcocked game hen, which came down the dumbwaiter, along with my Chilian Sea Bass over black rice and snow peas.

"Your glass is getting low," I said to the birthday girl. "Want another French 75?"

The cocktail she loved had her gazing at the tree lights forming a tunnel above the creek and below us.

"I would." She smiled back at me with a forced-to-be-happy face. "My hen was pretty good," she said. Translated in Texan, is the equivalent of, *'I couldn't possibly be more bored.'*

I didn't miss her pursed lips in the response. Maybe it was time to ramp up the party. I signaled for the Maître d' to bring the birthday present I had left with him. If anything could save the evening, this would be it.

Her long nails followed the edge of the brown wrapping paper like a knife. Folding the wrapping paper open, she winced at the oil on canvas painting I bought her. She laid it on its back and sat quietly across the table from me, examining it. "I see."

The Gauguin original was my most significant surprise ever. "Don't you like it? I'm shocked. You like paintings so much. It's Gauguin's *Queen and a Pipe* he did in Tahiti." My surprise gift was taking a nose-dive into the creek.

She twisted her mouth to the left, continuing to survey the canvas and gilt frame. She stood by the table, staring down at it, continuing to be slow to respond.

"Well," she started. "Are we gonna start collecting oil paintings now…I suppose?"

She missed a prime opportunity to display her pearly whites in gratitude.

"No," I came back, not to make it an apology but mostly to mask my hurt. "You like art. I hope you will like this one. I don't know. Why not start a collection?"

"I guess when we die, someone can sell it to a museum and pocket our hard-earned cash."

"As I said, I expected you would like it."

"I didn't say I didn't like it. There's the case when something is so ugly it can still be considered art—this might be one of them."

"Ugly enough to be art? So then…you don't like it?"

She positioned it up in a chair at the adjacent table, her eyes roving, her fingertips tracing over the canvas, following Gauguin's brush lines.

"Yeah. It's ugly," Laura said. "Very. Very. The queen's tits are younger than her face. Her legs are like crooked stovepipes, and she's missing one of her pinky fingers. Then there are her feet. They look like they belong to Sasquatch. But you know what, it would look good in the hallway to our bedroom. So let's hang it there."

She paused, and looked over my left shoulder, then said, "Did I tell you a man in Pittsburgh is setting up a party for my birthday on Tuesday? Would you mind if I accepted?"

Chapter 2

Dallas, Texas

I office in the penthouse suites of McDonnell Tower in Uptown, Dallas which my partner, Toby McDonnell, and I jointly own. He and I operated a government investigations company we started back in the days following the CIA and the Cold War. Of course, the facilities, equipment, and methods have changed since then. But the cases we work on haven't gotten any easier; governments kept growing, and the more they do, the more they screw up. So, it is a profitable business.

I stopped by Andi Weeks' door on the way to my office. She is officially Toby's assistant, who I sometimes borrow when I'm not on the road. Her office is the first one you come to when you enter the forty-fourth floor from its executive elevator.

"Has Toby come in?" I asked while passing. "We were supposed to meet at Einstein's Bagel for coffee, but he never showed."

Her answer came without giving up attention to her monitor. "He's at a urology check-up. You know Toby. If he has a tingle, he needs a pill."

Along with Toby and me, Andi dates to before Laura was born—meaning a long time before Andi's hair got a color update and that sassy flip.

She surveyed me as I passed her desk. "Is Laura on

the road today?"

I stopped. "What made you ask that?"

"You're wearing short pants."

"Hmm. Do I have any clean pants in the wardrobe? I'm lucky to have you watch after me."

By the time I got to my desk, I realized my comment was insensitive and out of line. Andi takes complete care of us, three boys on the top floor, and at the same time, raising a daughter and grandbaby.

I let out, "What I said was insensitive. I'm sorry."

"You sound like most men," came echoing back. "Oh, excuse me. Was that insensitive?"

"Yes," I said loud enough to carry down the hall. "You know what? Laura ditched the birthday dinner I planned. I took her to Abacus Jack. She kicked me to the curb for some shindig in Pittsburgh. Sucks. I don't think she even wanted to be there."

"You're too old. It's not the first missed meal for you, sweety."

She shut me up. That was true. "Once you're married," I said, "you're stuck with it."

"If that's what you think, quit your bitching. You'll put up with what Laura does to you until she pushes you out for a younger slab of meat." She paused for a second before returning to her outside voice, "Hang. It looks like an assignment is coming in with your name on it. I'll send it over."

Andi's email scrolled onto my curved monitor. It read, 'contact Ops Desk as soon as you get in.'

"Got it."

An annoying glare bounced to my phone screen from one of the higher buildings downtown. I pushed the base to a different angle and pressed their button.

"Mr. Haade," A professional female voice answered. "A job has come in; Mr. McDonnell wants you to handle it personally. It's from the Army."

"Local?" And then it hit me; it's the excess road time that's enabled me to put up with Laura's BS.

"Yes, sir. It's at the Grassy Knoll. The Army needs you to make a pick-up for them."

"What is it?"

"A backpack containing sensitive information. You are to deliver it to Security at Yuma Proving Grounds in Arizona. It's a new account."

I flipped my monitor screen open to show my calendar. "When do they want it picked up?"

"Tomorrow afternoon. Fiveish. Then take it to Yuma as quick as possible."

"I'll do it but put Harley Je's name on it instead of mine."

"Might I?...Mr. McDonnell wants you to handle this personally."

"Put down Harley Je." I hung up and checked the time on my screen; it was almost lunch. I dialed Je before he could escape the building.

"Something has come in from the Army. Toby wants you and me to handle it. Would I be able to talk you into taking the lead position?"

Having another lead assignment under his belt would make Harley a Certified Field Agent. "You sure can," he immediately assured.

Chapter 3

Flagstaff, Arizona
Kelly Lake

I thought. *A lady wearing a cactus print shirt. That should be easy.* Coming into the courtyard, I stopped on the terracotta sidewalk. Someone had wedged the kitchen door open. With the sun so bright, it was impossible to know who was watching from behind the windows. A waitress exited the open door and came toward me with a food tray. She veered away to two college-age couples sitting and laughing. The guys at the table examined each other's date with no effort to disguise what they were doing. The girls didn't seem to complain. Their waitress placed a beer in front of them, followed by subs. Three started with their beer. The heavy one, attacked his hoagie.

Next to a succulent pot wall, a geek sat, his eyes focused on his tablet, fingers slamming away. I paused for any sign he had an interest in me. He didn't, or if he did, he hid it. He broke his typing, downed a pair of potato chips, and returned to his screen.

That's her.

In the middle of the courtyard, the woman wearing a cactus print shirt grabbed my attention. I headed her way.

She nodded when I got there, as I dropped my butt

in a green wrought-iron chair. She held a quarter-folded Rocky Mountain Standard newspaper and then slid it in front of me, while saying nothing. Her eyes followed my moves—cold as a column of gray steel.

I opened the paper, and a cream envelope slid toward me, my name on its front in silver ink— 'Lake.'

Ms. Cactus continued watching as I put the unopened envelope in my pocket. Once satisfied, she stood and left, disappearing into the sandwich shop through the same door the waitresses used.

I returned to my truck, cracking the envelope's flap as I walked.

The envelope held a white overnight shipping claim sheet and a computer-printed instruction page. I was to take the chit to the Flagstaff Shipping Center tonight and arrive ten minutes before closing. Then, pick up a woman at the truck stop on I-40.

I love my vintage F-100. Last Monday I picked her up from being completely restored at the same body shop that has its show on PBS every Saturday. Before my effort, she looked like something that would send you to a hospital to get a tetanus shot. I'm told at one time, she was an excellent color of Ford black. Today (I call her Ruby) she's a matte cherry red with loads of chrome all over. The guys at the shop also added old forest mahogany boards to her high gloss bed. Inside the cab, they tufted her upholstery with hand-stitched palomino.

Ruby looked too good to risk getting dinged, so I rarely take her out. But for this trip, I want to impress.

Now, here is the idiot coming out in me. I kept the original engine. The problem is it is so worn it barely generates enough horsepower to climb the hills on Interstate 40. But, other than that one tiny thing, there isn't much about her I don't like.

At seven-thirty p.m., I pressed her parking brake in the shadows of the building by the shipping station. The sun still up, it baked the desert. I let the engine and A/C run so I could watch the place from the cool of my cab. The A/C is a new addition to my girl.

Commoners came and went from the store, bringing packages to ship, and others for pick-ups. When each entered, an overhead buzzer sounded as the door opened.

A native American man behind the counter greeted them by saying something, maybe, 'how can I help.'

A ceiling-mounted camera above the door recorded whoever came or left. Getting in and out without being identified would be difficult. From behind my seat, I fetched a wide-brim palm leaf Guatemalan hat.

I waited until no more customers were coming in. When the final woman left the counter, I put on the hat and pulled the brim down to block my face from the cameras. Then, I opened the store door and activated its irritating buzzer.

"Good evening. How can I help?" the man asked.

I kept my face under the brim, avoiding the inside cameras

Until I understood the nature of my new assignment, I didn't want any recording of me—especially if the cops could use it against me in court. So, staying in the hat's shadows, I handed the man the chit. He read it and strolled at his own pace into the back.

Then as slow as he left, he returned with my box— a shiny white, orange, and purple logo box about the size of men's slippers.

I returned to Ruby and we headed south toward I-40. My fingers vibrated on the gear shift lever as I ran the engine up through the gears to high—a raging antique Ruby machine off on a mission

Elbow out the driver-side window, *damn,* I jerked it in. A welt raised on my forearm where the bug met my 70 mph flesh. It hurt, but this was a night to enjoy the hour's drive. I let the old girl blow out her cobwebs while she chased like a dragonfly over the rises and valleys of eastbound I-40. Springsteen blasted loud through the dash speaker, rapping in time with the beat of the tar stripes passing below us.

Then, in my mirror, against the black wall of night, a pair of red and blue roof lights flashed, intent on catching up with me. The old girl, bless her heart, even on her best day, would barely stay even with the eighteen-wheelers. She would never be a match for whoever is driving that bullet gaining on me like an F-whatever fighter plane.

Volunteering to pull over might get me arrested.

A Flagstaff police car blew past me on the left as if I wasn't even there. His car's bow wake shoved me perilously close to a Mini Cooper, coming up on my right.

Then in a minute, an Arizona Highway Patrol flew past me, as did the Mini Cooper.

Shit. How embarrassing.

As I closed in on the dark hill straight ahead, the sky slowly faded from star-sparkling black to orange, flames going high above the cactus. A pair of Coconino County fire trucks were watering down an engulfed eighteen-wheeler in its death throes.

****

The exit I needed was before the flaming truck. I coasted slowly into the parking lot off the frontage road.

The truck stop's parking was full. Finding a slot where my girl wouldn't get banged by some ass-hole tourist would be almost impossible. I drove her to the outer edges of the pavement, next to the desert. Gear shifter in place, parking brake set, and windows closed, I slipped my pig-sticker knife into my back pocket and stepped out. Go ahead, count the number of times you've returned to your truck at night to find a spotted triangular snakehead in the passenger seat with his yellow eyes staring back at you. If your answer is more than never, that's why I close my windows no matter how hot.

Nuevo-Brave Wigwam truck stop was divided in two sections, the diner side and the fuel side. This Wigwam is the second of three between Nevada and New Mexico. Hostess Irene tried as hard as she could to persuade me to take a seat at the coffee counter. After scanning the patrons at the counter, I refused—no such lone woman sat there.

I asked Irene, "Has a single woman come in asking for Kelly Lake? That's me."

She scanned the line of sticky notes on her podium. While she did, I surveyed the joint for a solo mid-aged woman who might go by the name of Carissa Scaffe. Most of the women were with families and other people. The single woman by the window might be my target. Flames illuminated her face an orange color. She fidgeted—wiping crumbs from the vinyl table topper and organizing her pink plastic ware. The promo flyers on the table were no match. She placed them nicely in their stand. This lady is no regular truck stop customer.

I walked her way, dodging others mulling the sitting area. I like people touching me about as much as that snake in my passenger's seat.

My lady wore no makeup. Her uncombed hair framed her face. She wore a tee-shirt proclaiming her to be the world's number one beer-swigger, and her jeans sported knee holes in each leg. On her feet were two different colored tennis shoes, one red and the other green. *So is that this year's trend?*

I asked her, "Are you expecting someone?"

Obviously, she was scanning me up and down like a side of beef, stopping at my stretched golf shirt, chest, biceps, and abs.

"If by someone," she answered, her voice carrying an Irish lilt. "you mean yourself, then yes, I'm expecting someone. Sit."

I eased into the booth opposite her, pulling myself across the pink vinyl, and dragging the orange and purple box behind me. "Then I guess I'm it."

Irene's wait-partner, Patsy, made her way through the room, wearing a striped blouse of pink, orange, and white and a matching skirt. Her carafes were labeled '50 cal.' and 'blanks.' She stopped at our table. "Dead or alive?" She was turning my mug right side up.

"I don't need anything," I said, waving her on.

I asked my new best friend, "Would your name be Scaffe?"

"It might." She wrapped her answer around a sweet smile, the most becoming part of her.

I examined her eyes, *another ex-hippy seeking truth.* "Who told you to come here?" I moved the colored shipping box from beside me onto the table.

She answered, "This man on the phone said it would be worth $500 for me if I came. Did you bring the money? Is that box for me?"

Her soft face made her appear younger than I

expected. I asked, "Did the man say who he was? How do you know him?"

Her hand extended out for the box, but I pulled the parcel back.

"He's this crazy old man who I've known for a long time. He calls every year or so. He claims to have known me when I was a baby and wants to make sure I'm doing okay. I'm betting he's the same person who called you."

"Hmm." I cracked the tape wrapped around the carrier's box and took out an envelope hiding inside its flaps. Written in fat type was, *"Only employ the woman in this photograph."*

The black and white headshot stapled to the letter was the face of the woman across from me.

I flipped it so she could see and muttered, "It looks current."

She took it from my fingers and studied the person in the picture. "How did mister looney get this," she asked. "It's five years old. A friend of mine in Chicago took that. Sorry. She's dead."

"The picture is you. That's what's important."

Inside was another box about the same size—an aluminum one, black and locked.

Reading again from the handwritten page, *"Make sure this box remains locked. Ms. Scaffe will deliver it to Dallas when I say so."*

"Looks like you and mister looney-tunes are going to be spending time together."

From the unwelcome look on her face, I figured she caught me checking down the top of her tee-shirt. She said, "Did you see anything you want down there? Do they meet your approval"?

How do you answer that?

****

Without notice, a sweat-soaked twenty-something trucker staggered from the counter to our table and interrupted, his speech slurred in tune with his staggering walk. He smelled like stolen clothes from a decomposing corpse.

With that intro he came on to Carissa. "Hey, sweet thing, you need a real man—not old grandpa over there." He twisted and poked his finger at my cheek. "I got my sleeper outside." He raised his brows like a clown about to puke.

Before anyone in the diner could react, my pigsticker was against his belly button, pushing it in. "You best fuck off, sweety," I commanded of the boy, "and take your piece-of-shit farm truck with you…unless you want these fine coffee patrons to watch your guts pour out of that filthy ass shirt of yours."

Inside the Wigwam, the place fell silent, and the staff stopped like statues.

I pushed kid-smelly back against the wall to where he couldn't go any further. His head bounced from the wall abutment.

"Is that something you can do?"

I took Carissa's arm and pulled her from the booth. "Let's get out of here."

Chapter 4

Dallas, Texas
Rick

Like Je, I had no idea what I was doing during my twenties. Crawling through the tunnels of East Germany and snatching commie scientists from the bad guys was fun. If Toby said to do it, I did. When I made it to my thirties, I convinced myself that what Toby and I were doing was for the bigger picture—national security. We were saving the country from them pinko Bolsheviks. I didn't have a family, nor did I want one. My sister was enough to wart a man to death.

By my forties, I came to understand the ideas of my thirties were idealistic bullshit. Being a spy wasn't about protecting America; it was about safeguarding capitalistic wealth, which I more and more admired and wanted. In leaving the C.I.A., Toby and I were making a personal statement. Some American wealth that we were saving should be ours, if not a lot. No matter how big we could imagine, our goals were do-da compared to the governments we were protecting. If they couldn't think as small as us and we couldn't think bigger, why not make it real? They get the protection they want, and we get the luxury we were risking our lives for.

It was a turning point for us. We possessed a skill only a few in the country, including government employees, understood. We needed to make it profitable. If done right, we could set up a legit company to sell our services to the free world. But it wouldn't come cheap.

In my fifties and now moving into my sixties, I found I enjoyed what we are doing.

I walked down the ramp to the building's garage and motor pool, to the slot holding our company Chevy S.U.V. I tossed Harley Je the car key and got it clear with him, "It's been seven years. Put this Army gig to bed, and the position in London is yours. You'll get someone to tag along behind you."

Harley Je's usual deliberate and safe handling techniques went right in the waste can. Our tires squealed in the garage with his cornering and acceleration. He hit more than one curb bump coming out of the garage. And then came this little red traffic light running ordeal with the Dallas police. Je's nerves were on his short sleeve.

Soon I came to realize why my high school driver's education teacher lived with colorless knuckles…son.

But this is about how Harley designs a process to take possession of the backpack and return it to the Army—all essential if he has a career as an independent agent. Yes, it was a small case, but he needed to demonstrate he could handle whatever comes up and succeed and delight our clients.

He pulled into Dealey Plaza, parking on Houston Street a block or so from the Grassy Knoll. We could see everything happening on the hill. Harley started going through his checklist of what needed to be ready in the SUV for audio and video recording pick-up.

Knowing most of the hundred or so people in the apprentice pool, I did not recognize his guy up on the knoll. "Who's your huckleberry up there? I don't know him. He's got a TCU horned frog shirt on."

"We've overused the students from SMU. I think we need to mix it up a little."

"Still, I don't know him. Are you sure he can handle this?"

"How hard is it to sit on a hill, eat a picnic basket, watch the chicks and take a box when someone hands it to you?"

"Well, it's your future. I wouldn't be taking the chance. But it's your London."

The five o'clock Big Red Bus would be coming from our rear on Houston Street, opposite the evening rush. But traffic on Main, Commerce, and Elm would be backed up in the opposite direction during rush hour.

I asked Harley, "You've been tailing me for seven years. So how will it be going out on your own? Toby and I reckon you're ready, but in the end, the decision is up to you."

Harley Je adjusted his car mirrors and used a joystick to tweak the car's two rear cameras for the best view down Houston Street.

He radioed Sven Johnson on the hill. "Back up higher so you can see better down Houston Street. You're too low."

"Right."

"You've got three assignments," he said to Sven. "If you want to be used again, be inconspicuous. Let me know when the Red Bus turns onto Houston Street. When she gets there, delay the woman giving you the bag long enough for Rick and me to grab her. Anything you don't understand about that?"

Harley said to me, "This should be simple. Why do I feel it isn't going to be?"

I answered, "Things are never simple until they're over. You're right; it should be simple. You got a plan. Let it play out. Once we have the woman, you can say it's simple. Your man has moved. Can you still see him clear enough?"

Harley kept the SUV engine running. "Not so much. He's partly behind the tree."

He radioed, "Sven...move right toward the depository another thirty feet and act invisible."

"If you can't see," I said, "you can't tell what he's doing wrong."

Harley Je finally figured out the rear bumper camera was not giving him the coverage as he wanted. So he switched the primary image to the one coming from the roof.

He said to me, "You said you wanted me to handle this, so sit back and watch."

Right. I kept my eyes on Houston Street and checked my watch for when the bus should arrive. "It's you who wants London, so what you do is up to you. I'm only here to observe. But there are limits, don't stretch the rules so far they break."

"Break?"

"Traffic tickets? Unproven assets up the hill? And a new client?"

"And a new Case Leader?" he followed with, "Wait and see how the case turns out. You never know. Maybe my new school isn't so bad for the company. I'm following your footsteps with a younger spin."

Je persisted in adjusting his mirrors and videos for an improved view down Houston Street. The downtown Dallas rush hour came on time—meaning prolonged traffic like most big cities. Harley Je glanced up toward

Sven on the hill. Sven remained in place, a thin athletic young man sporting a cropped TCU shirt. After finishing his sandwich, he began focusing on the tourist babes strolling the sidewalk below him.

"Shit," Je said. He keyed up the radio and told Sven, "Stop worrying so much about the tourist tits and pay attention to the red bus coming on Houston."

Sven's voice returned rather quickly. "I wasn't…okay, okay…I was. Now I'm watching for the bus."

I said to Je once they were unkeyed, "Back then, when noobs wanted in the business, like you and junior up on the hill, we were little more than alligator bait. We got thrown into the swamp, like stinking chicken meat. If we didn't get eaten or maimed, we were a success, and we got another bullet for our gun. They kept throwing us in until a real job came along. For me, mine came from Toby. At least that's how it was when I was in your britches. Too much, I guess."

The architectural Romanesque windows in the sandstone courthouse were closed to the north and above us. On the clock above us, a scrolled black hand crossed five p.m. with a gong.

It was show-time for our bus.

I opened the black SUV door, stood to stretch my legs, poured the dregs of my cold coffee onto the blacktop, and got back in.

A Yellow Lines tour bus passed us on time, stopping at the Big Red Bus Lines' pick-up and drop-off signpost.

I wanted to distract Je at his busiest. "Tell me something about yourself I don't already know."

He ignored me, focused on what was happening. "You know everything. Let's don't play games now. I need to concentrate."

"Come on. One thing. There's got to be something in there." I needed to know if he could get back on the mission when the time came.

"Okay," he snarked. "I'll tell you something. The coffee you so casually tossed on the sidewalk was brewed at my house by me this morning specifically for my consumption."

"Nope. Nope. Nope. Something else, something real."

"No. If you're going to insist we play your stupid game, it's back to you. I told you something. It's your turn."

"Hmm," I tossed back to him and scratched my cheek, "How about my ace in the hole? How about since we're here in Dealey Plaza, "I was standing right by John Kennedy when he got shot. Part of his brain splattered out on my shirt. See the white X painted on the road over there? That's where the bullet hit him."

Je completely lost his attention on the guy on the hill, the mirrors—everything—and said what he doubted. "I've known you for over seven years. That's not true. Proof. What proof?"

"Okay. Check frame 284 of the old Zapruder film. That's me with my mom and dad on the other side of the street. I was a little boy. Now it's your turn."

Je paused for a moment, assessing the passing traffic, which was slow. He examined the mirrors and the video cameras. The cars behind us were stopping. He made sure the DVR was recording. "Something better than Kennedy's brains," he said, "Okay, I can beat that. I got hit by a piece of the Space Shuttle Columbia when it exploded and crashed out in East Texas."

"No, sir, you didn't."

My friend dug in his front pocket, bringing out a keyring holding two keys. Between them dangled a jagged piece of white aluminum metal, terribly worn. "This is my proof. This metal chunk hit me. I stole it. I'm guessing it's from the shuttle's wing. There's a scar on my head."

"No, there is not. Let me see."

Je put a crease in his coal-black hair above his right ear. The remains of a scar were there, exactly where he said.

"I do swear," I said.

****

Sven's voice urgently came over the car's speaker ending our game. Je immediately focused on why we were there.

Sven announced, "A Big Red Bus is turning onto Houston, heading your way. There's one woman on the top level."

Je, no longer interested in me, found the image on the SUV's video screen, his new focal point. The zoomed-out picture showed a woman on top, as Sven said.

"Where's your O'Doul cap?" Harley barked over the radio to his man on the hill. "Put your O'Doul's on. She won't know it's you." He checked once again to make sure the DVR was recording, and the remote zoom was locked on her.

I adjusted my passenger side mirror to scope her out, too. I couldn't help it. Regardless of what Je's next-generation stuff said, I still cautioned him, "Don't depend on the damn TV. You'll miss her too easily. Use your eyes. You see more with your eyes."

Je ignored my advice and used a joystick to pan the camera back and forth on the bus. He zoomed in closer. "There she is," he said, "on top, where she's supposed to be."

I twisted in my seat to see her, focused my digital camera, and started snapping shots until the bus caught up with us and passed. She was a face I recognized from somewhere. She focused back on me with a mystic look. I fired a final burst of frames as the bus moved away.

I uttered, "I know her." Then, I released the Nikon's shutter, stopping the rapid burst of photographs.

Je pressed the microphone button. "The bus is about to turn your way on Elm St. When it stops at the School Book Depository, the woman on top will get off and come your way. She's got a blue tee-shirt on with a white yacht picture on the front."

"I see her," Sven answered with his O'Doul cap in place. "She's standing up. Don't get your crotch knotted in a wad."

"Save the smart-ass for TCU," Je urgently said. "You make damn sure the woman comes your way. Take the backpack and detain her until Rick and I can get there and grab her."

"You want me to take her down?"

"God, no. She'll scream, and everybody for a block will start taking videos. You detain her. We'll take care of the rest."

The woman we watched grabbed the chrome seat rail before her as the bus stopped. She draped the white backpack over her left shoulder and inched toward the stairs. She was searching the sidewalks around the bus. Before she descended the spiral stairs, her attention focused on a big man passing her hand instructions. They appeared to be telling her to stay on board.

He was an oversize dark man, standing half in the shadows. I got a partial snapshot of him.

The lady in the blue tee-shirt nodded and plopped back down in the vinyl seat, backpack between her knees. The remainder of the stop-time she spent glaring back at me, my telephoto lens focused directly on her face.

"I got her," I said to Je, pleased with my shot. But, I knew, probably more than Je, how bad it was that the woman hadn't gotten off.

Je ignored me, managing to emit out loud, "Fuck," as he slammed the Chevy Express into rocket ship gear with no regard for traffic or the line of cars beside us.

I lowered my large black lens, being pinned back into my seat. "Okay, where are you going? Do you have any idea where the bus is going from here?"

He snapped at me, "What?" jerking to find an out-path in the traffic. He drove the driver-side front wheel over the curb, regaining control and accelerating around the stationary bank of cars. However—we needed to be going right. By us was an orange Volvo on Elm. Je sent it off the road into a light pole. "There's no catching her if we slow up with this."

I repeated, louder this time, "We're obviously going somewhere. Do you know where?"

Je, focusing on the pole the Volvo hit, answered, "The AA Center, I think that's the next stop. Something about basketball."

"And that's where we're going?"

"A-yup."

"Then you're wrong. The next stop is the Poirot Museum. After that, they go to the AAC. You're the leader. You should know this without thinking. Turn left up here, and you're back on track. You never plan for things to go right; plan for things to go wrong."

Je threaded perilously close to a crowd of curb-walking Asian tourists, sending them near a bloody Dallas welcome.

"This is all wrong. This was supposed to be a simple drop. How stupid can I get?"

I repeated what I told him before, "It's never simple until you know the answers."

My upper body got sent with his jerk of the steering wheel. The Chevy SUV skidded sideways, leaving parallel black tire marks behind us. Then he again jerked the wheel into a parking spot. "Did we beat 'em?"

I challenged, "So, what made her back out of the drop-off?" I unbuckled my belt and opened my front door.

He answered, "That big black man by the Depository waved her to stay on the bus."

"But why? You're going to get asked that when we get back to the office."

Silence came in the Chevy SUV. "Whoever is behind this figured out she was about to be caught and was afraid she would spill the beans. Sheeze—let me think."

****

I followed Harley to stand on the center stripes of Field Street, the Big Red Bus blowing its horn for him to move and him flagging it to the curb.

The driver opened the front door, but before she could start in with her rash of the lip, he shot past her, the length of the bus upstairs and down. He ended where she sat. Then, panting, he said, "The woman with brown hair carrying a white backpack, where is she?"

"Hell, if I know." The driver's hips exceeded the width of her chair. She added, "The bitty-bit ho kitty-hawked out of here a couple of blocks back."

"Kitty-hawk where?"

"Ross and Houston. Boom, she ripped the door you're standing in wide open and was gone with the wind. To hell with her, I say."

Chapter 5

Dallas, Texas
Rick

Andi entered Toby's conference room where he and I were and placed Berry's rum by him at the end of the conference table, an Old Fashioned by me. Then, to the right, a nine-ounce pour of Grenache for our Director of Operations, the greasy fat Brit, Mark Gower.

Toby placed his hand atop Andi's. "Thank you, my dear." An elder crack came in his bass voice.

I inconspicuously scanned Toby to ensure my senior partner was up for the debriefing. Mark Gower (the Brit with the belly) was invited even though he brought nothing to the case. Mark covered Operations. The Operations Department was the element that failed.

Andi circled the long end of the table, laying a yellow folder by each of us. Toby opened his and spread the internal pages across the table exactly the way he liked. Gower drank his wine.

Toby asked me, "Where is Harley Je? Shouldn't he be here?"

I answered, "Toby, why on earth do you resist moving into the twenty-first century? You could have saved Andi a bunch of time by not making her print all these damn reports. I told you already, Je is not coming because I told him not to."

Toby corrected the orientation of his sheets and grunted. "If I were much further in the twenty-first century, my boy, Ricky, and I'd be dead. And why did you tell him not to come?"

"He doesn't need to be here. He's busy building leads on this Grassy Knoll project we gave him. It is his project. Don't tell me you don't remember that."

Mark Gower took a Cuban Cohiba Behike cigar from his coat pocket, rolling it between his thumb and first two sausage fingers. "And specifically, who authorized Harley Je to oversee this project, anyway? I am Operations." Mark asked me, widening his big gray eyes. His mobile phone started vibrating on the table. The three of us let it dance to where it stopped against his yellow folder.

"As a matter of fact, I approved him," Toby answered in no uncertain terms. "And kill the god-damn vibrating distraction while we're talking. It's disrespectful to Richard and me." He sipped his Berry Rum to about half. "Je is our lead candidate coming up the ranks. It's time we certify him so he can take the load off Rick and our London team."

"Still," Gower went on, "I'm the executive officer. It should have been me who made the decision. Personnel assignments come under my lamplight."

I couldn't help it. That lamplight shit of Mark's irked me every time. "You keep saying 'lamplighter' this and that. What the hell are you trying to say? You're a lamplighter?"

Toby separated his fingers from his glass and held up a hand. "Don't you two start that again. As the firm's senior owner, I overrode you, Mark. And as co-owner, Rick overrode you. Understand how simple that answer is? Now can we get on to business?"

I agreed with Toby with a nod, sipping my Old Fashioned. I began to debrief. "You've both read Je's report, so I won't go through it, but there are a few items I find curious—if this case is real."

"If it's real?" Toby wrinkled his brow. "Listen up, Mark. You're Operations. If this is real."

"First," I led with, "the woman failed to make the drop even though Je executed every detail of the drop, per the Army's request. I was there. So, why? Je's theory is whoever sent her never intended to make the drop; he thinks we're being gamed. It's possible, I guess. But if that's it, we got a lot of analysis ahead of us to find who could even do it, and why."

Toby grumbled again, peering over his rum glass, watching me, "I don't like that possibility. Who would game us? Who even knows about us?"

I agreed, raising my brow with his, again nodding. "A second idea coming to mind is, that they were returning whatever is in the backpack. Unfortunately, whatever it was, was illegal, meaning someone was going to prison. So instead of them doing it themselves and risking getting caught, they hired this woman to do the dirty work. They realized we would break her once we got our hands on her. So calling her off at the last minute kept them out of brick-city and the chow-line.

"A third possibility could be, maybe the woman got a better offer from a higher-paying confederate. If this is a possibility, it's more likely than not that the guy in the shadows was her new customer, and the signal was him saying not to give us the box. So she didn't get off. She didn't have to. And we didn't get the backpack."

Toby's jowls grew long, his age over me catching

up. Finally, he tightened his jaw, dissatisfied at number three.

Mark Gower, who hadn't as much as cleared his throat, leaned back and listened.

I went to number four. "Number four is an extension to Je's number one. This lady's boss, whoever he is, never intended to make the drop in the first place. They were rubbing a message in the Army's nose…who knows…they're saying they beat the government at its own game. Why? Who knows? It's a possibility."

"Or," Toby turned his attention toward me, "number five might be, she stole from the Army herself and is trying to escape that big man chasing her. Harley Je saw him in the shadows. Her getting off would send her into the big man's arms. So, she went on. The backpack is somewhere in a trashcan. We'll never see it again."

I hissed air between my front teeth. "The Army's not gonna give us a bronze plaque if that's what she did."

Gower finally entered the conversation, clearly in doubt. "I don't think anyone is gaming us. We're like the guy who discovered that icebergs are deeper than tall. Who cares? Who in the world cares about us? No one cares."

Toby took another sip of rum. "I think that's obvious, Mark."

Given those as five viable scenarios, I moved on to my next curiosity. "Let's hold those for a while. Overnight, I asked Rory downstairs in Information to search for active Army personnel currently serving. This project was contracted, Mark, by General Legg. He called in through Front Operations. The problem is, he doesn't appear anywhere in the Army system. So, since he doesn't exist, it leads me to think someone created him as a front. And if this is what happened, we have no idea where the next move is. There's a non-person making plans to not drop off a backpack for an unknown reason. The only thing we know is a woman was on the five o'clock Big Red Bus with a backpack, as we were told she would be."

Toby placed his highball on the Teak tabletop, in a place where Andi could see it was empty. He then made a loud "Hmm" as if clearing his throat, but really to draw her attention.

I finished by telling them the strangest part of it all, "I got a real close look at the woman's face. I think I should know her."

Toby furrowed his forehead, quickly flipping through the pages to the full-sheet photo of her. "You think you know this woman?"

"Or," I said, "I should know this woman. Her face is out there in my memory somewhere."

Toby and Gower studied her zoom headshot.

Gower removed his forearms from the table and sat up straight. "I think I might know her as well. I didn't recognize her until you said you might know her."

Toby thumped against his glass like a bell. "Well, I don't know her. And I need a refill. Andi."

I, too, tapped my report. "This woman stood up on the top floor of the bus. She saw us as the bus stopped. I got a distinct impression she recognized me. Then, the man in the shadows signaled her to stay on board."

Gower assumed, "Well then, for whatever it's worth, we know she's not in this by herself."

"Do we?" Toby doubted that statement.

"I'm stuck." I paused. "This much coincidence can't be by chance. Someone has picked this woman to jerk us off, knowing I would go crazy trying to identify her. There are billions of people in the swamp; why did an alligator spit this one woman out to us?"

Toby took his fresh rocks glass from Andi and leaned my way. "Things like this are never an accident, my boy."

In his unexpected British way, Gower knotted his brows and made a point, "You have an interesting point, Richard. When Legg called in his case, he was smart enough to know how our company works—that he would not be able to open a new contract. So instead, his order came in as an addendum to an existing contract. That's concerning. Who knows how the government does business with us?"

Toby peered into Mark's bulging eyes. "You're the lamplighter. Are you implying an insider?"

Mark scoffed, "Who knows, maybe. It's as good a hypothesis as anything Richard has said."

Given we had no more to work with, I said, "'Maybe' isn't good enough, Mark. I say we sit until we know more. Let's see if the general contacts us again."

"But—just in case," Toby added, "I want us to continue tracking that backpack in case there's something to the story. I don't want any gaps to come back, and the Army blamed us for them."

"I can go with it," I voted. "Je will stay with it full time. It's his case."

****

We moved the meeting to Gower's office to give Toby a break. Mark's executive aide navigated the vermeil pastry cart effortlessly past Gower's zebrawood privacy panels, large conference seating group, and imposing mahogany desk. She stopped by a pair of antelope leather chairs where we sat.

I remember when his interior designer, Linn Leigh, decorated his office after we took over the building. Mark's office suite occupies one-third of the top floor, the same as Toby and mine. When you hear people talk about the God-Pod, you're standing in it. So, our reaction to the remodel was a pure surprise when we walked in. He had ordered the designer to make his unit like a London City investment office—as if he was still a royal subject. Above his desk hung a framed photo of Queen Elizabeth II between smaller black and whites of Edward Heath and Margaret Thatcher to its left and David Camron and John Major, his right.

He called his aide, *My Love.* She said, "When I'm through here, is it okay if I go home?"

"Yes, my love." Even after decades of living in Dallas, his English accent still contaminated his speech. "We'll be working late." Gower examined the top shelf of the trolly. "Are there chocolate éclairs tonight, love?" When she nodded, he took two for himself and passed one to me, asking, "Crème in your coffce, Rick? I think not."

I shook my head.

Gower arranged his lap-linen and dissected his first éclair. "You should be ashamed for sending a rookie out on a new contract."

His reprimands were starting to come my way more often. So, I asked, "How do rookies quit being rookies if we don't test them? They either grow to Field Agent, or they die and fall off the vine. Je's got seven years on him."

"But, my boy, you know better than to expose a rookie to a new customer. All sorts of things can go wrong. You should have come to me. I would have correctly directed you. Sometimes I think you don't see the bigger picture of my position."

"The longer you're with us, Mark," I observed the oversize man stuff his face, "the bigger fool you become. I sometimes think you believe the dribble you spew out."

"You know, Mr. Haade, you're an unclassified asshole. You have never respected me or my judgment. I don't like you."

"Interesting. You loved me when Toby and I hired you from MI-6. What a waste on our part." I pushed his éclair to the side. "Now, tell me how it is; you know the woman on the bus."

My Love refilled the black Jasperware cup with Ethiopian Yirgacheffe coffee.

"If we lose this account," Gower jeered at me, "it will not be Mr. Je's fault. It will be yours. Our company is not familiar with losing accounts, especially this way."

"That's crap, Mark. You told Toby and me you think you know the woman on the bus. How?"

Gower jiggled his little head above his fat belly. "I think you said you recognized her as well. How did you know her?"

"I said I should know her."

Gower added more cream to his Yirgacheffe with three sugar cubes and stirred. "Her name is Carissa. Carissa Scaffe. She was a young girl in Londonderry when you met her. I have no idea why you don't recall that. You used to have a mind like a trap."

Mark slid a sheath of documents toward me. It had printed a black Army War Office logo in the center, with a bright red Top Secret stamp above that. "These pages arrived a few minutes before you arrived."

I opened the tan inter folio and thumbed through the security warnings.

"The pick-up ordered yesterday," Mark's jaw extended, "came from the Army Proving Ground in Yuma. They think there could have been a micro-SIM card in a metal box in the backpack. The chip contains formulas for stuff. They believe the person who stole it tried to pass it to a buyer. That was the big man." Mark said, "I came to know the girl when I did fieldwork in Northern Ireland."

"You didn't do fieldwork. You were a desk mannequin with MI-6."

"Like it or not, Mister Richard, I've done fieldwork, same as you."

"Not at all."

Chapter 6

Uptown, Dallas, Texas
Laura

Being the wife of Richard Haade became a problem the first time I saw Brian from a distance. It made me tingle inside like a string of little crystal bells. I was aware of my teeth shining through my smile. I forced a frown to make it look like I hadn't noticed him, but I still kept a firm look out the corner of my eye at him. I set my tray at the cafeteria table by myself so I could watch him.

One of my material buyers was escorting Brian through the Pittsburgh company cafeteria. He told her he came from Kansas City. He kept their conversation focused on a line of gelatin we could use to make medicine capsules, cosmetics, and candies. Was it love at first sight? Some around me said yes.

I changed my hairstyle over the weekend, bought a younger, not-so-stuffy work wardrobe, and had Botox injections in strategic creases.

I admit, Brian looks a lot like Rick—muscular, six-foot-plus, gray feathers outlining his face. *He would never be interested in anyone my age.* Nevertheless, I found myself talking silently about him at my desk. *He holds his fork and knife so cute.*

When I finally met him, I found he could listen for hours telling stories about his travels. Around him, I would absolutely lose track of time.

****

I had told Rick a tiny lie about going to Pittsburgh to celebrate my birthday. I could read his face. He was sad, but he bought my fib. Instead of going to Pittsburgh, I built a plan to invite Brian to our townhouse and see what might happen. What was under his shirt, his naughtiness. Somehow the thought of getting caught by my husband made the plan even more exciting.

Rick was on a new project. His projects took him anywhere around the world, or maybe in town. Tonight he could come home at his regular time. *I wonder what would happen. Would he like to see me under another man?* That tickled.

I opened the front door and shook my hair. Brian stood opposite me on the stoop. I stepped back, holding in my tummy nerves. Then, instinctively, I scanned outside to see if Rick was watching.

I put my arms around Brian's midsection, palms tight against his ass. His pants were moist in the right places—from anticipation, I hope. I took another peek to make sure no one was recording.

Brian whistled softly, waltzing me backward into the townhouse, his toe closing the door. He nuzzled his right cheek into my hair. It turned my mind into a stem of red wine. I broke his firm hold. *What happens if I get caught?*

I nudged him away, saying, "I found a new drink. It's called a Bee's Knees. Do you want me to make one for us? It's enormously good." *Quit breathing so hard. Calm down. Your fingers are shaking.*

Brian slipped his bare feet out of his loafers. His toes pushed them under the bar's toe stop. He wandered around the townhouse. When I glanced up from the bar, he was at the Gauguin hanging in the hall. "I love your place."

"My husband gave me that for our anniversary. I'm not sure if I like it yet or not."

"What's not to like? Did he tell you what he paid for it? Even the cheapest Gauguin is in the millions. For millions, you can overlook its uglies—crooked tits. And, by the way, where is your husband? I don't remember you saying. Rick, isn't it?"

"Believe it or not, I have no idea. Rick works internationally. We're not allowed to talk about his projects. He could be anywhere on the planet or off." I warmed honey in a ramekin and sliced a lemon twist for garnish.

"What does he do?"

I laughed out loud. "I don't know. Let's not talk about Rick. It's my birthday. Let's have fun."

He answered, "Sure, but you don't know if he's in town or not?"

I followed his fingers while they moved over the oil painting. Then his body leaned in to see the image. *Jesus, I could get on that and ride it till it's worn out. Why are you scared?* I've wanted Brian more and more since the cafeteria. *Why have I waited so long, my hedonistic libertine?*

He came to the bar and held me, rocking my bum against his tool. He blew soft, warm breaths into my fine hair. His fingers caressed the lobes of my ears, and he nuzzled into my neck. *Rick never does this.* I closed my eyes, blacking the world out, and melded in the feeling.

"Let's go to the bedroom," he whispered in my ear.

I had already become so moist. *God, I want him on*

me.

I twisted out of his arms. "Let's not rocket our way to Boardwalk. Let's finish our drinks. Then we can enjoy...."

He pointed to the living room. "Why don't we sample your drink?"

I dropped the remaining Bees Knees ingredients into a hand shaker, gave it a vigorous mix, and poured the yellow concoction into a pair of martini glasses. "Okay," I said. "Let's buzz ourselves up with a few of these."

I don't know if I can.

He took his martini glass, and I lifted his shirt to see if what was in there was as good as my dream. Exactly, it was. I lifted his shirt over his head and tossed it across to the back of Rick's recliner.

Brian's chest was smooth, and his fifty-something abdomen remained remarkably tight.

He said, "I need some assurance."

I focused on his eyes. "I'm past that."

"Your husband. How do you know he isn't going to walk in on us right now? People get killed for less."

"It's part of the excitement," I said, "Isn't it— Rick walking in while I'm making you cum gives me goosebumps. It makes me tingle. Maybe I shouldn't have said that."

Taking down another taste of Bee's Knees, I snickered and went on. "That's part of the thrill. When I do it by myself, I pretend he's walking in on us."

I encouraged his fingers to lift my blouse. He lifted the bottom. My alabaster skin was there for him to enjoy. "That's so pretty," he spoke quietly.

"You shouldn't worry. When Rick gets on one of his projects, he can stay away for days or weeks."

I tipped my glass against Brian's moist lips. "What do you think?"

"You're spilling it on me."

"Here, let me lick you dry."

Chapter 7

Phoenix, Arizona
Kelly Lake

Landing at Phoenix Sky Harbor airport, I stayed up with Carissa leaving the baggage claim area. The squeak from her green and red sneakers echoed down the hall as she shuffled her feet against the polished floor. On the other hand, my leather Bruno Magali heels clicked as if a Gestapo Officer was chasing her. Ahead I could see the exit sign for limo pickup.

As we approached the sliding exit, Carissa peeled off for the women's room.

Today was another of those hundred-plus temperature days. Outside, a little past the limo area, a TV Channel 10 news crew set up to record a segment, lights, and lenses aimed at the hood of a shiny black Lincoln. The egg trick is shown every year on the six o'clock news when the summer heat gets so sweltering. The cameraman focused his attention on the tiny video screen. A stagehand then cracked an egg and poured it out on the hood. The whites of the egg immediately spread and began turning white.

Carissa's voice startled me from behind. "They do that every year. I don't believe you haven't seen it."

I sucked in the wind and jumped. "I've seen it."

"No, you haven't."

"People get stitches for sneaking up on me. So don't you ever do that again."

"Right." She sniped, holding out her palm. "My money. The gig's over."

Over? What balls...tits. "Sugar, this gig ain't close to being over. It's over when He says."

In the passing crowd, short Carissa tried to stare me down. Her disapproving face was more silly than serious. She threw her carry-on to the bench, opened it, and pitched the metal box my way. "It's over," she said.

The box came toward me, and I knocked it from flight onto the floor. A kur-thunk came from its inside.

"Running your mouth off like that's gonna get you hurt." I took an envelope from my coat pocket and frisbeed it twirling toward her. Then picked up the metal box.

She had replaced her holey knee jeans from Flagstaff with a pair of tight David McQueen's. The mounds of her butt filled then about right.

I said, "You might want to know there was nothing in that box except a dummy weight. You passed."

"Passed?"

"He wanted to see if you would go through with something that made no logical sense, without balking. You did."

"You're saying I went through all that shit for nothing more than to see if I could follow instructions. You people are weird." She opened the envelope.

"He needed to know for sure you wouldn't back out if we told you to do something and you didn't know what—if you would work purely for the money."

"I do money as long as it doesn't involve you putting your hands on me."

"You might not know this, but half the people in this world come wearing women's bodies. Trust me. There is nothing special about yours. So I can't imagine why He wants you."

"Go to hell. Was 'He,' one of those two men parked in that SUV in Dallas?"

"There was no SUV in Dallas."

"Two men were taking pictures of me from it. One of them seemed familiar."

"I doubt it. There's one more task for you to do, and you'll be paid a year's wage if you pull it off."

"I'm interested. If I'm going to be part of this, who is this 'He' person?"

"He's 'He' is the only thing you need to know.'"

Chapter 8

Kirkland AFB, Albuquerque, NM
Tommy Begaye

Master Sargent Tommy Begaye did what the US Air Force asked and never balked about hazardous duty trips or HazMat pay. With tribal black hair and bottomless dark eyes, Tommy marched across the motor pool's gravel loading yard. He had on the Base's uniform of the day—a pressed pair of summer green OCPs.

His dangerous duty pay went straight to the fund he designated for rebuilding his tribal land on Sandia Mountain. This trip would add another two-hundred and sixty-eight dollars to the pool.

Kirtland billets a half-dozen long-haul drivers for aircraft parts, wings, engines, etc. Tommy came into the duty officer's favor by volunteering for trips others didn't want to take. He got the highest paying routes because years of crappy loads taught him to become the best driver.

In a way, he studied the rolling gray sky rubbing against Sandia Mountain as if he was worshipping his ancestors. He did this daily. The Sandia Mountain grounded him as to why the gods had assigned him to Kirtland—to build back the land the tribal elders lost.

Outside he found his unit at the loading dock, a Stoughton trailer number JBHU211960 that matched the flat white JB Hunt tractor attached to it. Trailer 211960 was painted with an orange 'J.B. Hunt' ribbon high and forward. He checked out his girl. Was she ready for the trip? The rig wasn't 'his,' but Colonel Wright had dedicated it to the Kirtland to Patterson Air Field route. By tradition, this was his route, so she was his.

The gods began scattering sprinkles on his high-altitude tribe's land, marking the beginning of fresh summer water riding the winds from the Pacific. Tradition had it Pacific winds were the nurturing winds, benefiting Sandia's endless miles of pinto and cayuse pastureland. So, in early summer, red columbines and blue Jacob's Ladder were up there painting the land.

With the exactness of an Air Force One pilot, Tommy slowly rubbed 211960, checking every box on the safety sheet as he went. He pulled on hoses, poked tires, and tugged at electrical connectors, inspecting every aspect of his rig for dependability. Only at that point would he certify 211960 to be road-ready.

He noticed a single tapering column of white smoke lifting from the back of his girl. The smell irritated his nose. As he made his way to the rear of the trailer, he took a double squirt of Afrin Spray from his pant pocket for each nostril, then peeked around the end to see a pair of closed eight-foot-high doors. A ladder leaned against them with a bony airman stretching atop, wrapping up his job of welding the doors closed. The boxes inside were sealed in place.

The airman asked Tommy, "This thing's hauling men's slippers. Why the hell is it getting its doors welded?"

Master Sergeant Begaye explained to him, "They're Officer slippers."

The airman shook his head and climbed down from the ladder. "Like everything else in this Air Force—nothing makes no sense, whatever," he said as he made his way out of the morning sun's building heat.

****

Carissa Scaffe stepped out of Colonel Wright's administration building like a woman on a mission. Tommy eyed her. A female of any sort leaving Wright's office meant something sucked or was about to. He instinctively measured her body; then, he put her shape aside. The lady came using a civilian walk to the front of his rig. She was not American. No, she wore a non-uniform uniform, some green fatigue jumpsuit with an unfamiliar badge stitched to her right shoulder. She carried a travel bag. The nameplate above her chest pocket said she was *Scaffe, Carissa*. An Irish flag had been printed on her left shoulder.

Scaffe asked Tommy in a firm Irish lilt, "Is this the rig taking me to Ohio the State?"

Tommy Begaye did not answer; instead, he opened the cab door, readied for the short jump up, and climbed into the cab. Security of the load takes precedence over whoever the woman might be. And now that the doors were welded, the rig was his responsibility.

She held out a flap of unfolded white paper which she extracted from the pocket under her name. "I have instructions to hook up with a native man named Begaye." She wiggled the form so the sheet would unfold itself.

Begaye wanted to resist but stepped back and read it, raising his brows. The paper appeared to come from the Secretary of Defense and was co-signed by his airfield Commander, Colonel Wright, out of whose office she came.

"You're mistaken," he said. "I'm sure you want a different load. Let's see. Which one might that be? … I don't know, but you aren't interested in this load."

Colonel Wright, coming to join them, sported the newest flashy Master of Space Badge, dangling from a silver missile pinned on his shirt. Tommy realized the inevitable. *Wright's about to dump this leprechaun on me.*

Wright gave a Cheshire grin. "Tommy, I see you've met QM Sergeant Scaffe. That's good," Those were the words, but the meaning was don't give me any shit.

"Not so much, sir."

"Scaffe will be your co-driver to Patterson." He smiled, facing her.

"With due respects, sir …" Tommy said.

Colonel Wright missed the opportunity to give a courteous pause in his speech, "She is developing a black-load operating procedure for the Irish Government. Chief of Staff Dungee wants us to aid her."

"I can't say I agree with Chief of Staff Dungee, sir." Tommy squirmed, knowing better than to contradict. "Procedure states, one-hundred percent, against letting a foreigner in the cab of a black-load. It says never provide a foreign government the advantage by giving knowledge central to the United States. And on this load, sir, it doesn't get any more central."

"Hold it, son. If the Chief of Staff directs us, we will help Ireland."

Wright smiled apologetically at his guest.

The redhead in Irish fatigues and curled sideburns said, "In all my years, I've never seen a trailer that's welded closed, Colonel."

"It's one of our steps to secure the load," Wright answered like a father, air writing what he said with an imaginary pen.

As Wright flailed the air, an inbound flatbed entered past the security shack carrying a load of construction rebar and rolled by the three of us, shaking the ground.

"You're right, Colonel." This was a battle Tommy was not going to win.

"Good. Then the two of you climb up there and let me see some smoke."

****

JBHU211960 made it to Interstate-25 on time in 1:27 hours; Tommy Begaye turned the five-hundred horsepower Peterbilt north and lined up for Denver, quickly putting sticky blacktop and stripes behind him. Over his head, he pressed a white button. It was marked '*Weather.*' A digital weather screen slid open on the dashboard showing yellow and red lines—a storm coming from Arizona. When it got there, 211960 would be far north as the storm passed to the south. But the screen also showed the distinct green arched line of outflow winds preceding the downpour. If that catches up with us, it could spell trouble in the form of an overturned trailer and officer slippers scattered all over the embankments. Tommy touched Denver on the screen, and the navigator box calculated the likelihood the wind would catch them. It would be close. They could have no delays. But, for now, he enjoyed the smooth ride north.

For the first time, he spoke to her, "I love a strong air conditioner and loud cowboy music. Make sure you put it in your little black book. Long haul drivers got to have good air conditioning and better cowboy music."

Quartermaster Scaffe stopped slouching, bored, and she sat up. "I'd like to drive sometime," she said. "I'm certified. What do you think about that, us breaking the trip into shifts?"

Tommy scowled across to her. "You should have read the Ops manual. I'm guessing you didn't. Did you read any of the Ops manuals?"

"It sounds like I should have." She adjusted the A/C to flow away from her cold arms and face.

"Hmm. If you're in this cab, you should have. You'd know I'm completely responsible for the load back there; it's no matter what. So, until we get to Patterson, I'm in command of everything between the bumpers, good or bad."

"I didn't mean to light your butt."

"Understand, sweety; this rig ain't no funhouse. We're dragging hazardous stuff."

Carissa replied. "Jeeesus. Give. It. Up. I get it. When we get to Raton, I need a lady break. That's the reason I want to drive."

Tommy sucked in a slow breath of dry desert air and exhaled. "If you'd read the Ops manual, you'd know this is scheduled to be a solo drive. You'd also know black loads, and this is a black-load, don't do lady-breaks or any other type of breaks. Black loads stop for meals and pee breaks at places the Air Force designates safe and only those places. I warned you in the yard not to come. When we left, security locked this coffin, inside and out. We can't get out even if it burst into flames, so sit there, shut up, and thank the stars you're not a black-crispy."

She tested her door lock and frowned.

Tommy took the white and blue Afrin bottle from his road bag and gave himself a couple of sniffs to clear his nose and calm his nerves. "I tell you what…when you need to go, there is a pot in the sleeper behind me. You can use it. Make sure you pull the drape shut. I don't want your stink up here."

Carissa puffed up. Tommy was not as welcoming as Colonel Wright assured her he would be. She snorted back, "I'm not having you sit out here and listen to me potty. You're a pervert. We stop in Raton, or I call Colonel Wright."

Begaye shrugged. "Call anyone you like. These rigs block cell phone signals coming in or out. Looks like you're in a communications desert with a pervert. And as for urinating, that's up to you. I don't care either way. You shoved privacy in the shit can when you signed the secrecy papers. Underline no privacy in your little black book. Kirtland monitors this rig down to how many times you blink in that jump seat. They take no chances."

****

Just before Raton Pass, elapsed time of 2:54 hours, the I-25 northbound traffic lanes slowed to a crawl. Where they were, the weather was dry, with cumulus clouds leaning against the mountains in front of him. The winds were calm. Tommy envisioned no reason for the stop. He pressed the red-and-white emergency call button above his head on the ceiling.

"Kirtland here."

"Traffic on I-25 has stopped. We're south of Raton," he quizzed the control operator.

"We're watching it. There's an accident two miles ahead. New Mexico Troopers are on location with a helicopter ambulance."

"Thanks. We'll wait." Begaye released the button.

Out the corner of his eye, he could see Scaffe

drawing lipstick from her purse.

She cackled in one more attempt. "We've got the time. Let's exit and go into town. I want to see the place. My friend in Ireland told me it's fun. We're not moving anyway."

"What does the manual say? No. There is one in the map box. Read it. We can't ever leave the highway for any reason except where designated. We've got double the food and all the fuel we'll need to get straight through to Patterson. Besides, there's nothing to see in Raton but some rathole motel."

She removed the bottom part of her lipstick.

"What are you doing?" Tommy could see her expose a needle from the bottom.

She lunged at him like a shark. A syringe in her hand pierced his neck below the ear.

The liquid burned. "Wha—?" He drifted unconscious, then died, his head falling into the bowl of the steering wheel.

****

Carissa pulled the parking brake and changed positions with his limp body. Then, she pressed the red-and-white button.

"Kirtland here."

"Say, I think your driver guy here is dead. After he talked to you, he fell into a slump. I don't think he's breathing."

"Are you reporting MSgt Begaye is incapacitated?"

She replied, "He's pretty damn incapacitated all right, that's right, and stuff is coming out of his mouth."

"Maintain your position. I'm dispatching New Mexico Troopers and medical."

That was not the response she wanted. She pressed

the red and white button again.

"Kirtland here."

"You need to let me out of this cab. Your guy has liquid poop coming out with farts and urine. The stink…I've started throwing up."

Kirtland replied, "Ms. Scaffe, this says you are freight qualified in Ireland; is that right?"

"Six years."

"Directly in front of you is a road turning east, US Highway 87. Make a right onto it. You'll see a rise. Drive for two-point two miles after it. Then turn right again. Drive for one point four miles. You will see an abandoned RV park next to a canyon on the left. Park the rig there behind the trees where no one from the road can see you. The driver-side door will open. We're sending a medic and fresh driver."

Chapter 9

Dallas, Texas
Rick

Waiting to get into my parking lot after work, I pumped the engine a couple of times to a few thousand RPMs, and the power roar cleared the crowd. They waited and watched as my yellow Enzo pulled into the parking lot and my garage.

Earlier that afternoon, I visited Dallas City Imports to see if a much hotter McLaren 720S fit me. It had seven hundred ten horsepower and two hundred twelve miles per hour top end. The lady was more than I could resist. So, yes, my Enzo had one more night parked in my garage. Tomorrow it would be available to serve someone else via Dallas City.

"Where do I sign?" was my only meaningful comment to the salesman.

"You can pick it up tomorrow morning," was his answer.

As the garage door started down, a black RAM truck left our parking lot on the other side. I should have paid attention, but I didn't, probably because of the 720 on my mind. I will be parking her here tomorrow. The Enzo served me well.

Our inside door came from the garage where the kitchen, living, and dining rooms met. This evening the house smelled unusually bad from Laura's tobacco smoking—blue stripes tilting down in the sun rays between the curtains. Had Laura been trying to burn down the place with them damn Chancellor cigarettes again?

And isn't she supposed to be in Pitt?

I pressed the rocker switch, awakening the Smokeeter. It came to life with its welcomed cleaning roar and wind. I dropped my wallet and keys on the table by my chair. Laura's blouse lay on the floor.

Why's that ... hmm?

The smoke was coming from down the hall. She was in bed, drapes closed, lights dark. A glow came from a porn movie showing on the wall television. My lady leaned back against the headboard, her pajama top, and bottom laying on the floor on her side of the bed.

Her hands were under the sheets. I forgot about the cigarette smoke.

She spoke unusually off guard, "Aren't you supposed to be on the road? I, ah, didn't expect you home for a few days."

I answered, "And I understood you were in Pittsburgh. So what happened to your birthday party?"

Seeing the TV, I paused for a bit. Her favorite usually had three or more people in bed. This one had two younger men with ear-to-ear grins and an older woman playing a game of choke the bratwurst.

I suggested, "Would I be too late if I got a cold bottle of bubbles and some chocolates?"

"Have you ever?"

I returned with a pair of flutes balanced between my fingers and a bottle of California Blanc de Noirs bubbles in my hand. I sat them down and rested myself on the bed, slipping my shoes and socks off. In the glow of the TV, there was a depression I could see in the freshly vacuumed carpet. Someone with a considerably sizeable right foot had stepped out of bed.

I drew in a long breath. "Did you enjoy yourself?"

"I did," she said softly. "I'm going to start taking off more time." She snuffed her cigarette in the ashtray on the nightstand and pushed it back from the table's edge. "My meeting in Pitt got called off. You'll never believe it, but Sunday evening, a researcher threw a chair through her 10th-floor office window and followed it out. She worked on my team. They sent us back home."

I fixated on the carpet impression. "Jeez," I said. "Dead?"

Laura shot me her 'how stupid can you be' look. But she raised her covers to provide a flash-view of her fresh Brazilian landing strip. "Does big daddy want a little happy-happy before beddy-bye?"

"Actually, uh," I paused. "I'm wiped out. Maybe tomorrow." I accidentally bumped one of the empty flutes, and it fell to the floor in pieces.

****

At six a.m., the townhouse's front door creaked, waking me up with a who's foot is that headache. Emilie, our German au pair who had recently changed her short hair to neon green, returned with two paper bags from the farmers' market. She buzzed our bedroom to notify us breakfast was underway. Medium fried eggs with biscuits and country gravy she ladled on my plate and a poached egg with toast and berries on Laura's. Emilie then retired to her private quarters.

My much younger wife sat across from me, perfectly calm, hands of steel, no indication of a problem between us or any secret. I was not her man anymore. That hurt.

Trying to bounce away from the issue, I smoothed the gravy across my biscuit. "Do you consider yourself happy?"

"I do. I have rough periods, but overall, I'm happy." Laura's soft egg yolk ran the distance from her toast past the berries to the rim of her plate. She dammed it with toast before it dripped off.

"What a strange question. Aren't you happy, Ricky?"

"I guess."

"That sounds dangerous."

I paused to admire the woman across from me, the one I loved no matter what. Her corralling the golden egg yolk put me at ease.

"It's work. I've got pieces right now, and they should connect, but they don't. It's early yet. I seem to be losing it. Hey, no fret. Solving a puzzle feels better the harder it gets."

I poured my first cup of coffee, wondering if Bigfoot ever sat with Laura in my breakfast chair.

Laura went further. "I'd ask what the problem is, but I know you can't tell me."

I'd stayed up all night pretending to be asleep, wondering who the man was. I was short on what to say to keep the conversation alive. "Do my long hours pose a problem for you?"

"No, I work long hours," she answered with her usual word bounce. "Maybe not as long as you…what brought this on? Are you starting to get tired of McDonnell's? Say yes."

"It's this puzzle—I'm curious…Toby said after you

went north last week that he's retiring. It got me wondering. That kind of stuff, you know."

She brought her toast closer to her lips then stopped short. "I like it when we can talk this way. It's like we're a normal couple. But, do you know I don't even know what you do for sure? Fourteen years I've lived with you, and you've never said what you do? You said in the beginning, international solutions. So what the hell is that?"

"I can say the same about you. You're gone most of the time. We simply can't talk about trade secrets and government contracts. Usual people aren't like that.

Laura was about to say something when her right upper eyelash came loose. "Damn…it." She grabbed for the tiny string of hair before it went into her egg. "I didn't tell you, but Natasha at the Plano office asked me what you do, and I couldn't tell her. So all I could think to say was International Solutions. She rolled her eyes, *what the fuck do international solutions do?"*

"Easy." I flashed my grin across the table, the same grin that initially won her heart. "Just tell them I'm an investigator."

She chirped back with a small laugh. "Investigator? Why didn't I think of that? But, of course, people will assume you're a private eye."

"In a way, I am. So how about you? What do you do?"

A half wedge point of toast remained on her plate about to be eaten. She moved the butter knife across it for a quick slather. "My official job title is Master Chemist of Quality Control. Why did we wait so long for this conversation?" She grinned, her pearlies shining at me. "I love you."

"Me too. We don't seem to have the catalyst to keep it alive. Now, about Toby, he cornered me when he got back from the doctor. He said he's ready to retire."

"Rick, no Toby talk, especially this early," she came back, "can't you ever remember that? When he dies, I'm going to throw a party."

"Toby is your father, and he has cancer. He doesn't want to talk about it, but he's telling people he's stepping down as soon as he finds a replacement."

Her happy wife façade cracked. "Well, isn't this fucking great? Toby's going to give his job to you. I'll never see you again. For twenty-five years, my father didn't give a shit about me. And to end it, he's going to make sure I don't have a husband. The only thing good Toby can do is die. Thank God for cancer. I'm sorry, he can completely rot in hell as far as I care—that is assuming you want my opinion."

"I do. I'm only saying if you ever want to settle the difference, this is the time."

She fiddled with her egg white. "You killed my appetite."

I put my biscuit and gravy down. "Well, Toby and I go back long before you were even born. He's going to need someone to help. It might be nice if it was family."

"I tell you what, if you like the bastard so much, you take care of him."

Chapter 10

New York City
Kelly Lake

I rolled down the back window of my GreenScene taxi to enjoy the morning breeze coming from the Atlantic. It brought with it a fog to lubricate the city and obscure the base of Lady Liberty, Governors Island, and Battery Park. It had crept inland by daybreak, filling Wall Street, Madison Avenue, and Times Square. My GreenScene, like the yellow ones around me, ground to a horsey stop. The morning TV news predicted lunch would bring a brief clearing to the ground clouds.

My driver's dash-mounted taxi permit said he was Raj Bhavesh. His permit photo matched the face watching me in the rearview mirror—he had a thin olive face with a brow bridge. Yes. I want him to remember me. That's why I prodded him to talk and look at me. I want everyone to remember me.

Raj read the sign crossing the road above us, 'Welcome to New York City—Home of American Business.' He went on. "America is my new country. I'm raising my family and me here."

"Good luck. Take me to Fifth Avenue."

I took the brass and marble building elevator to the Sixty-Seventh floor. My destination was the glass door marked *'William, William and Morris Agency.'* A doorman greeted me, escorting me to Mr. Morris's office in the far corner. The inside of his office was decorated like an entertainer's hall of fame.

Covering the walls within Morris' domain were headshots of some of the business's most notable clients: Neil, Hawn, Strickland, Armstrong, and Minnelli. And there were two platinum albums from Jackson and Nelson.

Morris sat at his desk in the middle of the room, a dark-suited man with yellow-gray hair and a red tie. He extended his hand.

This guy is going to be a push-over. Chit chat in the past, I began with why I was here. "I need to hire a player to act the part of an Army General. I want him to give my customers the impression of experience and decisiveness. Above all else, he must be convincing."

"There's fortunate timing," Morris said. "I have an actor I'm thinking about who recently completed a successful three-month General Patton run at the Bosley Theater, off-Broadway. I will ask and see if he's interested. Did you bring a script?"

"In due time. It's a one-night job in Dallas."

"The man I'm thinking about has a guaranteed ten performance minimum. That's going to be expensive for a one-night show."

I ventured to the window side of Morris' glass office. Planes above were aligned like pearls going to JFK. "I wouldn't call what I need a show. It's more real life. I will coach him through a contract negotiation I want him to make on my behalf. I'm testing two colleagues. It's straightforward. My pay will be more than worth his time."

Morris tapped a dagger-shaped letter opener against

his jawbone. He reread my calling card. "I don't know who you are, Mr. Lake, but our firm can't be a party to illegal activities. Unfortunately, this sounds like your proposal may border on that."

"No," I assured. "In the end, there will be no contracts signed. I want your man to act the part of a negotiator. Nothing in writing."

Morris got up — walking toward the door, preparing to end our conversation. "I will talk to him, but I can't promise any interest."

Out the window, I pictured one of the planes possibly being mine. I followed Morris. I could see that being cordial was not working. So I said, "Listen to what I'm telling you. Your man will be in Dallas next week in full uniform. If there is any hesitation on your or his part, think about the horsehead scene in Godfather. Except I won't be as nice to either of you."

Chapter 11

Dallas, Texas
Rick

The image of Laura's body flashed through my mind when I heard the garage door lowered. Her Jag had been in for brake repair. And, thumbs up, it didn't make that damn squealing when she stopped.

She elbow-swung the dining-room door closed behind herself, aligning the bottom of her grocery bags with the counter. Then, she came to the TV room where I was watching the Texas Rangers game.

"Who's winning?" she asked.

"Sounds like they got your Jag fixed. Houston, damn 'um, three to two. We got time. It's the bottom of the seventh." I glanced around her rear end toward the screen in time to see Beltré at-bat and getting hit by a fastball. He took first base.

I told her, "I picked up my McLaren today. It's beautiful, isn't it? Did you sit behind the wheel? It's so better than the Enzo ever was; I mean, I did love the Enzo, but man, this thing is hot."

She moved a couple of steps away. "I got you some canned anchovies and jalapeños. I'll get Emilie to fix you a pizza for dinner. I fly to Pittsburg tonight for a crack of dawn meeting tomorrow. Julianne called me on my way home. They need me to rejigger our project timeline.

That lady on our team who went Tinker Bell out the office window needs to be adjusted. I expect I'll be there all week."

"Why can't you do it from here? We've got the setup." I finally took notice of her face. "What's wrong? You've been crying."

"Nothing."

"Babe, I keep telling you, that job ain't worth it."

"Beyer is important; I need to be there for the rest of my team."

"The team can live without you. So let's take off to Casablanca, get drunk, and stick our necks out for nobody. We've never been there."

She pulled away and went back into the kitchen. I could hear her sorting through the bags. Then she knocked on Emilie's door.

With my voice volume way up, I asked her, "Do you recall me telling you a story about an assignment Toby and I were on in Northern Ireland? There was this family that had a daughter named Carissa. Her dad bought guns from us from the black market. Anyway, it was the same day I got shot. I'm sure I told you."

She came back, her voice recovering a wee bit, "I can't say so. No, I don't think I remember." She tossed a bag of popcorn into the microwave. "Julianne said the police told her the chair went out the window first before she did. So they think she committed suicide."

"I know you remember me telling you about the girl, Carissa. Her father led an IRA militant group the police ambushed. Toby and I sold him the guns for the attack. We convinced him Gaddafi was supplying the guns to get back at the Brits. Anyway, the girl was in Dealey Plaza this afternoon. She's all grown up now—and looks like her mother."

"Sorry, I don't recall."

The microwave ended the popping, with a delicate machine chime. I said, "For some reason, Mark Gower seems to know her too. Go figure."

"Since when did you start believing anything Mark Gower tells you?" She sat my popcorn on the coffee table along with two Shiner Bock beers.

And, without hesitating, she kissed me on the crown. "I'll see you when I get back," she said. "The company plane is picking me up at Love Field. Fingers crossed; your Rangers pull this one out."

Chapter 12

Pittsburgh, PA
Laura

I knew my eight o'clock Aussie appointment was soft, depending solely on him making the connection between Sydney and Dallas. From there, he needed to catch the hop to Pitt International—assuming he makes the trip at all. If he shows, I figure, he'll be the weird-dressed bloke in the lobby waiting for me.

Computer bag over my shoulder, I rotated the revolving door, and my eyes widened with surprise.

My estimate of his dress was correct. He moseyed around, reading the lobby propaganda about plants and medicine, and had, apparently, been doing it for an hour. The State Department's letter said his name would be Bill Himbury. Almost cliché, he sported an Aussie snakeskin vest with brass buttons, and jeans pulled over the tops of rough cowboy boots. He held a wide-brimmed black cowboy hat by his side. And there was a knot of sun-bleached blonde hair positioned on the crown of his head.

"Dr. Himbury?" I approached him.

"Bill Himbury." He turned, facing me. "I'm the bloke from Alice Springs, down under."

****

With him solidly in tow, I led my self-proclaimed

'bloke' to the department's work center on the tenth floor and into my office.

"You've come a long way, Dr. Himbury," I said rather stupidly, directing him to the armchair in front of my desk. *Do not stare at his topknot.* Indeed, there was no way Himbury could have known how out of fashion that is in America. "I received the State Department's letter on your behalf." *I'm looking at his topknot ain't I?*

Himbury wiped his hands, front and back, across his vest, reaching to take a spare copy of the letter I offered him. "That's right. A long way it was, but it's worth it. I need to see you."

I said, "I understand."

He went on, "Yep. I learned about your new drug through that American Ambassador of yours in Sydney. My Australian Government contracted me to take back a means of controlling our overpopulated animals outside the black stump."

"Black stump?"

"They're no more than your regular 'ole variety—Roos, Dingoes, Wombats, Rorybills, Tazies, them sorts. Just about anything shows up in places they aren't supposed to be. I'm trying to say any beast who makes a nuisance of himself."

A curl of hair fell to the side of my face. Returning it behind my ear, I nodded yes to Dr. Himbury. "Your wombats, rorybills, it's possible. I suppose there's a possibility we might be able to help."

"I was hoping you'd tell me that."

"What the State Department is talking about is an experimental drug we've developed that would likely work on your Black Stump brood. But it is dangerous. Your people administering it will have to follow every specific safety precaution—at least until we have more data, hopefully, coming from you."

Himbury eased back with a pleased look on his face. He started spinning his hat by the brim between his knees and leaned forward. "I have to tell you, that's a mighty load off. The wilds back in the Springs were betting on you blowing me off—pardon my expression."

I repeated, "You need to understand, the drug I'm thinking about is a new class of chemistry and poses dangers to everyone associated with it. Its name is Eight-Five-Four, we call it Klearance, and you're going to have to respect it down to the last degree."

Himbury sat back seriously. "Well, I think you'd be proud of the safety posts we've situated in the outback. I'd say they're straight-up dinky-di."

"Dinky-di," I responded with a smile. "That could be, but to get this drug, you're going to have to conduct your clinic the way I tell you. The State Department said we're to give you a trial quantity of the medicine– if I think you can administer it without killing yourself."

Himbury's shoulders slumped, and the twirling of his hat stopped. The outback sun marked his skin a doe color and formed deep aboriginal wrinkles. I reread the card attached to the State Department's letter. Research Operations—no Vice President or Executive title, only Dr. Himbury.

"The other thing," I said as his eyes scanned me, "in return for letting you have the sample of Klearance, we want you to tell us how effective it is on life outside your stump thing. By that, I mean, are there any unintended animals or livestock injured while you're doing your Tazies, or whatever? No data, no meds."

"Yes, ma'am. London to a brick. I'll see to it you get

your data."

I took a deep dive into his eyes. They were dark, bloodshot, but honest. His hands showed wear, callused, the way hard work leaves them. His vest had been recently oiled and weatherproofed. It smelled of tree oil. The dungaree scuff marks below his knees probably came from horses working the scrub brush. And there was a missing wedding ring.

"Tell me," I asked, "how much Klearance do you need? I may be able to source a small quantity from quality control stock here in the laboratory."

His chin rose. "Enough, I'd say," his eyes lifted as if numbers were going through his head, "to handle, say, fifty in the bush. I'd think that would be enough for a trial. Yeah."

I said, "I wouldn't know, but for fifty large animals, I can source that from our Quality Control stock. I'll have our team containerize what you need for transportation back. I'll include all the equipment you'll need to dispense it. But, you'll need a charter-plane home. Flight laws say Klearance can't travel on commercial planes."

Chapter 13

Dallas, Texas
Rick

"Pittsburgh? Was your trip good?"
"It was. I met a new client."
I swirled my Old-Fashioned glass and examined the concoction spinning inside. "Anyone, I might know?"
The restaurant head waiter gently placed a fried shrimp and calamari plate before Laura, then a half-dozen wood-roasted tarragon oysters before me.
"No talking about work," was all she said back.
I chased a sip from my Old-Fashioned glass. "You seem in excellent spirit."
"I am. I got done what I needed to. That's nice." Her hanging pearl earrings swayed as she spoke, her eyes on the young ones outside playing pick-up soccer on the green.
"I wish I possessed such luck. I gave Harley Je the most straightforward job on the planet today, and it flung itself out completely wrong."
"No work talk, right?"
But being with her for fourteen years told me something else was going on. I couldn't put my finger on it—something on her mind, something she didn't want to discuss. Sometimes it's dangerous knowing too much about your partner's mind.

An incoming text message made my phone buzz in my pant pocket. I read it and, in no way thinking, said out loud, "Shit. Toby wants a meeting at his house in thirty minutes."

Laura followed my comment with, "Well fuck, yet again your inconsiderate asswipe of a boss screwed our evening. God, please fast-track his cancer or at least gun him down with a tank."

Calming. I summon the waiter for a third Old-Fashioned. I appealed to her, "Chill, okay? Let's go on and enjoy our meal. He'll have to wait. We'll go over to his place afterward, and you can take the McLaren home. I'll get an Uber. Whatever it is shouldn't take him too long."

"Did you know about this already?" she sat back in her chair, holding her breath for an answer.

"Nope, I did not."

"I'll be so glad when we can get our lives back again. You can't possibly know how much."

I said, "Even more than what's been preoccupying you this evening?"

"Preoccupied? I'm not preoccupied."

A few minutes after ten, I stopped the tires of my McLaren from rolling in Toby's circle drive. Antique gas lamps lined his parking area, spilling golden circles of light over the shrubs, on the ground, a perfect atmosphere for strolling. It's just the people of Armstrong Street spent most of their evenings indoors, in silence and darkness—broken sporadically by the odd couple enjoying the twinkling of the moon through the trees. Toby's crystal chandelier hanging on his porch was gas-lit like the yard lanterns.

Maria, his housekeeper, came to the door.

Laura slipped into the driver's seat. "Don't say anything. I know I've been unduly rough, blasting Toby. I didn't mean to unload on you. Work has me on edge right now. I'll find something to occupy myself."

"If I'm not too late, I'll ping you."

She spun the tires on Toby's concrete and left—her red rear lights disappearing down the twinkle of Armstrong Avenue.

****

Maria directed me, "Them in the study."

Toby bounced from his home office into the foyer. The entry floors had mirror-polished black streak marble and stained wood on the walls. Post oak timbers lined his formal dining room. That was supposed to aid digestion, dark hickory in his office for focus, cream-washed walnut in the reception hall, and relaxing living rooms.

He whispered in my ear, "I've never met this guy before, have you? I don't think you have. He doesn't seem to know anything. Major General Legg, may I present Richard Haade. Rick leads field solutions for us."

The general responded, arm out my way, eager to take my hand, "I think I have met Mr. Haade earlier. Happy to see you again."

I examined his face, torso, uniform, and replied, "Ah, I don't think I remember. Or it must have been a far while back." We shook hands. "Maybe at the Fort Ord conference on Asian strategy."

"No." Legg tilted his head to the negative. "I'm afraid I wasn't there."

So, I took the chair next to Toby, opposite the general. Toby's oversize conference table of mirror-polished resin over natural cypress.

"General Legg," Toby opened, "Rick was assigned

the Grassy Knoll pickup. His charter was to collect your product and deliver it to your Yuma Proving Grounds. You're here, so you know the McDonnells Corporation has more work to do in that regard."

The general leaned back.

Then, Maria, who waited in the doorway, asked us, "A drink for each of yous three, sirs?"

"Without a question," Toby answered boldly. "Yes. I'll have a Berry's Guadeloupe, neat. And Rick, one of his Old Fashioneds. General?"

"A Staten Island Pale Ale, if you have it." He smiled respectfully toward Maria.

Maria answered him, "No, sirs, I don't tink so. So you like Dallas Blonde instead? Dallas Blonde, it's good."

"A Dallas Blonde would be fine."

She stepped out.

"Mr. McDonnell…" General Legg removed a paper of talking points from his coat pocket. "…I would like to accomplish two things at this late hour. First, share what we know about the woman on the bus. Second, get assurance your firm will follow through and capture her with our stolen property."

Maria came back with Toby's rum. Toby said, "Then, General, let's hear what it is that you know."

Legg leafed down his notes. "Well, a theft took place at our Yuma Proving Grounds not too many days ago. The thief took a memory chip containing several formulae for a new heavy equipment armor. It is a material we've been working on for a long time. We believe the theft was done by a civilian employee named Kelly Lake. He took the memory from a technician's workbench at the end of his shift."

"And," Toby interrupted Legg. "it's safe to say you've not seen Lake since?"

"That's right. The woman you witnessed on the bus is a mule for Mr. Lake...Lake called us before we contacted you, saying the whole thing was an accident. The memory unit fell into his bag as he passed on his way home. He says he wants to return it. That's when we contracted you to coordinate the pickup."

I said to Legg, "Then, why all the theatrics? Why didn't Lake himself drive up and return the part?"

General Legg checked his paper. "The micro card contains state metallurgic secrets. He was afraid of the secrecy; we would arrest him when he showed up. In fact, he is the person who insisted you two handle the exchange."

Toby tightened up with a wrinkled brow, "Us? How would a blue-collar worker know about our firm?"

I said to Toby, "The general's not going to know that." So I asked the general, "The woman. Did the man indicate how was she selected?"

Legg again checked his sheet. "Fair question, but I can't answer that. I can tell you we believe the woman has a connection with a Columbian cyber cartel called Gente Libre. She works with a big, dark man. You might have seen with him."

I said, "I'm sorry. But, what's a cyber cartel?"

Legg stuttered, referring to his sheet. "A cyber cartel, yeah. It's a white-market business moving black-market data from the western hemisphere to central Europe. We've known about them for some time but have elected to leave them intact."

Like Toby, at the same time, I raised a brow. "Your reason?" *Who is this goober? Why would some guy come here this late and read us this load of shit?*

General Legg went on, "We've inserted several intercept points on their network. So we know what information is flowing in each direction without the cartel being aware of us."

I sponged his story in, then suggested, "So why don't you simply intercept the memory card's data when it goes through them and kill it?"

"Well..." Legg's voice warbled a tiny bit. "It's not so easy. They still have the physical chip. If we kill the transmission, they will switch and physically move the data to Europe by courier."

Toby said, "You give me the impression all is lost. The data on the chip is in the hands of the cartel. Any minute now, it's about to be flashed overseas. So why did you even bother us?"

"You accepted the contract. Do you want to know the story or not? We made sure they discovered one of our interception points. They have shut down their pipeline for a while until they can map around our security breach. For a few days, the pipeline is out of business."

Our conference room quieted until the General spoke again. "We believe the woman was flashing the chip to the Army because they found our disruption. She was running the device past us on its way to Europe. The cartel's way is saying gotcha."

In a subtler tone, Toby echoed back, "Gotcha."

My BS meter flashed white-hot with every progressive word from this guy's mouth. Finally, I said, "So, tell me if I'm wrong here, you sacrifice your monitoring site. They shut the data tunnel down until they could rely on its security. You time this to happen before the data chip can be transmitted, giving them something to rub in your face when they move the data chip by surface transport." The pieces were now coming together in my mind. "What you didn't say is while they are down, our government can move even more secure data across our national networks and not risk the cartel finding out. Tell me if I'm wrong."

Toby added, "So some nonphysical thing has come up within the government. You want to be sure the cartel is out of the data business while you process whatever information it is?" He tipped an empty glass toward the man. "Another round of drinks, Maria."

And I added to Toby's reasoning. "The only way to know your new information isn't getting picked up and retransmitted is to keep the cartel's data lines down for some time. And you're willing to do whatever it takes to make sure that happens."

Our guest, General Legg, squirmed his butt around the leather cushion. "You're talking in areas I can't discuss. But, if they try to bring their capability back before we are ready, we have other monitoring stations we will sacrifice to keep them off-line."

I stood and backed away from the table. "So, what's your deal? Do you want us to hand you Kelly Lake? Or find the real story because, frankly, I don't believe the one you told us, or do you want the memory chip back? Or all of it?"

Legg took a draw from his pilsner glass. "Mostly, we want the memory chip. Kelly Lake would be nice, but not as nice as the chip. We don't think anyone has been able to decrypt the data yet. If we could prevent anyone from doing that, it would be good."

"And the woman?" I asked.

General Legg pushed away from the table, putting the paper back into his coat. "That's up to you, but I don't want you getting the War Office involved."

****

I waited alone in the glow of Toby's gas-lit circular drive. The day's warmth had given way to a chill in the night air. Our meeting went longer than I expected. I didn't want to disturb Laura, so I checked my phone. My Uber driver was still some four minutes out. That was four minutes that needed killing. So, I activated McLaren's security tattletale with my phone to see a map of where she had gone after she left.

After dropping me off, she traveled a beeline to the Quarter 'til Bar on McKinney Ave. Fifteen minutes after, she drove it to a place we rarely went, the Uptown Pub on the first floor of a multi-use low-rise, a few blocks from the Quarter 'til. There she stayed until midnight.

The car now sits at home in our garage.

****

I dragged myself into the townhouse through the street-side front door. The house lights were out, and the Smokeeter was on full blast. *Finally—a flow of air to breathe that's free of cigarette smoke*. Surprising. Refreshing.

In the valet on the table next to my Texas Rangers chair, I dropped my wallet and keys then went to the bedroom where Laura was watching TV. I unbuttoned my shirt when I entered the hall.

Laura asked as if she cared, "How did Toby's meeting go?" She positioned herself with the duvet tucked under her chin.

"Not bad. A new Army contract came in. And, no— I can't talk about it." I answered as I kicked my shoes off. "I truly wish Toby didn't feel so compelled to hold these meetings this late at night. The poor fellow we were with about fell asleep sitting there."

"I could use that tactic," she said. "It would sure take the edge off negotiations. Go, Toby."

"He's keen like that, but that's not me." I tried to think of anyone living in the apartment building over Uptown Pub. No one came to mind. "How did your evening go?"

"Uneventful." She had a poor fake for grogginess. "I stopped at the Quarter 'til Bar for a frosty margarita, then came home. Did you notice? I flipped on the Smokeeter."

Grateful, "How could I not?" I said, slipping out of my trousers. "Did you stop and see the guy you've been entertaining in our bed? I think he lives above the Uptown Pub."

She jerked upright.

I held my eyes fixed on her. "Would it be the guy who leaves large footprints in Emilie's freshly vacuumed carpet?"

She took another of her long cigarettes. "You seem to know a lot. Would it help if I said you're mistaken? Maybe Emily has a boyfriend."

"I think we're too brainy to play those games." No, I shook my head. "The tattletale on the McLaren said you were at his place until midnight."

"You don't know it was *his* place. I hate technology." She dropped her cigarette lighter on the duvet and exhaled a cloud of fresh smoke. "Isn't it too late to get started with this conversation? We both have to work tomorrow."

"I'm fine. I'd like to know how old Ricky, here,

figures in this *ménage a Trois*."

The cherry end of her smoke burned bright red as she steadied her hand. "I can't say I'm surprised this didn't make you explode. You're always so cool. That's the way you are."

"Should I explode? Is that what you want? I can if you need that. I've known of your nighttime antics for a while."

"Daytime. Daytime antics."

"Daytime, then. I was hoping you could give me an idea of where we are and what's causing you to do this. I'm not feeling good."

Laura rolled to her side and got out of bed. "If we must talk about this, let's do it under the veil of alcohol. We're going to need it." She slipped into her house slippers and led the way to the TV room, where she poured herself a double Woodford Reserve.

"Would you like one?"

"Bring the bottle."

She sipped her drink and circled about like a vulture eyeing her prey. Was I dead or alive?

To break her strategy, I told her, "Sit down. You're making me dizzy. I can figure out the obvious, but for right now, all I care about is where I stand. Is there a Ricky in this equation?"

She brought me the bottle but remained standing. "Now, that's the stupidest thing you've said in some time. Assuming it's not obvious, my whole world revolves around you, Richard Haade. It always has. I love you. It's that simple."

I took a long draw from the mouth of the bottle. The script I had worked out in my head these last few nights no longer sounded right—not with her there in my face.

A glug of Woodford from her glass, and she spilled, "The obvious data are his name is Brian Hunter. He is older than me but not as old as you, somewhere in between. He is and has been my weekly escape from the horror of my job, all the while blaming you because I have it. He's my 'I'll find something to do.' He travels a lot for work like you do, and he lives on Cole Avenue, but you already know that."

"Weekly?" My stomach was already wrenched in a knot. "How long has this been going on with…Brian Hunter?"

She cleared her glass like a sailor licking the bottom and poured another deep bowl, taking my Woodford bottle. "You're making what I'm doing sound all wrong, honey, maybe because it's not normal. Brian is my sauna, my Zen, a way to relax from my job. I like my job, but I hate it. Brian mediates."

"You are running around and talking like I'm the ogre. What the hell is it? Brian Hunter is your Zen?"

"What I'm trying to explain, and I'm not doing it well, I suppose, is my project at work has me under crushing pressure. It's destroying me. I can't go on at times."

I closed my eyes and slowed my breathing. *Who's been telling Laura to quit every Saturday since when?* My lips tightened. I wanted to make this point. "I've always been here for you, hell or heaven. Whatever you've needed, whenever you've needed it, I've been there. And I'm talking since I found you at the Navy shipyard."

"But," she bounced back, "I can't talk with you about my work. Does that make sense?"

"And you can talk to him about it?"

"That's my entire point. Brian doesn't care what I do or how I get things done. He's only interested in me for one thing. We both get what we need. I get relief because, for a little while, there's not a world of problems out there spinning around."

I took Laura's long cigarette from her fingers and sucked its smoke deep into my chest, feeling the instant nicotine buzz. "I don't mean this to sound crude, but you sound like a slut."

"Maybe that's the point. Brian doesn't care about judging my work. Maybe that's right. Maybe I am his slut. All he's after is sex. And that's the same for me. Two people who know nothing about one another, wanting to fuck. He has the one unrestrained thing I want, and for one hour each week, he gives it to me."

"And you can't get that here? I'm not man enough? Our home isn't a place you can come to relax?"

Laura shook the bottle to see how much was left. From what I could see, we'd done away with half.

"Honey," she said softly, "Our struggles go on here. We're hosting an au pair. There are a plethora of issues needing daily answers. When we are together, we can't get away from living. We can't share stories about our work-life. We can't joke and laugh. Life has become too complicated. I need a break."

Then she took a long drink—as if our discussion was paining her more than it was crushing me. "I don't want you or me to change a thing," she said. "We have a happy and prosperous marriage together. We love each other. Brian isn't about you or love. He's a lightning rod. I can empty my mind and enjoy the euphoria, even if for a little while. His sex erases my Beyer sins and buys me another week of breathing."

"And him?"

"I don't know and don't care. When I leave, I leave with a smile."

I emptied the amber liquid in my glass, and straight down it went. "I have to say that's the strangest justification for anyone having an affair. You're cheating because your work sucks." I stubbed the unfinished cigarette into a partly filled coffee cup by my chair. "It's hard enough to face the fact that your wife is sleeping around. Then you say the guy you're doing it with doesn't even care about you, and you don't care about him. It sounds like a pen full of pigs rooting around on top of each other."

"That's not what I said at all. I think Brian cares for me, though certainly not with the intensity you do. He's morphine. Think of him as our family friend, except he gets extra benefits. That's how he is for me."

I couldn't think of a better argument than it's morally wrong. *So why isn't the whiskey coming up with some good answers?*

I said, "Would you consider another outlet? Something else closer to us to get rid of the ugliness of your job. It's no secret; my release is alcohol. I make a good drunk. How about doctor counseling? Church? A women's group?"

I held my hand out for the fresh rectangular bottle.

She laughed. "Are you becoming a bible-thumper? Every one of those alternatives raises questions I can't answer. You know that. I'm not going to pay some counselor to ask me what I do for a living: *Uh…I plead the fifth amendment…What about your husband?*" She gave me some from the top half of the amber liquid. "A couple of hours a week with Brian is all the therapy I need. I'm not a sicko. I get off, and I come home. I see you, and I'm happy. We're happy."

"If I asked you, would you stop seeing him?"

"Without question. In a second." She laid a hand on my restless knee. "But I hope you won't."

When she asked, my chest tightened and made it difficult to exhale. My mind blacked, and not because of the bourbon. "Well, at least you've been straight with me. If you were making up a story, you'd surely have come up with something more realistic than this." For some reason, I focused on my shoeless feet. "Give me some time to think about it. I haven't always been the best of husbands, I know. Or even a friend." I raised the Woodford bottle as a salute as I stood.

When I left for the bedroom, she snuggled into my warm buckskin Texas Rangers chair.

Chapter 14

Dallas, Texas
Rick

Minutes shy of another crystal summer daybreak, the sun draped the floor of downtown Dallas. Lines of pinks and oranges sent diamond sparkles up to the windows of 'Rainbow Hanks' office. When I arrived, I found soft-spoken Hank in his desk chair facing the gold-tint window watching the sun stripes on the ground below. One of Toby's early finds, Hank wore an apricot mohair cardigan wrap with an empty Earth Grown juice bottle resting on his thigh.

"Morning," I said, using tai-chi softness. We took Hank out of European field duty, placing him here handling office audits. I wanted to know but never asked why we were here before the traffic reporters started their morning's broadcast. I figure he will tell me when he's ready. "I have to say, Hank, your floor is the easiest one to navigate in our building."

"My floor, you probably know, is fashioned after Alexander Girard's design for Braniff Airlines in the sixties. Each hall is one of its seven rainbow colors. The carpeting is authentic Herman Miller to his day."

Once the sun broke the horizon and killed the drama, Hank swiveled, facing his desk, and hurriedly covered a brilliant green folder to block its contents from my eyes.

"It might be better if we go out to Einstein's Diner to talk this over. What do you think?"

I took that as permission to sit down. "Not this morning. I have things."

My 'happiest of all men' opened a drawer and extracted a packet of flavored coffee. "Let me make you a cuppa coffee then. We can sit on the sofa and talk to each other properly."

Toby and I took Hank in during the cold war. That was a period when anyone willing to get shot at, stabbed, or electrocuted, could return with massive amounts of moola. We all made good money in those days. Depending on the customer, Europe, the United States, or Russia, delivering one senior East German scientist would bring more moo than the average American worker earned in his life.

Hank passed me a steaming mug of joe from his one-cupper. "Well, are you still a gambler, Ricky, like the good old days in Germany? I know you were a big gambler back then."

"Jeez no," I answered, "and I would hardly call crawling around wet tunnels, kidnaping East Germans gambling. Unadulterated idiocy comes to mind, being pushed on stupid people. So, what's going on?"

"It's these huge international bank computers, they hold lots and lots of information on their depositors, and I've found they have zero respect for an individual's privacy. They say not, but it's true."

I snickered. "If you're talking about my account, Hank, I'm going to be offended. We have rules you know about peeking into peer finances."

Hank laughed, a good hearty laugh—a good thing to see from him. "No, no, Ricky. It's not that. I have a point to make—you and I know, we all know, how the world works. Occasionally dust turns up a few gemstones too beautiful to pass on. I'm honest enough to admit I've found a doubloon or two that I brought home. That's true for you too, I bet. But you and I know, don't we? When we find a nugget that belongs to someone else, we leave it alone."

I would typically let Hank work at his own pace, but I needed him to get to the point. Today is going to be a busy day. "What the hell are you talking about, Hank?"

"I'm not talking about anything," he said. "I more want your opinion. I read things, you know. About things, you know. Sometimes about people we know. Sometimes it's people we don't. It's part of the job. It happens all the time with you, I'm sure. We read and hear things, and we don't know what to do about the information we get."

I tried to pick my way through his word salad. Despite the brain damage, he was a monster at crunching numbers, and I admired that. "Okay. What do you have on who? And why are you telling me about it?"

"I must tell you. That's why. You'll see."

"So far, you've said nothing. All I'm seeing is nothing." Instant regret for acting that way sizzled through me, so I took a deep breath to go with my instant coffee.

Hank fingered his way through various brightly colored folders until he came to an orange one with Mark Gower's name typed across its tab in bold. "You're right; you're so right. That's why I get bewildered by this. I need your help. There's this ugly thing I've found, and it isn't going away, maybe never."

"You're driving me crazy, Hank. Give me the

folder. Let me see what you got."

He pulled the folder back to his chest. "I can't. We have rules. You know that, Rick. You wrote the rules. I'm sure you understand, I'm sure." He paused, fixed on the neat pages in front of him. "Do you ever do anything with Mark Gower off duty, by any chance? Do you have any idea what his life is like outside the crystal palace?"

"Mark Gower, outside of here? I'd rather sleep with an Ebola goat." By the quizzed look on his face, I'm sure he had not understood what I meant. Damn on me.

He returned his attention to the file in his hand. "Would you think Mark Gower worked in the field long enough to collect bank accounts in multiple countries? Would you say that?"

"As far as I know, Mark Gower never worked in the field. He tells people he has, but I bet your orange folder tells you we vetted him, and the only thing he ever did was British Space Operations. He's a four-walls with a window worker."

"You're right. It does say that. And later, it says Gower played heavily in British and IRA funding activities. Did you know about that? Does he ever talk to you about those days?"

"That's news. But I'm impressed you found it. You still got field agent in you after all."

"I do. Sometimes I get inspired, and it comes out. Does Mark ever talk to you about the British funds he carried into Northern Ireland? Large sums? Does he ever talk about that?"

I thought about Carissa. "Again, that's total news."

"I'll be honest with you, Ricky. Maybe you should buy him a few drinks. See if a bottle or two of Shiraz will crack open those shadows he keeps in his past. See if he'll tell you about how his foreign accounts got so well-funded."

"Why are you so interested in Gower suddenly? Who's told you what?"

"It's Whitehall. They're talking to Washington, and Washington doesn't want to talk about things like that. So now they're talking with Toby. And Toby is talking with me, and now I need your help."

"If it's money, let me save everybody's time." I sat my less than perfect cup of coffee syrup on the corner of his desk and pulled over a piece of paper. I started writing on it and gave him my instructions. "Rory, in the data center, has a computer program called *Dark Pipe*. He uses it on IRS Tax contracts. You tell him what money you are interested in, and his program can trace it back to how much and where Gower got it. He can tell you where every deposit came from and when. The IRS used it to convict that, what's his name, Giovanni."

He took my paper and tapped his pen on his calendar blotter. "I don't know, *Dark Pipe*."

"And now you do. Tell Rory the bank account number you're after, and he'll give you everything you want to know. Tell him I said to help you asap."

With a faint nod, Hank agreed, "Okay, Ricky. But if Gower did abscond with the money, where would it have come from?"

"Mark never told me anything about it, but lately, he's been bragging again about fieldwork crap. I don't believe him. On the other hand, if he did run money for the Brits, he could have tucked millions away."

"I suppose the Brits maybe want it back. What do you think?"

"It would be so un-British. I don't believe it." But I

did need to ask Hank something. He stayed connected with people he, me, and Toby worked with when he went underground. I changed subjects. "Let me ask you something. Rory's data center is connecting our servers to the NSA and Defense Department Information Networks for a new Army contract we got."

"Yes, I know. The government is so obstinate; you can't get anything done. They mess up everything. All they care about is keeping their people from blabbering on Channel 8 news. Loose lips, all that."

I got closer, as close ranks made Hank feel more secure. "Would you poll your friends in Europe and see if there's any scuttlebutt about a new metal alloy our Army has developed?"

"I don't need to. No need, indeed, Ricky. I received a message this morning from my partner in London. He wanted to know if I could tell him anything about the memory deal. Of course, I told him, No." At which point Hank fetched me a violet two-ring binder containing overnight communications he habitually printed from offshore email. He thumbed through and removed a single sheet, passing it to me. "Some electronic components," he said, "are to be hand-delivered to Cardiff in Wales. Our London office is planning to kidnap it. I don't think they know it's yours."

I read his sheet. "Did this come from Cardiff or London?"

"These things are never easy, never. It came from Cyprus, somebody in Nicosia sent it to our office in London, and my friend sent it to me, and now I gave it to you. He's good about doing that. These things are never a straight arrow for us anymore, are they, Ricky? Nothing is simple."

Chapter 15

Miami, Florida
Kelly Lake

The Atlantic breeze ruffled my salt and pepper hair. My watch moved a total of three minutes from the last time I checked it. It said eleven fifty-eight. Now it is saying twelve oh one. *I'm busy. Where is this Captain I hear so much about? That rust-bucket piece of shit out there better not be his boat.*

Anchored midstream, the rusty trawler rocked on its hook. It was primarily white with an equal amount of rust-red on its hull and superstructure. I mentally questioned; *Could I push my finger through that hull? One big wave and the floating white turd would crack open and make a beeline to the bottom.*

Personal watercraft and small yachts plied the brown waters of the Miami River, heading downstream to the Brickell Key outlet.

Mark Gower was beginning to scrape my nerves. No matter how I suggest we get the box out of the country, it wasn't his idea, so he vetoes it. *Well, I'm doing the job. I decide. Screw him. If San Juan's all that important, I'll get it there any way I want.* The secret black box rested safely in the rucksack by my side.

I leaned over the weathered gray rail of Queen Seafood Grill and Bar to examine the river under the

Lucy Q. I rubbed my lucky '21 Morgan silver dollar—hmm. I've left enough clues that Rick Haade will expect me to dock next at Harbor Island, Bahamas. Ha. I'll be in San Juan.

Behind me, a slumped and weathered seafarer spoke. "Are you Kelly Lake?" I turned. The man was a seasoned seafarer—scruffy white whiskers, wrinkled skin face, sun-browned arms, curly white hair, carrying the smell of diesel.

"Are you my man?"

"Spot-on, mate." Captain Webb spoke with an 'I've smoked too many cigarettes' gravel cough.

"If that's your boat out there," I said, "I don't think I'm interested."

The captain sucked wind back through his nose. "Because she's a couple of brushes short on paint? She's a workboat. Paint her, and she'd probably sink on me."

"Well, I'm not renting a boat I can push my finger through."

"Yarr. Oh, *Lucy* there, she stands right on her own, all right. She's hauled plenty of heavy loads between here and Havana—quite regular she does. Her regular talk is cane and rope, but she hauls people once and again."

I waited. *A flashy ride would increase the chances of getting me caught. That's what Rick Haade and the Coast Guard will be hunting.* I shook Webb's callused hand. "Let's get a beer. I'm going to San Juan."

Webb's eye twinkled. "Sir, I'll never pass a good bottle, especially when you're a' buying. You need ta know *Lucy* don't run no drugs or underage children without an extra fee."

The cold Buccaneer Max Lager, dripping frost and

did my throat good. "I got no kids or drugs. I will have a woman. How much?"

"Women can be all right. How much depends on how bad you want'a go."

My Buccaneer Max bottle left a sweat ring on the bar. "I also might need to disappear for a while."

"Disappearing is what you're a wantin'. Yarr, for that, *Lucy Q* runs five-thousand the first day, two-thousand a day afterward. That's if you can afford to pay, and the good Lord keeps the *Lucy Q* a-floatin'." Webb aimed his brown longneck bottle toward me and wiggled it. "If ya wont'n to completely ghost, like a sandfly, fifty-thousand'll settle you in nice on an unmarked atoll for a month. It's a place I stake claim to. After that, I'll haul you ta San Juan or wherever else you wont'n ta go."

That bent-over shyster of a man amuses me. *Or would he take us out there and leave us in the sun until it bleaches our bones dry?* "Fifty-thousand it is, but you don't get it until you pick us up. I don't want you getting any ideas of free money."

"It'll take us a day to get to my island. I'll put provisions on board now. I'll need two thousand up front. We'll sail on the tide in the morning."

"Two-thousand? How much food do you think we eat?"

"It's the carrying charges, yarr."

"One thing," I said. "When we leave, we start by setting course to Nassau. Then, once we're out of range of Florida radars, turn to wherever your atoll is."

Chapter 16

Dallas, Texas
Rick

Monday morning, I caught Harley Je in the lobby, biscotti in hand. I asked my younger, "What do you know about Carissa Scaffe?"

Je waited for the elevator door to open. "Who is Carissa Scaffe?"

"The woman on the bus you're chasing."

Harley Je tightened his face in a quizzing way, his brow furrowed. "You mean Morgan Flatley?"

"No," I corrected. "Her name is Carissa Scaffe."

Je said, "I sent you an email. The Dallas Police found her in a stupor Saturday night in Deep Elum, smelling like Maui Wowie. They took her to Commerce Street and locked her up until Sunday afternoon."

"Our girl? Arrested?"

"She's out on bail. The dark guy in your snapshot bounced her to the street."

"Morgan Flatley?" I repeated out loud. "No, I don't buy it. She's using a fake ID or something. Our woman is Carissa Scaffe."

****

And the day didn't turn any better.

I walked into the house and dropped my keys on the table by my TV chair. Jeopardy was on before the ballgame, but no one was watching. I poured myself a Woodford Reserve at the bar and carried my rocks glass out onto the balcony.

Laura was out there, French doors wide open. She came my way, saying, "I didn't handle my part of our conversation well last night."

"Me neither."

"Infidelity is wrong," she said. "My cheating on you is wrong. Brian himself is wrong. But I stayed home thinking about it today, and you know what I figured out? I figured if you agree to let me keep Brian as a friend, I'm not cheating anymore. Cheating is when I hide something. Now that you know, everything is out in the open. There are no secrets; I'm not cheating, assuming you agree with our private parties. Everything is aboveboard. Would it be okay? I'm trying to find a way to keep seeing Brian. No more sneaking around."

Her conclusion balled a knot in the bottom of my stomach. "We already don't have enough time together. You've said it yourself. I mean, are you going to tell me we can't have dinner together because you and Brian are planning a private party—that's not going to work. And there's that little thing you're doing at these parties."

She topped her glass from a half-emptied Sauvignon Blanc bottle.

I tightened my lips against my teeth and tried to quieten my breathing. "I assume me being negligent in our relationship is what's led up to this, me being gone so much. And there's the fact we don't talk like normal muggles. Neither of us has a social life—at least, if you discount getting drunk and growing old, I don't have one."

"Don't talk like that. I'm the one who did this, not

you. It's…Brian wooed me, and I fell in the pond like a college preppy. It started innocent, but the further I let it go, the closer and closer he got. Finally, he put my Beyer stresses aside, and I became a new woman, at least for a little while. We got comfortable together."

I stepped outdoors to watch the people on the sidewalks below—primarily uptown professionals stepping faster than the five o'clock rush hour cars beside them. "Believe me," I said, "I'm trying to understand the dynamics of this. I guess what you do with your body is up to you. But, I'm having a hard time getting past what you're doing with it."

She clinked her glass against mine. "Most committed people aren't honest with their partner like you and me. We've never been normal."

"What you're asking—is for me to bring Brian into my life. I've always been the man, and you've always been my girl. Now there'll be two guys, and you'll only be half my girl."

"That's not right. I'm still fully your girl. I'm his denigrated slut." Laura held her hand out for mine. "Are you leaning toward, yes, I hope?"

I reluctantly nodded, yearning to give her the world she wants after what I've put her through.

****

Rory groused around in the thirty-fourth-floor office breakroom. "Pricks. Everyone at NSA has an asshole he can hide his face in."

"What do you mean?" I said, walking into the room from the elevator. I wanted to get a Heath Bar from the vending machine.

In Rory's shirt pocket, an ink-stained pocket protector stood prominent. Rory paced around the breakroom like a bull about to attack. "I told them fucks that General Legg authorized us to lay a direct node on their network. This guy comes back, '*who is Legg?*' For real? There's no Legg in their system, he says. Nyet. Nope. Nada. I'm to disconnect, or he'll pull out the government guns and start shooting. Well—fuck—him."

"You knew that. How about the Army network? Did you try them?"

"Now, what'd you think? Don't look, but I'm breaking McDonnell's number one sin, hacking a US government system. If we were Russia, the Army would kick us in the ass. But, no. So, here I am, having to route around a whole bunch of pricks. Not to worry. We're in through the Watson's defense link. So, take that."

I stepped a distance back, asking the one question I rarely ask, "Are you sending me to jail because you got mad over this?"

"And who cares." He stopped, then rephrased it, "Not today."

I offered a cautious grin of approval. "One of these days, you're going to sink me. But, I'm glad I found you. The woman on the bus, were you able to match her face through the Washington computers? Any idea what her real name is?"

He got to the system terminals on the breakroom wall. "Let's find out." After a string of characters went in, Carissa's image came up. "Her name," he read, "when she entered the country was Nora Scaffe. She came from Belfast by way of Canada eleven years ago. She settled in Chicago, where she lived with Betsy Rosen until five years ago. Rosen died in a boating accident on Lake Michigan. Scaffe changed her name to an AKA and moved to an apartment in Phoenix."

Rory cut and pasted her Phoenix address into a text message and sent it to me. "She has been living here as a single person ever since."

"What's her new AKA?"

"Morgan Flatley."

"Okay, you need to go back further. See if you can link Flatley with Timothy and Victoria Scaffe in Londonderry, Northern Ireland. Timothy is dead, but I think her mom is still around. Figure this a priority."

"You're the man."

I brought two coffees from the vending machines as Rory logged off. "One more thing, it may be too soon—but does the Army have anything related to that Yuma robbery out there?"

By now, Rory was calm and blew a column of steam from his green paper cup. "Yuma is all over the place, coast to coast, top to bottom. They've isolated a prime suspect but haven't caught him. He's a civilian worker named Kelly Lake. The story is they can't find him. He's cut out, running, but if you want, I can find him for you."

"Have you seen anything that links Kelly Lake to our woman?"

"Not yet."

Chapter 17

Dallas, Texas
Rick

Baseball game number eighty-two for the Texas Rangers played loud on the overhead TV screen. I enjoyed Louie's Henderson Street News Bar. Two-thirds of its patrons claim to be writers for the Dallas News. Their cigarette butts overflowed a scattering of throw-away aluminum trays throughout the joint. The stink corresponded. I pressed my belly against the bar rail, resting my tush on a red swivel seat and my elbows on the oak railing. Any night that involves Old Fashioneds, warm pumpkin seeds, and the Rangers is a good evening.

Laura asked if she and Brian could be together this evening.

A trim early thirties woman, new to Louie's, sashayed in my direction. Somehow, that night, she'd managed to squeeze herself into a skin-tight crop-top and poured the rest of herself into a pair of black elastane shorts. *And who could even walk in those heels?* She rubbed her hand against my leg suggestively as she mounted the high stool next to mine and slid her empty glass toward the barkeep. "Another Gray Goose Martini," she slurred toward him.

Her butt remained resting against my hip, firm, and got me imagining how good it would feel to push back.

And, given what Laura was doing, why not?

But our agreement didn't extend to me. The deal was for Laura's benefit and her mount. And up until now, the arrangement had not been a problem. So my question evolved to should Laura and I stick with the threesome arrangement, or would it be okay to push the envelope for my sake in cases like this?

No, I shouldn't. The woman's tight ass made me relocate my glass and wet napkin to a table away from Louie's bright bar lights to a dark corner booth reserved for lovers.

I said to my favorite barmaid, Gaynelle, "Limit me to two more Old Fashioneds, then kick me out." She helped to get my stuff to a black Naugahyde banquet in the corner, in a place I could still watch the Rangers.

Gaynelle had barely graduated and could make Sildenafil unnecessary even in the oldest farts like myself. As usual, she tied a knot in her plaid front shirttail tonight. Cowgirl blue jeans caressed her perfect Vogue butt-form. I don't deny the pleasure I got from watching her buns flex on her way back to the bar.

The play-by-play man on the TV declared, "That ball is forever gone. That will be the second walk-off homer in as many days for the Rangers. The Rangers beat the Angels 4 to 3. Tonight's win puts the Rangers two games over 500 for the first time this season."

"*That's right,*" I declared in my mind. "*And the play-offs are barely around the corner. How cool? An actual October in Texas for a change.*" I flagged Gaynelle to get me another. "Make it a double in one of those tall glasses."

Laura had not messaged me that the coast was clear, but I figured, by the time I walked the distance home,

Brian should have finished his thing and be gone. The last thing I wanted was to walk in on a man sacking my wife.

I waited for my tall drink. Then by the door, Toby's silhouette appeared in the light of the foyer. Jake's joint was not a dive Toby would frequent if he could help it. *So, now what's wrong?*

Toby came my way, and I stood. He asked, "What's this I hear about you owning a parrot? You don't have a parrot, do you?"

"A lot of stuff but not a parrot. Jake has a treasure trove of rums here. Can you have one with me?"

"Rumor has it; if you give me a rum, I'll demonstrate how to make it disappear. I'm hoping we can talk."

I answered, "Disappear? Did you learn how to do that on Broadway or on a battleship? And what makes you think I would want to talk on my night off? I might not. How did you find me?"

"A parrot told me. The tattle-tale on your car."

Gaynelle's figure approached us with Toby's drink on her tray. Toby took out the ice block using his finger and thumb, dropping it to the carpet below us. "You and I chose a long time ago to hire Mark Gower because of his experience. He would be able to build our company operations faster than you or I could. He's done that. So, I want to know what you think about him now; I mean his integrity?"

"Are you talking about Gower getting caught stealing the British cash-ola earmarked for Ireland?"

Toby had a Havana in his jacket pocket. He clipped it and fired it up. Despite the no-smoking sign on the table, his was not the only tobacco burning in the room.

"I wasn't going to jump right into that cesspool without at least a little chit-chat. But yes." Toby swirled the glass around and took a deep whiff of the dark West Indies distillate. "Good."

I kept an eye on the post-game video narration going on over Toby's shoulder. "There's no way to know Gower's thinking in those days. But I think he stole the money. That's my opinion. It's not uncommon today, but it was guaranteed back then. So if he worked in the field, he stole the money."

"But," Toby said, "he assured us he never left Vauxhall MI-6. He worked straight on Russian space programs. SCC was it, totally."

I shook my head. "When have you ever known Gower that he didn't lie? It would help if you were in the office more often. Nowadays, he's out spouting off about how good he was at fieldwork. I don't see it, but that's what he's saying. He's telling everyone he was a pinch-hitter for the Brits. That's what he's saying."

Toby kicked the block of ice he dropped to the table next to us. "You think this happened when you and I were over there? If it did, we would have seen him. Don't you think?"

I said, "Maybe we did and didn't know it. Do you remember the night before Loughgall, when Tim Scaffe got killed, he and I were dunking pints, and he confessed a British agent and his wife were having an affair? I'm betting that was Mark Gower. How else would he have recognized Carissa on the bus?"

Toby said, "Looks as if my Guadeloupe is about gone."

Gaynelle came again without being asked, minus the ice. "I made your Berrys a double. Once the morning paper is put to bed, we don't allow work talk. You're about an hour overdue."

"What's she talking about?" Toby asked.

She focused on me, one of her regulars. "Would your friend here like some munchies?"

Toby gave her a sick smile.

I added, "Call me a conspiracist, but when is the last time the British Government admitted guilt for a screw-up twenty-five years ago—especially over money?"

Toby inhaled with a nose-whistle.

"I don't believe Whitehall gives a damn about a few hundred thousand pounds," I said. "Even a million. Especially two decades ago. Hell, you and I walked out of there with more than that."

"Maybe."

"Not maybe. That's the money you bought the Armstrong House with."

"And you bought the damn banana car," Toby retorted.

Chapter 18

Dallas, Texas
Rick

Where had we parted ways? My house slippers had gone missing. Usually, it happened somewhere around the bed. So, what's up? I do remember I couldn't get Toby to shut up. He was on one of his good old-day story rampages. Eventually, my liver clogged with Old Fashioneds, and I was a goner. My pants came off. I found them by the bedside with my shirt. I would have put my slippers on then...hmm. Oh well.

I resorted to my backup slippers and shuffled to the breakfast table. Emilie expected me and commented, "You're up early."

"I am." I nodded. "But I wish I was dead."

She placed my plate down. "Your work phone has been buzzing since four o'clock. The red light is on." She handed it to me.

An urgent message had been put on my message board. "Excuse me," I said, subtly needing Emilie to leave.

The message read, "S*omeone is shopping your scalp. Guess who. Kelly Lake.*"

I cleared the screen, paused, wrinkled my forehead, and sat for a moment in silence, Emilie watching from the kitchen. *What the hell does that mean? Kelly Lake?*

How the hell does Kelly Lake know my message board?

Emilie tucked a folded tea towel under her apron string. "May I join you?"

"Yes. Do." I pressed the side button to turn my phone off. Its screen blackened.

Vegetable juice came in her glass. "I wanted to tell you something. Ms. Haade seems so much happier these days. Incredibly."

"That's good."

"I think so. But Ms. Haade concerns me."

"How's that?"

"It seems she's always happiest on my days off. It used to be she would come home and throw her bag on the table, then break out the bourbon—gripe for a while, and by the time you got home, she was woo-woo. You know?"

How should I respond to that?

Emilie glanced at me unexpectedly, seeming embarrassed she had brought the subject up. "That sounded lame," she uttered. "Never mind."

"No, it didn't. Ms. Haade is happy recently."

A moment passed, and wearing an Asian floral house gown with white thong slippers, came Laura into the kitchen. "What's all the talking? I smell coffee."

I covered one of my biscuits with white gravy when she slipped in. "I got an urgent message from work last night. I need to go in early."

Her hair in disarray, Laura headed to her place at the table, Emilie making way. "I could hear you're talking about Ms. Haade. That's me. What were you talking about?"

Emilie gave Laura coffee and a plate of fruit.

I spoke to relieve Emilie of any discomfort, "We've

been talking about how happy you are these days. We're glad to see it."

"I am happy."

****

Andi Weeks arranged my office for an early meeting with Rory. She booted my machine, signed in, and made sure it was mirrored on the conference board.

"Are you sure you don't want Toby here?" Andi asked.

"And wait until ten-thirty to get started? He doesn't need to be here."

"Your choice." Andi placed Wedgwood footed cups with saucers on the service cart.

This was an odd time for me, which I swore only occurred in books, seven-thirty. The room smelled of fresh roasted Elefante Nigerian coffee and freshly baked almond-apple croissants.

I projected up the message that came in on my phone this morning.

"*Someone is shopping your scalp. Guess who. Kelly Lake.*"

Rory asked, Is this the same Kelly Lake as Yuma?"

"I'm hoping you'll tell me. How does anyone outside know how to drop a message on my board without my permission? What's happened to security?"

Rory studied the wallboard, the gears under his wavy Scotch hairline grinding away. "Click the dot by your name. You are assuming this came from outside. I'll defy anyone to penetrate our security."

"Okay then, tell me who inside McDonnell uses the name Kelly Lake?"

"Just a guess, somebody named Kelly Lake?" Rory examined the embedded routing instructions now showing in the document's header. "Well, the donkey screwed Humphry. Your message did come from outside. Someone encoded it, so the mail system thinks it came from inside."

"Meaning?"

"Security." Rory leaned back, tense, his mental gears still grinding. "Someone knows mail good enough to create a ghost message server, it looks like in Nevada. They configured their system to look like a node on our internal systems. The routing says it came from Carson City. Our servers should have bounced this."

None of it sat well with me, even if I knew what he said. "The systems should have. Or was it somebody inside coding the message to look like it came from outside?"

"I don't even want to think of that possibility." Rory took my keyboard and made a few more keystrokes. "It behaves as if it came from our internal mail server. But no. It went through the logic level translator, which only works on outside material. We use three-level logic. The rest of the world uses two. This came from outside. You want me to take your Wisenheimer offline?"

Should we take him offline and prevent him from coming in again? Or leave it the way it is on the chance he'll attempt to send something in, and we catch him? "Do you have enough info here to know where the hole is in our system? We need it fixed."

"No. Not yet."

"Then let's let this guy through again so we can find the hole."

"Ok. I'll put a trap on the translator and watch everything trying to come through."

I took the laptop offline and closed my door. "Let's

talk about something else. A while back, there was a backdoor app we used to tap phones without going through the courts or the telephone company."

"We still have it," he assured. "It's an easy download from our apps library."

I navigated to the app's library on my pocket phone and scrolled.

Rory said, "It's quicker to search for its name, '*Marconi*.'"

"Ah, here."

"Once it's installed, *Marconi* will ask what number you want to monitor."

I guess I was feeling defensive, "What I'm doing is totally innocent. I want you to know. I need a little bit of info. Does it listen even when the other person's phone is off?"

"It does. And you can see through the phone's camera, if you want, without your target knowing anything about it."

"Video?"

"I've never found the video useful." Rory shrugged his shoulder as if *Marconi* was an application he frequently used. "Phones are usually in your pocket or in a purse. Not much value."

He stood, ready to begin the search for our security hole. But, before he left, he asked, "It's none of my business, but I presume your interest is Laura. When *Marconi* starts, put her number in, then click the 'monitor' icon. When you figure out the guy's number, put it in there too. It'll notify you when they talk with each other."

"Why do you suppose it's a guy?"

"I doubt you care about what she says to the dry cleaner."

Chapter 19

Phoenix, AZ
Rick

Assuming all hung to schedule, I would be in bed by midnight and ready to see Carissa Scaffe face to face in the morning. In my front pocket, my phone vibrated. It would be a text message from Rory, relayed to the Phoenix Airline gate at Love Field. He forwarded Carissa's address for me; 801 Meridian Rd, Apt 111.

My boarding number put me at the head of the queue. In the morning, I will listen to her version of why she was on the bus in Dallas. I suspect it will have nothing to do with what General Legg said. And while I'm with her, I want to know why she ran and what was in the box.

The following text came from Rory, "Confirmed Yuma thief was Kelly Lake, your message man. He lives in the Phoenix area. Working on his exact address." *Kelly Lake is moving up the list.*

Before boarding, I decided to call Rory rather than play this text game. "Rory, I'm going to Phoenix to talk with Carissa Scaffe, or whatever she calls herself. If you can, send me Kelly Lake's address, and I'll find out his background while I'm there."

Rory came back, "When you do, decide if he's the one who sent us your message. If it was him, bring him to Dallas. I want to hear how he did it."

"Done."

Rory then finished, "Your Irish girl? So far, we're not finding anything on her or her family. Londonderry records from back then are near impossible to get across the internet."

Outside, the baggage loaders sweat under the Dallas summer sun, throwing bags into the belly of the plane and rushing back inside the terminal. "Well, don't give up," I said. "I need to know if Scaffe is who I think she is. Her father got killed in the Loughgall massacre. Loughgall is all over the internet."

Rory added, "Now some good news. We discovered a message coming from a Welsh outfit calling itself Car-Park Managers. They're complaining your memory device has not arrived yet, and they want their money back."

"Who were they communicating with?"

"Some group here in the States, Salt Lake Research."

Chapter 20

Dallas, Texas
Laura

Rick being on the road tonight gave me the opportunity for an extra one-on-one with Brian that can go 'til sunrise. I readied our place, adjusting the low ambient lights, putting on a bump and grind playlist, and made Bloody Mary-oyster shooters lined on the island. I dropped '*Little White Lies*' fragrance on my living room scent sticks and started a soft rolling flame in the fireplace—orange beams danced in the room.

"To us and tonight," Brian said as our glasses came together with a delicate touch. But he gave me the impression something was wrong in his mind.

"To us."

We sipped, then he started strolling, fidgeting with small things lying around the townhouse.

He said, "You actually told Rick about what we're doing? So you're joking, right?"

I snorted. What a buzz kill. "I didn't exactly tell Rick. He's an investigator, for Christ's sake. He figured us out on your first visit. That's my good old Ricky boy."

"Well, shit."

Brian studied an oyster that settled to the bottom of his red drink, then tossed the glass back, and down the slimy fellow went. "How much does he know?

Particularly, what does he know about me?"

"Well, I'm pretty sure he can tell you the size of your right foot; by the way, the one you left imprinted in our carpet."

"You're pretty damn casual. I don't like your husband knowing about us. Especially while I'm having an affair with his wife, Rick worries me."

I checked him over. Half of Brian's smile was missing. I assured, "Don't go there. I only told him your name is Brian…Look…Rick has ways of knowing what he wants. He doesn't need me to tell him anything. Ricky knows where you live. If he wants, he can tell you where you buy your shirts and any policy riders you have on your life insurance policy. Whatever Rick wants, he has a scary way of finding out. That's his job."

The other half of Brian's smile dropped away. "Then, I should leave."

I lifted my second shooter and clinked it against his third. "Don't go there, babe. If there's one Rock of Gibraltar thing about Ricky, he is absolutely a man of his word. If he promises me something is okay, then he'll live by it. He told me partying with you is okay. So, let's drop it."

Brian raked his fingers through the side of his hair—and stood up for shooter number four. "I think we should call this off. I'm not eager to meet my maker at the hands of some government thug."

"Chill." Tonight was about to vanish. "If Rick wanted you dead, you would already know it. You'd be stored under a refrigerated sheet at the morgue." I chuckled aloud. "I'd be surprised if he isn't listening to our conversations by now. Sit down. You're not in trouble."

Chapter 21

Phoenix, AZ
Rick

A deep gray thunderhead boiled up from the west as my Flight 777 neared Phoenix Sky Harbor Airport. White lightning zigzagged across the desert cloud's edges, traveling miles before it could reach us. Below, winds churned against the desert sand, lifting a fierce red dust storm. Ground visibility went to zero. The pilot announced over the cabin speaker, blaming Air Traffic Control for waiving us off from landing.

Of course, there was nothing for the passengers to do except doze. I awoke over Mesa Verde, Colorado. That's what my phone GPS said, Durango township lit the edge of the forest like a jigsaw puzzle below. We banked, and the pilot came on the overhead again, announcing a change in our destination. We would temporarily land at the Durango La-Plata County Airport to replenish our wasted fuel dodging the night's storm.

I drove north the following day, leaving my Phoenix hotel. When I arrived at the address Rory sent, Carissa's apartment gave me the impression of arriving in a homeless village. Her ground floor unit contained two broken glass windows, dented aluminum furniture with brown stains, torn seat cushions throughout, and floors coated in the trash. Of her four white kitchen cabinets, three were empty with missing doors. No photos or tchotchkes were displayed anywhere.

From what I could see and the missing clothes, Ms. Scaffe abandoned the hole rightfully.

A teen working the rent office with glasses jacked on her skull and Screw-You stenciled on her midriff top pretended to help me. Not personally familiar with Carissa, she searched the company computer to answer my question.

"Ms. Flatley," she read from the green screen, "vacated because she didn't renew her lease."

I said aloud, more thinking to myself, "I can understand no one wanting to live here. Do you have a forwarding address?"

She pointed to the two words emblazoned on her shirt. "I don't own the place, Gramps. I rent them. Your lady went to Colorado Springs, General Delivery."

"When?"

"Two weeks ago. There was this stiff about like you helping Flatley load a trashed-out VW Rabbit."

****

I pointed my white over orange Bronco, rented at the airport, toward Yuma. Immediately I noticed the car rental company had not subscribed to XM radio. So, I was stuck, blowing through the desert and listening to earth-based radio. Then sixty-five miles from Phoenix, I lost my last FM station. From there, I had to rely on a scattering of low-power AM stations operated mainly by Native American families. I touched the AM scan button to break the wheels' rumbling monotony of endless white stripes flashing to my left.

The man's voice on the radio made sure I heard that he was "Radio 1380 AM, KLTZ, Now Country Radio,

Parker, Arizona. Tomorrow's high will be the same as today; 114 degrees on the pavement at the airport. Tonight's low isn't low. Let's get back to the music. Here's King George Strait from his new album, *Love In, Love Out*."

Strait wasn't my rammer-jam, but I cranked up the volume and pressed the wagon's accelerator. Hours of switching stations kept the road roar from hammering me crazy. But then, watching the white stripes coming and going gave my head a falling buzz, and the hot desert air converted the rest of me to crispy bacon.

Finally approaching Yuma, I selected the first motel displaying BAR and OPEN on the same sign. I adopted the red adobe building to be my home for the next few hours. Dirt crunched under the Bronco's knobby tires as I pulled off the half-melted blacktop highway. Interestingly, like many buildings this far from town, this one's hand-painted outdoor wall signs were all but faded by the sun, except the magic word BAR.

Inside, the desert sun had not been friends with the only person I saw. She was behind the bar, adorned in native-colored wrinkles crisscrossing her face, enough for three or four people. But, at some time, she must have been a beautiful woman. She gave me a napkin that matched the hole in her feed sack apron, and dropping it, like who cares.

Once she started talking, she kept talking. In her pauses, I squeezed in my Old-Fashioned order. Her ink-black hair hung straight to her waist, tied with a Cocopah family ribbon. First and foremost, in her speech, she wanted to know the individuals in my family.

"Ah," I said. "I'm from the Frank and Gladys Haade

clan in Port Isabel, Texas. I have one sister in Phoenix, and I'm from Dallas. My sister and I are the only Haades alive. Frank and Gladys are warring with the gods."

Then it became her turn to talk. She walked to the bar to mix my drink, never missing a beat. She told me of her uncle in jail for robbery, some man living in her clapboard community house who makes repairs on roads for the state, and her half-brother. He owns a filling station and garage out on the highway.

She came back with something I'd never seen before. She generously called it an Old Fashioned. It came in a honey mustard jar with no ice. At best, it tasted like cheap moonshine spiked with sugar.

I nodded at the right time as she continued and politely made my way out to the front porch. The Old Fashioned made its way to the sand. I slid the switch on my phone to the satellite and dialed Rory's number in time before she followed me.

"Yes, yes," he said. "I do have something you'll be excited about."

"I'm listening."

"The memory chip you're chasing, it hasn't left the United States. It's on the Miami River in a boat named the *Lucy Q*. The boat's registered with the Coast Guard as a part-time freighter, part-time fisher running the waters of the Upper Caribbean."

"The *Lucy Q*," I rhetorically repeated. "Whoever it is, is taking his time to get the thing out of the States. Could the *Lucy Q* be hooked up with Legg's data cartel?"

"I don't know anything about a data cartel."

"No worries. Can you lock onto the boat's location-chirper?"

"Either the owner of the boat has it off, or *Lucy Q*

isn't fitted with one. I can't tell. It's an old boat. It may not have one."

"Get your team juices going. I need to know where the *Lucy Q* is every minute."

"Are you going after it?"

"I need to know where it is, so if they run, I can get ahead of them."

Rory stopped talking long enough for a new idea to surface. "The Coast Guard has a new over-the-horizon drug radar we might be able to use. It's digital. Maybe I can get into the Coast Guard network and tap into it."

"That's good. Now let's talk about your Morgan Flatley. She headed out of Phoenix. Her apartment manager said her forwarding address is General Delivery, Colorado Springs. See if you can find an address more specific than that."

"Can do."

"Okay. How about Kelly Lake? Have you found an address for him?"

Rory's voice grumbled as if he hoped I wouldn't bring that up. "Your Kelly Lake is something else, my friend. I don't think there is a Kelly Lake. All the hits I'm getting are dead people."

"Wrong answer," I said, "don't give up."

****

Morning came, and my coffee disappeared fast. The motel's front-desk clerk spat on the tip of a golf pencil and drew a map to US-95 heading northeast out of Yuma. The old man shook the pencil toward the soda machine. "There are two cannons you'll pass. I swear you could hit New York from here. Turn left, and you'll come to a nest of rockets. The proving ground is a few miles beyond—it's about the size of Mexico."

I arrived at the Fort security gate, parked, and flashed my US Senate Defense Audit identification badge. It was powerful enough to make muggles worry about not doing what I said.

"How do I get to Admin?" I questioned the soldier wearing his chromed helmet and green fatigues. "I have a meeting with the fort commander."

Sixty minutes later, I had my answers. The most notable answer was that Yuma has never billeted a soldier named Legg. I exited the Admin building and walked to the softball field to meet my so-called general. Legg was waiting on the bleacher seats near first base, wearing his general's uniform.

I was sure the Army Police would want to talk with him once the fort commander told them of my conversation.

I glared at the pale man. "What the hell is going on? Why are you wasting my time? I spoke with the fort commander. There's never been a theft of any material like you say. He says there's no super battlefield armor on the fort or any secret microchips anywhere. And mostly, there's no General Legg, to his recognition."

Legg glared back at me. "You shouldn't have done that. Colonel Kent's security doesn't go as far as my area. I lead research and development, not him. His group measures how far a cannon can shoot. My group finds ways to shoot it farther."

"Bullshit," I said. "There's never been a Kelly Lake working here. Never. I'm not even sure there is a Kelly Lake alive."

Legg answered, "Kelly Lake. You're an investigator. You should know he worked in research, not out here on the proving ground. Colonel Kent wouldn't know Lake if Lake walked up and grabbed his ass, much less any details of my group."

That tipped it—enough. "And what fucking general would set a meet in the blazing Arizona sun on a softball field in the middle of the day to talk about some darkshit memory chips? You're full of shit. I don't know your game, but you're wasting my time. Unless you come up with something real, McDonnell has spent all the money we're going to spend on your game."

General Legg stiffened and pulled a phone from his dress jacket in a huff. "Give me Kelly Lake's address and phone number." Legg scribbled in a small black notebook and ripped the page out. "That phone number may not be in use any longer, but the address should be real enough for you."

"We'll see."

The address proved to be a local Yuma location, not far from the fort. This man's game still churned my guts. Legg was a waste of time, no doubt, and the trip here proved it. But, if it weren't for Lake's message piercing our veil of secrecy and that damn mystery box, I would mark this as a hoax and head home to figure out how to handle Laura.

I stopped at the address Legg wrote on his paper. It would have been an apartment building at one time, but now it's a burned-down gray heap of ash on a concrete slab. A Mexican flag drawn on a man's work shirt across the street caught my eye. He sweated while singing songs and clearing dead frons high in a palm tree. Nearby him, a boy, roughly ten or twelve years old, stacked the fallen fronds on a trailer.

I called to the man up in the tree, "When did this place over here burn down?"

The boy stopped and yelled back to me, "He doesn't speak English."

I examined the heat cracks in the concrete slab of what used to be a 1950s eight-unit apartment building.

The boy came to my edge of the road. "But if you have five dollars, I know when it burned down." What a tyke.

"You want five dollars to tell me when this place burned down?" I couldn't help but laugh at America's latest member of capitalism. "I could go down to the newspaper and find out myself, you know."

The boy eased toward me in his dirty tan shorts, his hand held out. "But your time is your money, and you're too busy to waste time. Now the price is ten dollars."

I flashed the lad a stern face, but it didn't work. "You're a crook, and you know it." I retrieved two fives and paid before the price went to fifteen.

The kid examined my fives to make sure they weren't counterfeit. Once satisfied, he disclosed, "It burned down a couple of weeks ago. On my birthday, June 19. My apartment is there, up the street. So I chased the firetrucks down here."

I dialed Rory while I stood in the middle of the slab and kicked a burned 2x4 to watch it slide through the dust and fall off the edge. "Legg gave me Kelly Lake's address. It's a burned-out apartment building. I need you to check the Yuma obituaries around June 19 for Lake's name. See if there is anything about arson or anything."

Rory spoke back, "I'm in Watson right now. Let me check…It shows the closest one to you as a park ranger, along with the other dead Lakes. He patrolled the Cabeza Prieta National Monument, it says."

"A park ranger? Where's that park?"

"South of you. He was in a gunfight with a group of illegals coming over the border. He got shot. It looks like he came out of the cactuses wearing a toe tag."

"How reliable is the story?"

"The source, it says, is the Park Service Human Resources Data Center. Reliable enough, I'd say."

"When was it?"

"A year and a half ago."

Stress pulled at my temples, adding to my gray hair, I'm sure. "Crap. Whoever is yanking us around has been setting this up for a long time. I need you to do two things for me. First, see if you can come up with another name for Kelly Lake or anyone else who might have stolen a research facility memory chip. And have you been able to hack the Department of Defense system yet?"

"I gave up on the DoD. So far, Watson is giving me what I need."

"Then find me any billet anywhere in the Army where a General Legg might be assigned. I doubt it's Yuma. It occurred to me any good Army/Navy store can dress a man like a general."

"It'll take a while."

"In the morning, I'll be heading to Colorado Springs to meet Laura. I'll catch up with Flatley or Scaffe or whatever her name is on Monday, so text me her address when you get it."

Chapter 22

Colorado Springs, CO
Rick

For once, I didn't complain, letting Laura enjoy her first post-coitus cigarette in the bedroom of the Pinemoor Hotel. I jumped up and pulled the balcony door open, washing our room with Pikes Peak's piney smell, freshly mowed bluegrass, and a box of European summer flowers.

Sheets off, she said, "You're magic. It took a while, but you completely did it for me."

"I hope that's a compliment."

"It was meant to be. Thank you for putting up with me."

She flicked her ash away, carefully keeping it off the bed, then sauntered to the balcony, where the mountain breeze raised the tiny hairs on her bare arms. "A toast to us and a great day and life together."

I raised my Pinot Gris glass high. "To us, today, and to Brian."

"And Brian?" Her laugh came across Bacall's sultry.

I wrapped a thick terry robe around her bare body. "To Brian. I've been thinking about it, and I'm comfortable with what the two of you arranged. It does you good, and I'm learning it does good for me too."

"You continue to surprise me. But I have to say I'm glad to hear you don't want me to stop. I was afraid you would, and that's why you invited me up here." She took in a puff. "So, how's it good for you?"

I hesitated, unsure why I had included that part. "I'm not sure I can put it into words, but I find it…erotic…when you're off somewhere enjoying sex. Having you with someone else gives me a charge."

Her lips tightened into amusement. "I don't love Brian, you know. Not the tiny, littlest bit."

In the distance, our balcony at the Pinemoor overlooked Cheyenne Lake. A service cart made its way over the bridge, coming toward us. Rambunctious children shouted across the sandy beach on the lake's south. Opposite us, to the other side, patrons milled at the hotel bar.

"Regardless of what you say, you and Brian are not about your job. That's a byproduct of him reducing your stress. I think now that we have it out in the open, you'll start getting a thrill of having two men treating you special. I think you'll feel sparkly."

Laura smiled sheepishly. "Maybe it does. There's nothing wrong with that." She planted an extended kiss on my lips and wrapped her arms totally around me. "I love you for no reason other than you're my Ricky to take care of."

The balcony proved an excellent place for a kiss, holding each other, and caressing.

I refreshed our Pinot Gris. "How long do you think you'll want to do this?" Then I hastily added, "No more than wondering."

"I don't know. Sometimes I see it ending this week. Then I see the three of us going on forever—if the dynamic is right. You're happy. I'm happy."

"Does he travel with you?"

"Occasionally."

"What's type of work is he in?"

Her grin returned as she humored me. "Aren't you the husband with all the questions? I think you know already, but he sells gel for capsules, mostly in Europe. He's about to start supplying to Beyer, here in the States. So sometimes we meet up there. Are you okay with that?"

"I didn't know."

"Yes, you did. Sometimes I think Brian's on the road more than you…if that's possible."

"Is he traveling with you when you leave here?" My robe began to bulge, thinking that might be the case.

"I'm going back to Plano, but no, he's not." She guided me by my bulge. "Let's go back to bed."

****

Laura called for luggage pick-up and checked out of the Pinemoor to catch the first direct flight back to Dallas.

Alone, I nursed my breakfast coffee, absorbing the sun and aroma of fir trees and bluegrass growing up the expanse of Pike's Peak. When I dialed Rory to get my morning update, I was surprised.

"Anderson Weeks here," the lady's voice said.

"Andi?"

I checked the number I dialed to make sure I dialed correctly. Andi answering Rory's line could not be right in any way. "What's wrong?"

"Toby came in the office today. He's called an all-hands meeting. Everybody's down in the conference room."

Toby hates staff meetings. "What's going on?"
"You're gonna have to hear it directly from him."

Chapter 23

Plano, Texas
Laura

My mind spun about Brian. It spun about Rick, and it spun thinking of the three of us together. But I need to keep my mind on the Quality Control run from last night. On the screen, the report showed a significant production failure. It suggested that metal somehow contaminated one of the liquids mixed to make Klearance. Contamination was no good at all. I'd entered instructions for the entire batch to be taken offline and filtered, then resubmitted for acceptance testing. The other runs were clean.

Peter Bach, my Chem Lab supervisor, knocked on my door and entered without an invitation. "Did you see the Turboluken numbers from last night?"

I frowned at his unannounced entrance. "They were hard to miss."

Peter Bach continued, totally ignoring what I said, "The production tech said a piece of a nozzle broke off in the tank."

"Except for the metal contaminants, the rest looks okay. I sent instructions for them to filter it off and send it back for another sample." Truthfully, I was a bit taken back that Peter hadn't already ordered the lot filtering.

"I'll tell them." Peter Bach flipped the cover page to

his notepad. "Another thing you need to make a decision about is we need to find more storage for Klearance samples. I'm told you're holding several batches back. Are you all right if I incinerate them for more space?"

"No, I'm not. I want you to get me an accurate inventory of what we have. Then make some small dose containers. I need fifty inhaler-size tanks topped with 90% xenon and 10% helium. Have them containerized for international shipment. An Australian outfit is getting Klearance for data collection."

****

For the sake of safety, I rested Dr. Himbury's attaché on the banquette between me and the window. Thinking back, I'm not sure why I agreed to meet the Aussie here anyway. Junior's 24/7 Café never struck me as one of the safest night places for a single woman.

I ordered a glass of tomato juice with Worcestershire sauce and waited. Then, cigarette in the ashtray, elbows on the table, my phone in my hands, I went through my after-work email.

The waitress assigned to my booth beamed with a smile when she brought my drink. "Hi, darling," she said. "Would you like a croissant and some marmalade to go with your virgin Bloody Mary?" Then she leaned in and whispered, "And sister, you look a little overdressed for a hayseed joint like this. Are you in trouble? You need me to get you some help?"

"Oh, no. No, I'm fine. I'm waiting for a gentleman."

"Well, if you find one, sugar, don't forget to share. But…" The waitress stopped as a citrus-orange Volvo with one working headlight skidded into the handicap spot by the door.

Wearing a kangaroo vest, my sinewy man with his

cowboy hat squeezed out of the driver's side door. He tried slamming it a few times, then finally kicked the wobbly door shut.

The gingham-dressed waitress met him at the door. "She's over there. You be a gentleman, you hear, or my boys, we'll see you do."

The daily blue collars parked on the same diner stools they use each evening eyed the skinny Australian. He strutted across the room and swung his butt straight to my red vinyl booth.

My jaws, being clenched, should have told him all he needed to know about the uncomfortable situation he put me in. But then, the spectacle he made of himself coming in with that fancy little strut said it all.

"You seem to be the center of attention," I said. "Best we make this quick. We had less Klearance than I estimated, but you'll still have enough to put down your fifty stump animals or wherever you keep them. Tell your friends, when you get home, to covet what you have and use it wisely. It's going to be a while before the next production run."

I pushed the attaché across the table, then took out a demonstration dosing unit from my purse. The tiny cylinder stood upside down on a protective frame. Out of it came a flexible tube to route the medication to wherever it was needed. "Hold it like this, remove these red safety pins, and press the container down to dispense the drug. I had some instructions drawn up. I'm sure you can adapt them to your needs. Don't forget your masks."

Chapter 24

Worldwide News Wire
(AP) Associated Press
Bishop Joseph Ferring of Montgomery Dead
By Starla Hamp
(Montgomery, Al)—The Montgomery Diocese reports Most Reverend Bishop Joseph Ferring has joined the Lord following his untimely passing at 77 years. The cause of his death is unknown currently. Parishioners found the Bishop in the confessional of Saint Agatha's Cathedral this past Monday morning. His Reverend Bishop Ferring's Mass will be on Wednesday, followed by interment in the cathedral crypt.

Bishop Ferring was named native 9th Bishop of Montgomery.

Before his appointment to the Alabama diocese, he served as auxiliary bishop in Anchorage, Alaska.

Born January 14, 1942, Joseph Longfellow Ferring was the oldest of four children born to English-American baker Daniel Ferring and Rita, his wife. Ordained by the Archdiocese of Chicago in 1969, he served in pastoral and youth education assignments until appointed apostolic administrator of Anchorage, AK, following Bishop Lawrence Gamble's retirement. In October, he became bishop of Anchorage.

During his time in Rome, Bishop Ferring earned a licentiate in theology from the Academia Alphonsiana and a Doctor of Theology from the Pontifical University of St. Thomas Aquinas. A moral theologian and history lover, his parish knew Bishop Ferring for his humility and vibrant teachings of Jesus Christ, his frequent outbreaks into song, and his concern for those less fortunate. His spirit increased local enrollment in the seminary by two-fold to 18. At his death, he ordained 32 men to the priesthood.

He was a member of USCCB's Administrative Committee on Doctrine and Bishops' Life and Ministry. He also served as chairmanship to the Committee on Science and Human Value. In addition, he headed a series of annual lectures on the relationship between science and religion.

The Church rejoices in his passing.

Chapter 25

Colorado Springs, Colorado
Rick

As much as anything, I wanted to ascertain that the woman Je and I came across at the grassy knoll was the same little girl I knew from old Londonderry. And assuming she was, how did she get mixed up in this ugly game? How did Kelly Lake come to select her? I was reasonably sure of the answer to that one, but did she have an idea what was hidden in the box? Rory messaged me. Her apartment was nestled in the Rampart Range foothills before getting to the Garden of Gods. I drove northwest out of Colorado Springs in the direction of the mountains.

Exiting a half-dozen switchbacks, the secret service-style SUV I rented strained against the repetition of long hills ahead of me. Its engine groaned, needle pointing to the top of the tachometer, a spot inferior to the McLaren I wish I had with me for these hills. My satellite phone vibrated. I jabbed the answer button. "Yeah."

"We made progress." The call came from Rory.

"Tell me."

"First, let me ask, have you spoken to anyone about Mark Gower?"

"What happened?"

With a fusion of glee and remorse in his voice, Rory

started with, "At the all-hands, Toby told us the police arrested Mark Gower last night at his home."

"Arrested?"

"Yeah. US Marshalls and a British Ministry of Something busted into his house and hauled him off. They've already deported him to the UK."

While I didn't care for Mark, US Marshalls breaking in and hauling off anyone without due process bristled my spine. "They've already taken him out of the country? Can they do that?"

"They did," Rory answered what was obviously a rhetorical statement.

"Who was it from the UK?"

"Somebody official, I guess. He's gone. Why does it matter?"

Like him, I, too, started imagining a world with *Gower finally out of our hair. Let them have him.* "I'm not complaining. I'm surprised someone can break into your house and snatch you. I'll get with Toby when I get back. You said 'first,' what else?"

"You were right about General Legg. There hasn't been a General Legg in the US military since World War II. This guy's an imposter."

"Figured. Were you able to get another name for the person who did the Yuma heist, or am I stuck with Kelly Lake?"

Sometimes he did this. He prolongs my anticipation intentionally. And when he did, it pissed me off. "You're not going to believe this, but if you remember, when we were sniffing around for Kelly Lake last week, the military networks were covered with articles about him. Now they're gone—no articles—nothing anywhere. Kelly Lake is nowhere on DoD Net."

In my mirror, an ambulance was coming up the hill behind me with his flashing red and blue lights going but no siren. "You're saying he disappeared? Why? How long does it take to clear something from their systems once they realize they've been hornswoggled?"

"Apparently, not long."

"Okay." I paused, reviewing my conversation at the Proving Grounds. Had the fort commander triggered the data purge?

"What about *Lucy Q*," I asked. "Do you have any updates on the memory device?"

"So, here's the last thing I have. The Coast Guard shows that *Lucy Q* filed a float plan for Nassau Bahama. She sailed yesterday out of Miami. Our guys have been watching her on the Coast Guard's radar. She's staying on course."

****

When I got there, an EMT had already readied a gurney. Its legs unfolded; the man laid straps across the cushion where he figured someone would need them.

A senior woman with auburn streaks outlining her gray curls stood on the front porch of a two-floor apartment building behind a screen door. She appeared to be questioned by a suited police detective, gesturing toward the ceiling of her unit and the wall of the victim's place.

I stepped out of my SUV and made a stealthy walk around the corner to the side of the old lady's half-timber building. According to Rory, this is where Carissa would be found.

And there behind the blinds, he proved to be correct. Carissa Scaffe peeked out with an eye on the flashing ambulance, her gaze going back and forth to the front.

Then, with me standing by the window watching her, she caught a glimpse of me.

"What do you want?" She yapped a defensive yap.

I answered her much quieter, not raising interest in the detective. "I think I know the answer to this," I said softly, "but does Morgan Flatley live here?"

The vanes of her blinds open, and she responded, "Why?"

"I simply want to know. I'll come back."

Curling back toward the SUV, I stood in the grass near the sidewalk to watch the investigation unfold. One of the CID men wearing a white paper moon suit came out of the front door dangling a large zip-lock bag. A revolver packed with vials of white powder and empty gun casings lay in it.

Several uniformed cops made the round trip in and out of the victim's apartment. Others craned for a peek in at the crime scene. The rest of them stood as busy as lampposts, kibitzing back and forth among one another. Then the gray-suit detective finished with the old lady and addressed his collection of peers, apparently breaking up their chit-chat. Then, he disappeared inside the crime scene for five minutes or so. When he exited, he pointed toward me and barked something to one of his men, who made a straight line to where I stood. That one ordered me to get back into my SUV.

The gurney came down the sidewalk with a white sheet concealing someone. The EMT rolled the deceased head-first into his ambulance. Then, with its flashing lights off, the ambulance drove away. At the same time, other officers dressed in white brought evidence bags out, cameras, and tripods. Finally, a female officer sealed the apartment door with yellow tape, and with her peers gone, she too left.

My turn.

The woman with the auburn-striped hair responded when I knocked on her screen door. Inside, her mint color living room was orderly enough and clean from what I could see through the screen and the cracked inter door.

I flashed my Senate Inspector ID badge, anticipating she would associate me with the cops leaving the murder scene. "I talked with Morgan earlier. Maybe you could let me in."

The older woman tried to read my brass badge as it passed. "You stay outside. I'll see if I can find her."

It occurred to me Kelly Lake might be the next face I see. If so, *should I take him down and haul him somewhere?* On the other hand, if it is a man, I have no way of knowing if he's Kelly Lake or not. I've never seen Lake, and no one has ever given me a good description of him. He'd have the advantage, so I locked my knees and braced.

Instead, the older woman nudged a younger woman's face toward me. Carissa finally stood face-on in front of me, behind the aluminum screen.

I checked her top to bottom, then behind to see if anyone else was in there before flashing my ID. "Once and for all, are you Morgan, Morgana, or Carissa—Flatley or Scaffe?"

She squinted in the sunshine. "I already asked, what's it to you? Who are you?"

"Richard Haade. This is official."

She studied my face. "I know you, don't I? Official what?"

"I doubt it," I answered in an all-knowing voice that

officials attempted to make. "I'm closing an active case. Can I come in and clear up a few simple bits?"

She hesitated at first, then unlatched the screen door and, in a drooping way, shuffled a path back to her kitchen—her feet hardly holding her slippers on. She poured herself a coffee from a cold pot and dialed up the microwave.

"I think I know who you are," she said. "What do you want?"

"I want to talk about your trip to Dallas."

"Never been there."

"You were on a bus I'm interested in, and you didn't get off at the book depository."

"I've never been there." Her neutral tone seemed dull and lifeless, not the voice she demonstrated at the window.

"Don't start that, Carissa. Things are getting worse every time you lie." For sure, this is the girl Toby, and I bounced on our knees in Northern Ireland.

The microwave timer sounded like a tinny ancient ding. "How do you know my real name?"

I asked her, "Who's the old lady?"

"Her? She's my mother."

"I know your mother. That's not your mother."

The elder made herself comfortable in a side chair and crossed her arms.

"You don't know my mother."

I said, becoming frustrated. "Let's pretend I do."

Carissa glared back. "Let's pretend you don't. My mother's dead."

"So, this isn't your mother?"

The older woman's voice came from the living room. "No, thank you, honey. None for me. I've already finished mine."

Puzzled, I stared at Carissa, then the older woman in the living room.

"Don't mind what she says. She's got rats in her belfry."

"You not getting off the bus got one of my friends in big trouble." I paused to watch her reaction, then added, "You may have made him lose his certification."

"I've never been to Dallas. I told you." She shook her head in total denial.

I showed her the close-up picture I took of her on the bus. "What was it in the backpack you were supposed to drop off?"

"What backpack?"

"That one between your knees."

"A Senate Investigator? There's no such thing."

"Lying isn't working, Carissa."

Finally, her fence came down, and she gave me a straight answer. "Listen. I needed rent and caught a break, so I carried it. Lake paid me $500."

"Kelly Lake was your man?" She piqued my interest. "Is he here in Colorado?"

"Phoenix. Why," she asked, "did you tell me you knew my mother?"

"I was in Londonderry when you were tiny. You and your mother stayed with my partner and me for a bit." Fond memories they were. "So, how close are you to Kelly Lake?"

"Not so much. I did the one job." She drew her arms tight around her middle section.

"How did you two connect?"

Carissa's surrogate mom fell asleep with a snore in her comfy chair. "We met over donuts at a truck stop. He came across as weird, but the money was right."

"Weird?"

She nodded. "Like a serial killer. Like a Unabomber. I don't know."

"Do you still think he is dangerous?"

"No."

"So, you and he wasn't a one-time thing?" My heart thumped at the possibility of this case starting to make sense. "Would you say you see him a lot?"

The old lady's eyes popped wide open, and she got up, heading to the back rooms, a tail of knitting yarn trailing the carpet behind her.

Carissa shifted attention. "Sometimes, I feel sorry. She used to be bright and giving."

It wasn't my place to say it, but I suggested, "Dementia?"

"Yep." She nodded.

"Sorry," I said. "Is this your phone over here?" I grabbed it from the table, wrote down the model and serial number, and thumbed through her call log. "I take it you're still interested in Lake. You have a lot of calls to him. How often do you see each other?"

"Not much."

"Take a guess."

She hesitated. "About every month or so, maybe two."

"That's a long time between visits for people who talk as much as you do. Now, Dallas. Did you ever see what was in the backpack?"

"It rattled is all I know. A black metal box was in there. Then Kelly told me to leave it alone."

"About how big would you guess?"

"I don't know. Not too." She held her two hands

several inches apart.

"Light or heavy?"

"Heavy. Several pounds."

I asked her, "Can you guess what it might have been, then?"

"Not an idea." She took another sip of yesterday's coffee.

"How about Lake? Give me some specifics: who he is, what does he look like, where does he hang out?"

Then from the table, Carissa's phone vibrated. "Hello? ... But," she said. "Okay." She returned the phone to the table. "That was him. He told me not to tell you anything about him."

"That was Lake?"

She nodded, yes.

I made a visual scan of the place, turning on my bug detector app. It pointed me to a DIY lamp vase. I found a taped microphone transmitter on the underside. I removed it and returned the vase light to the table.

"Kelly Lake," I said, "has been listening in on you and the old lady."

Unbelieving what I said, she blinked numbly at the little half-finger-sized cylinder rolling around in my palm.

I dropped the device into a zippy plastic bag before leaving and told her, "So, you know, I only believe about half of what you told me. We'll do this again after you think about it for a while. When you change your mind, here's my card."

I slid the two-and-a-half by three-and-a-half-inch card under her coffee cup.

Chapter 26

Dallas, Texas
Rick

"I'm bringing in the bug I found in Carissa Scaffe's apartment. Kelly Lake has been listening in on her and some old lady living with her," I messaged Rory. "See if an IP address is in it or anything else which might indicate where he is. I messaged you her cell phone's serial number a little while ago. Do your magic with Horizon Data and find her conversations. See what she and Kelly Lake have been talking about."

I picked the nonstop between Colorado Springs and Dallas-Fort Worth. When I got to our office on Central Expressway, I found Anderson Weeks micromanaging two painters who were refurbishing Gower's old office. After watching the three for a minute, I asked Andi, "Has Toby said anything to you about his health?"

Surprised, she responded, "I haven't seen him. Haven't you talked with him after he announced he's stepping down?"

I didn't answer.

"You should have." Andi hurried to the spot where the short painter dripped dark brown paint onto the floor. Had this been a Catholic School, Sister Andi would be working his knuckles over with a ruler, and they would be bleeding. She swore at him, "You stop that. These are expensive tiles."

The painter made a big mistake when he snorted back at her, "Stop what? Them little things? Babe, don't let that shit ruffle your panties." Andi was the wrong person to say that to.

She firmed like Medusa, her face becoming pepper red. Her eyes squinted. Her jaw clenched her teeth together, and she quivered from the arms up.

Oh, what a mistake. I told the man, "Shorty, if I were you, I'd high-step down and put some distance between you and her. You just unleashed the she-devil of the building. If she catches you, she's going to snatch your nuts off, and there's no telling what floor they're going to end up on."

Shorty, unsure, cleared his throat.

Anderson Weeks took a half step his way, staring up with those dark eyes, and made a throat-clearing growl of her own.

Before things deteriorated more, I distracted her. "Is Toby camping at home?"

Shorty on the ladder cowered, quickly coming down. Andi answered, "Yes, but don't bother him. He said he's going to take some medicine and lay down."

Satisfied I saved the man's soul, I admonished him, "Don't let this thing anywhere you. Professional wrestlers shake."

On my way back to the elevator, I picked Je as my next target. When I got to his office, he leaned over his desk, elbows locked. He was studying a three-dimensional model of San Juan Harbor covering his desk.

I interrupted whatever he might be doing. "Looks like my newest agent is ahead of me."

"According to Rory, the *Lucy Q* changed courses last night and is now heading to Puerto Rico." He failed to look up. "I figure we should jump ahead and meet 'em when they arrive."

"Rory said?" I asked.

"I bought him lunch."

I scanned over his colorful model. "Does the name Kelly Lake ring a bell with you?"

He waited for a second. "No. Should it?"

"He seems to be the one at the bottom of this." I took his one guest chair. "I went to Yuma where I was supposed to meet our General Legg. Well, not only is he lying about being the Post Commander, but the real commander also said there's never been a data heist there, ever."

Je relocated to his young man ergo desk chair. "So could Yuma be covering the robbery story to protect something?"

"Could be. Kelly Lake was all over the military networks until yesterday when he disappeared. Rory saved the specifics about the memory chip. Kelly Lake is the center of it." My mouth was going dry. "I could use two fingers of Woodford if you got it."

Je shook his head. No alcohol for this hombre.

"You're gonna have to put in a bar if you want your promotion," I teased with a grin. "There's more. Rory connects to the DoD Personnel System. It says there hasn't been a General Legg in the military since World War II.

"And by the way, the woman you know as Morgan Flatley, her real name is Carissa Scaffe. Kelly Lake paid her $500 to do the bus drop scam we chased downtown."

Je leaned back. "I'm sorry, but you lost me

somewhere around Woodford."

"It'll come to you. Someone is filling this case with extensive fluff, for what reason I have no idea."

"So, you're canceling our trip to sunny San Juan?"

"No. I think most of what we're seeing is a ruse. Still, some parts seem to be real."

"So, we're going. I don't think we can afford to let that boat and that box getaway, you know, in case."

"If the *Lucy Q* turns out to be a dud, I'm telling Toby we're killing the case out of lack of substance. We'll get something else for your certification."

****

Owning a McLaren 720S in Toby's neighborhood was barely conversational. Of course, the beef belting from its tailpipes does turn heads, but anyone who owns a house in Toby's area could have two of these if they want.

Maria stood in the door sidelight, watching me lower the car's gull-wing and pace up the circular drive. She wore a dust net over her hair—cleaning day. She opened the sculpted Mediterranean bronze front door before I knocked. "Shush. Master sleep. He not feeling so pretty well." Then she took my Texas Rangers ball cap.

"Has he said anything about why he's not feeling well?" I asked. "I think something's wrong."

"You, he friends. I not supposed to tell anyone, but okay, I tell you some things. Two days ago, I hear him say to his *medico*, uh, doctor, 'How bad is it?' He on his black pocket phone. He says, 'How long if I do nothing?' You know?"

"If I do nothing?" I repeated in the form of a question.

"Jes," she said.

Maria and Toby go back at least fourteen years to when Laura and I married. Toby hired her from some immigrant pool to help with our wedding reception.

"How long has he been upstairs in his room?"

Maria pursed her lips. "He calls his office this morning. He say he not coming to work need rest. Since then, he has been up there."

I knocked on Toby's door and pushed the golden lion head handle, cracking it to peek inside the darkened room. I kept quiet, stepped inside, and pulled a wingback chair to his bedside. "Why is it so dark in here?" I could see his eyes were open.

"There's no light. That's the definition of darkness. I don't like light today."

"Was yesterday a better light day?"

Toby whispered tenderly, "Yesterday, I didn't have cancer. The rule is, as long as they don't tell you, you don't have it."

I blinked, trying to think of something to say. "So, that's what Doctor Toby thinks?"

"Quit. My doctor said I have stage two prostate cancer."

I sniggered. "I was afraid you were going to say something bad. I got loads of friends with stage two and three prostate cancers. Some have both at the same time."

He glared me down. "No, you don't. There's no such thing."

"There is."

"No, there's not." Toby sat up. "Okay, who? I want to know."

I hesitated, thumbing idly through his TV Guide.

"You don't need to know."

"I do. I need to know who these people are. Give me two."

"Two? You don't need any. Okay, two…one is…John Lennon. The other is…Audrey Hepburn. They're not in our industry, so I doubt you know them."

"You're a moron. First, Lennon was a Beatle, and he got shot cold dead in New York about a million years ago, and Hepburn was an actress, and she's been dead even longer. You can't even make up good dead people."

I rebuffed, "Well?"

He kicked his covers off, and his brain changed gears. "You're pathetic; you know that? Let's go to the office."

****

Evening came, with it the opportunity to swipe an Old Fashioned from the pub. I found my way to the darkest corner of the far back. My hands quivered as I inserted my wireless earbuds. Guilt, I figure. Secretly, I wanted to hear Laura and Brian going at it without them knowing I was listening. What does she do when she's with another man away from home? How does she act in another man's arms, and what will she do to him? Voyeurism might be my new favorite porn.

Or maybe I should call it off.

A man was the first voice coming from the earpiece, maybe Brian's, and in the background, it sounded like wine pouring. "You've stopped wearing a bra."

Laura would never go braless. Self-conscious? That must not have been right.

"Do you like it?" she questioned.

"You know I do."

"Your fingers are cold," she said. "Stop."

"I'm getting your nipples hard." Brian softly responded, "I like the way your boobs effortlessly move when we walk. You have to be proud." Glasses clinked before he said, "And I like it when we're walking together, and other guys can't keep their eyes off your dancing chest."

She won't be putting up with that talk for long.

"Before you came along," she said, "I would never go to dinner without a bra. It felt dirty, having people look at me, but if you like it, I'm all in."

It brought a good laugh from Brian and planted a coldness in my chest. *For you? How about me?*

"Even without me," Brian's voice said in my earpiece, "you're what most women envy."

"Not at home. It's work, and whiskey, and Victorian life."

Victorian life?

Her sigh came as if it originated within his arms. A shiver crept down my spine.

"My god, you feel so good. Go slower."

"Should we take it to the bedroom?"

Laura answered in a baby voice, "Let's finish on the sofa tonight. Keep. Uhm."

A pair of pants unzipped, and a belt buckle hit a hardwood floor. This was enough. I pressed the disconnect button. *God damn, that was fun.*

Chapter 27

Dallas, Texas
Rick

I opened my eyes, head on the pillow, and stared at the ceiling-diamonds sparkling from the rain outside. Finally, I kicked my covers off sometime through the night. With Laura in Pittsburgh and me on the road so often, I've gotten used to the loneliness. Last night I indeed hung lonely. My phone woke me.

Laura's voice sounded like Brian satisfied her. Her voice bounced between words. She asked, "Are you headed to Puerto Rico? Make sure you pack some shorts and sandals. You never know; you might learn to enjoy yourself while you're down there. I know that's a lot to ask."

I sat on the side of the bed, slipping my house slippers on. "I know how to enjoy myself. I can be plenty of fun. But, on the other hand, I might be turning into an old fart. Is that what you think, too?"

"I wouldn't say an old geezer. Why? You've never enjoy yourself."

"Never mind."

I took the DART light rail to DFW airport to catch a 10:30 morning flight to San Juan. With any luck, Je and I will snag Kelly Lake on the *Lucy Q*. And if we're fortunate, he will have the metal box with him—another mystery solved. But I know catching Kelly Lake is more hope than expectation.

I picked up a cinnamon roll and coffee for Je at the DFW Admiralty Club.

Classless Harley Je dressed for the flight like a Hawaiian tourist. "I haven't been on vacation since," he said, "... well, I guess I've never been on vacation."

"This ain't a vacation. Let's grab the table over by the window." I put down my quarter-folded Dallas News and chugged my coffee. "If this is real, whatever is behind it's going to be so bad no one is willing to take ownership. I want to make sure you understand. This fake case could also be lethal."

Je played with his newly purchased diving watch.

"So, calibrate me," I said. "Is it so big discovering the United States has a new tank alloy? We always have new alloys. So what? If Russia steals the formula and starts making tanks from it, what difference does that make? We're never going to war with Russia. Or China, for that matter. We're not going to war with anybody if there's even the remotest chance we would lose. Whatever's in that box is bigger than Russia, America, and China combined—assuming it's not fake."

Not hearing a word I said, Je continued to tinker with his watch and first-class ticket.

I took the ticket from his hand. "Put this in your pocket and leave the damned watch alone."

The San Juan flight finished with a serpentine approach over the azure Caribbean. The plane pointed leeward, nose up, and made the short roll to the terminal after a bounce or two. Je hailed us a green-and-orange Island Checker taxi.

I told my partner, "I want us to find the *Lucy Q* first

before we go to the hotel. Lake will be relaxed. He thinks we took his bate and are waiting in Nassau. Let's make sure she's in one piece."

Salt air scoured our faces from the open cab window, hair blowing in disarray. The driver occasionally had eyes on me in his mirror. I said, "Take us to docks off of Old Fort Morrow."

As we drew near the channels and passed a string of docks, I spotted what proved to be bad news. "That rigging is sticking out of the water; I hope that's not the *Lucy Q*."

From behind the steering wheel, the driver broke his silence. "It came in yesterday. An American captain scuttled her where she sat."

"Scuttled?" I quizzed. *Did Lake know we were coming? Why sink the Lucy Q?*

Once the taxi driver stopped, I jumped from the back seat and rushed to the end of Rodrigo's Wharf, which extends into the channel. Our small freighter settled straight to the bottom, obviously backing up the morning's fishing fleet.

A weathered seaman picked through used cigarette butts lying around to find one with enough tobacco left in it to light.

"Bad deal, I'd say," he mumbled toward me with a voice abused by sun, liquor, and smokes.

"Do you know who this was?"

He said, "Some American fishermen…he docked yesterday."

"Is this the *Lucy Q*?"

"Yup. It is." He put flame to a stubbed cigarette butt he found in a wharf crack.

"So, what happened?"

"Captain pulled her in behind these others. They say he killed the engine, cut the cooling hoses below the waterline, and she went straight down."

Je asked, "The captain did it himself?"

"They say he took an ax to the hull after cutting the hoses, and the next thing you know, Davy Jones had him in the deep." The smoke died out, hitting the filter.

I handed Je a twenty. "Run over to the icehouse and get him as many cigarettes as twenty bucks will buy."

The fisherman thanked me with a lopsided nod, his whiskers brushing the curly hair on his exposed boney chest. "Some say another fellow swum free, headed to the other side of the channel, getting on the sandy shore over there. Divers brought the captain's body up this afternoon. They lay him here in the sun until the city came and carried him off. Some say the wet spot he left won't ever leave this dock, yup."

I asked the man, "Any idea who has jurisdiction over this shipping channel?"

He made a line in the air with a gnarled and disjointed finger toward Highway 1. "Follow the road down that way. You'll see the sign for the wharf manager."

Je called in a second taxi to take us along the only highway on this part of the island.

"Rodrigo's Sea Services," the sign read, and I said aloud. "That must be it." I handed the cabbie a ten for the short trip.

Inside a yellow-painted shack, a retired barnacle greeted us. A crop of gray hair strings scattered across a nearly bald head, and an unlit cigar waggled between his teeth. He gruffed a bark our way, "I seen ya out on my dock. Is *Lucy Q* your lumber blockin' my canal?"

"Maybe."

Rodrigo scowled. "When ya gonna get your timbers outta my way? You're blockin' men lookin' for a good day's fishing."

Harley Je interrupted, "Any idea what happened?"

"The damn thing sank." Rodrigo scratched over an anchor tattoo on his shoulder.

"We can see that. So why did it sink?"

"Too much water got inside." He snubbed down on Je. "When're ya gonna get it outta my channel?"

I couldn't help but share my amazement with Je via a me-to-him chuckle. "Has anyone claimed salvage rights?"

"I did," the man said, "now you showed up. You can have 'em if ya get it outta my water. I got traffic needs passage."

I let a slow, pleased grin show. "I'll take rights then."

"Done. Get your shit outta our way."

"Provided," I answered, "you haven't let anyone dive on her already. Has there been anyone?"

"Just them rescue bunch lookin' for the captain. Rest his soul."

I said to Capt. Grouchy, "My partner here will have a barge and cradle over her this afternoon. Word has it, there was a second guy on board. You wouldn't have a name or place I can find him?"

"Kelly Lake was his name. Port Authority lists him as a paying passenger. American with no address. He skedaddled soon as they let him loose."

The cabbie drove us to the Carlton Central Hotel, a mile from Old Spanish town, two miles from Fort Morrow. The lobby was always open. It had no front or back door, allowing a constant tropical breeze through for the guests. Varnished native wood went up the walls from white coral flooring. A casino was hidden in the basement with a guest bar between reality and fantasy. I chose fantasy.

After we got our drinks, I told Je, "I'm going back to Dallas tonight. You stay and get a local crane to lift the *Lucy Q* out of the water and store her in a rolling cradle. Get her out of everybody's way."

"It's getting late." He saw beyond me, through the hotel's arched backdoor, to the sunset Caribbean waters.

"You're going to find that people will work any time if they can make money. They'll work straight through the night if the price is right. So, find the right price."

Even though Je nodded, I could tell this was not how he wanted to spend his evening, but he said, "Okay."

"Once you get the boat on land, put armed guards on board and four more at the base of the cradle. Nothing is to leave the boat without you giving the go-ahead."

I could tell Je was still eyeing the pool and the path to the beach, both the envy of every tourist.

"I don't want to hear about you frolicking in the damn ocean until this is over. This is not a vacation."

"I'll get our maritime surveyor over here in the morning to determine exactly how it went down. Then I'll put a crew on to go over her for the box."

"Mast to the keel." I took a piece of paper from the hotel registrar's desk and wrote a phone number. "These people are in Fort Myers. Get them down here to help you find any hole a six-by-nine-inch box could hide. Then rip it apart."

"There's a company in Old Town that'll do the same," he updated my opinion. "I'll get them started tonight. But wouldn't you think, if Lake were smart, he'd have taken the box with him?"

"For this exercise, here, let's assume he left it. I don't think we understand the jerk enough to presume otherwise. So, from here on, wear your Agent-in-Charge hat."

****

A blue message light kept flashing on my phone, indicating a text message from Carissa. It read, "Check your email. You need to see these photographs."

My flight was crossing over New Orleans when I scrolled down the email to a set of black and white Denver News snapshots. The story headline read *'Seven Die in Keystone Pileup.'* The first snap came from a helicopter above eastbound I-70 showing heavy traffic stopped in both directions. The second showed a ground-level shot of snowdrifts in a mid-summer mountain snowstorm. The faces of the seven dead people are shown in the last image. Carissa circled the head of the man on the end. The news claimed him to be Kelly Lake.

She had typed under it, "I don't know who this man is, but he's not Kelly Lake."

First-class passengers exited before coach tickets. I smoothed my hair and made sure my Caribbean shirt was buttoned correctly. *Victorian? Who says I'm Victorian? Not me.* As I closed the gullwing door on the McLaren in the secure airport parking, I pressed Laura's phone icon on the dash.

"Hi, honey," she greeted.

"Looks like I'm going to be in town tonight," I said. "Maybe we can go out. I have open tickets to the Pops Symphony. Are you free?"

"Oh. You said you were going to be out of town. I'm

occupied right now."

"I got back early."

"Ah, Brian and I are at the movies. You didn't tell me how I could get in touch."

"That's okay. I got in a little early. Well, never mind."

She said, "I could come home when it's over."

"No," I responded, "stay. I'm going to drop by McKinney Avenue for a few slurps of Woodford, then turn in early." As I hung up, for the first time, I had the feeling of being a three-string banjo at a hoedown. *Well fuck.*

When I settled in at the bar, my usual tender asked me, "Your regular Old Fashioned, Mr. Haade?"

"No," I said. "Tonight, I want you to set up a line of shot glasses, start filling them and see if I can keep up with you."

By the time I found my feather pillow, my head had disconnected from my body. The room spun. On the one hand, I didn't want to, but I couldn't resist pressing the link to Laura's phone tap and placing it on the pillow next to my ear.

Those were not the sounds of a movie.

It sounded more like heavy breathing—thrashing between sheets—faster breathing—two people pushing against each other. Then there was a deep man's primal groan. The thrashing sped up. Then Laura's music started. I love Laura's song.

I tried to break through the spinning fog and focus on the phone's video screen, hoping what they were doing would get me going. Instead, the spinning stopped, and the bedroom faded to black.

Chapter 28

Madrid, Spain
El Pais Daily Newspaper
SUDDEN DEATH OF NEWLY ELECTED GUATEMALA PRESIDENT
By Hector Beirut
(Guatemala) Guatemalan President Brianmy Argueta, 44, elected for his second term, died Thursday in his hotel room near Villa Nueva's family compound. Police reported hotel staff found him alone in bed with no sign of struggle. Argueta led the Popular Party. The cause of death is unknown.

Vice President Otto Girardi accepted the position of president.

The State Medical Examiner ordered Argueta's body transferred to Guatemala City for autopsy. It has failed to determine the cause of death. Toxicology studies are underway. "Results," the police chief said, "can be expected to take a few weeks."

After his death, an internet video appeared from a previously unknown organization claiming responsibility for his death. The group, calling themselves Brahms 4, gave no reason for the president's death nor the method of his assassination. Still, the tape contained enough site details to make it credible. Police are investigating.

Highly regarded internationally, Argueta won his

second term in a landslide election due to the nation's gains during his first term. His party is credited with significant improvements in personal freedom, ownership of property, and tourism. During this time, Guatemala rose in the World Heritage Freedom Rating, now above Portugal.

The Chief of Guatemala City Police has assigned the nation's military guard to protect the crime scene until the coroner determines President Argueta's cause of death.

Argueta is survived by his nation; two sons, Santiago and Mateo; one daughter, Mariana. His mother, father, and wife Luciana Argueta preceded him in death. He also fathered three grandsons and two granddaughters. His body lies in state at the capital.

Chapter 29

Dallas, Texas
Rick

When Andi caught sight of me coming her way from the elevator, she jumped Tasmanian on me. "What the hell gives you the right to come in here like that?"

I dragged past her to my desk, now overlooking mid-morning downtown. "You squeak, Andi. Shut up."

"And what on Earth have you been doing, might I ask?

"I feel like Vesuvius and Pompei. Last night, I got my bartender to line up shots and told him to try and keep up with me. I'm pretty damn sure, somewhere he won."

She poured me an Ojo Rojo. "Laura didn't let you out this morning. Did she? Your wife would never have let you out in public, smelling like rotgut. Did she even see you? Have you showered?"

I slumped into my office sofa. "I don't know. I don't remember getting sprinkled. I think Laura is…somewhere."

"Well, she wouldn't let you out like this. She must be in Pittsburgh."

I realized then straightened up. "Where's my McLaren?"

Andi pointed her index finger at me and shook it, "Drink this Rojo and get yourself in Toby's shower. I'll put fresh clothes on the vanity. You're a disgrace to spydom."

"I want my car."

"We'll find your car." She pushed me in the direction of Toby's shower. "There's only so many half-million-dollar lemon sports cars that can park on McKinney."

Chapter 30

San Juan, PR
Kelly Lake

Toward the middle of this solstice Caribbean day, San Juan offered their tourist an average UV rating of 11 on the skin blister scale.

I approached the overnight freight counter, and a clerk in a brown shirt and cap greeted me. "How can I help you?" He was a muscular box thrower with skin about the same color as his shirt and home-bleached white teeth.

I passed four identical cardboard boxes across the counter to him and the weight scale.

"You've labeled them already," my instant buddy shared.

"Does it matter?" I answered. "I do need them to go out today. Has today's plane landed?"

"She's on the tarmac right now, a brand new 7-5-7. Your packages are gonna be on her inaugural flight." He slid each box across the scale and scanned my tracking codes. "Let's see where we're going," he failed to stop talking. "Boston, a freight forwarder…Dublin, rural delivery…Londonderry, a Chemist shop. That's what they call 'em over there and finally, the city of Cork. Is this a residence? …Yes …You're shipping everywhere."

I made an eye sweep outside and behind me before answering, "I make hobby parts. Internet sells."

"Sounds fun. Let's get them parts on the plane."

Chapter 31

Dallas, Texas
Rick

The shower didn't help. Forget being run over by the donut truck. Someone had lashed me to a tree and let a bear molest me all night. Against my will, I ached my way down the elevator to Rory's conference room on the 34th floor. I called Andi to bring me another Ojo Rojo. My head was filled with tuba and twangy Japanese Koto music.

Rory linked his tablet to his room's projector as I went heads-down on my forearms at the table. "Now," he said, "Let me show you something. Are you okay?"

"Just don't stop."

"That giant man leaning against the Texas School Book Depository—his name is Sampson—Maurice Sampson."

I reexamined the image on the wall. *He's a Sampson if ever I've seen one.* Rory walked around me, stopping at the head of the table near the image. He circled a second area on the picture with a blue laser. "This piece of the other guy's face matches Kelly Lake. So, you got both of your guys in one shot. Good on you."

"Do you have a front view of Lake?"

"No, but this side shot matches that photograph from the Denver News."

"Then he's not our Kelly Lake. At least, according to Carissa Scaffe. Besides, if Lake was at the depository, she would have told me."

"What can I say? You're getting too close to her." Rory shrugged off my comment. "According to the Draft Board, the IRS, and Federal Health and Human Resources, this face is his. You're too close to your lady—she's lying to you—Rick."

"I don't think so." I shook my head and shaking hurt. "I think she's level with me, at least to the best of her ability. The Denver News pictures aren't the man she's dating."

Rory gave me an incredulous stare as I returned to the heads-down position. "Even so."

I spoke from the cracks in my elbows, "The man you're showing died in the traffic accident. His name might be Kelly Lake, but he's not our Kelly Lake. Ours is alive and well, swimming somewhere in San Juan harbor." I moved a ballpoint pen from the middle of the table when Andi ushered in my tonic. "There's some other person Carissa calls Kelly Lake. To me, this case is starting to feel like some sort of corporate espionage scheme. Someone out there specifically wants a round of cat and mouse with McDonnells." I drank down her god's nectar. "See if you can find any record where McDonnells has stepped on someone." I slid the remains of the highball glass to the center of the table, where Andi picked it up. "Did you find out any more about the Army heist?"

"Not so much. The noise on the government networks is all about some Air Force mischief."

"Anything else?"

"I found on the Coast Guard Net that the *Lucy Q*

sank, but you were there, so my money says you know it already. I didn't bother deleting the *Lucy Q* if we have a mole. Let him think we're still following her."

"This doesn't have to be a mole," I reminded. "I did see the *Lucy Q* mast sticking out of the water yesterday. Je's with our folks down there now floating her and searching for the memory thing. I don't think he'll find it." I strummed my fingers across the tabletop. The potion started working. "Still, if I were Lake, I'd want to get the box away as soon as I could. I'd stash it in the sand until McDonnell lost interest. Do our in-house computers still have access to shipping manifests for big three overnight companies?"

"They do. It'll take a few minutes, but yeah."

"Then, see if you can find any shipments out of San Juan for a box; I'm guessing, six by ten inches or smaller. Have them search back a few days."

"That's a lot of boxes."

I raised my brow. "It'll be a lot of problems if we get it wrong. Have somebody put a query to focus on those dimensions. See if anything turns up. I know it's a long shot, but computing is cheap."

"I'll get it going—one more thing before you die on me." Rory held up a hand to keep me from standing and lumbering out. "On my own, I've been going through Mark Gower's company emails. A little more than a year ago, he sent several messages to someone code-named Brahms 4. He asked if they were going to honor his family contract. It looks like he has some interest in them. F.Y.I. Brahms 4 is claiming responsibility for the Guatemalan president's assassination."

****

I joined Toby on the third floor of Medical City

Hospital—the only hospital in Dallas exclusively decorated in original art, some important, some not. A nurse behind the glass window of the waiting room called for Tobias McDonnell. I got up to bring him the forms she handed out.

My phone insisted on buzzing a coded buzz I assigned to my sister in Phoenix. Once Toby finished his forms, I answered Esmee's call.

She bubbled over with excitement. "I'm going to be in Dallas Tuesday. Would you offer to take me to Medina's for dinner? I want to talk to you about something."

"Tuesday?" I checked my e-calendar. "I can be there. Any hints as to what your secret is?"

"Wait until I see you. Loves to ya, big brother." And with that, she hung up.

"Hmmm."

Also, while still playing caregiver to Toby, another instant message came in. This one came from Harley Je. "Lucy Q is cradled. Our team is onboard."

I reacted with one loud word, "Good."

Toby lost his attention on the forms and gave them to me. "What's good, my boy?"

"Je has the boat out of the water, and our crew is going through it."

"Are you expecting to find anything?"

"No."

Then, a few minutes later, another text message came through. Laura typed, "It takes a loving man to deal with what I've done, and you still love me. I needed to share that. I love you more."

****

Dr. Mathew Graves, with long fingers, and a

medium size torso, had thick, dark brows. He sat behind a minimalist glass top desk in a medical pose. "Tobias, how are the antidepressants and antianxiety drugs I gave you working?"

Toby grumbled a pitiful answer, "Things are better. As my partner here tells me if Audrey Hepburn can beat prostate cancer, so can I."

Graves quirked to one side. "Audrey Hepburn was a woman."

"That's not an issue, according to my expert here. He knows about all the stages of prostate cancer." Toby inclined his head in my direction.

Dr. Graves pointed to me, "This expert, is you?"

I tried not to show it, but I squirmed with an uneasy chuckle. "I had to tell Toby something. That's what dribbled from my mouth."

Graves must live without humor. "Hepburn aside, the sooner we start treatment, the better it will be for you. So many scholars believe there's no need to treat men your age, but if you follow my protocol, there's no reason you can't return to a normal life."

Out of turn, I asked, "Guaranteed?"

Graves pooched his pointy chin and responded, "Almost guaranteed."

"What do you mean by almost?" Toby got focused.

Graves demanded, "Do as I tell you, and there's no reason you can't be here slapping high-fives for many years."

Chapter 32

Worldwide Newswire
(AP) Associated Press
Vanuatu President Dead, Cause Unknown
By Danbury Golli
(Port Vila)—Michel Iwai, president of Vanuatu archipelago, along with five-armed security guards, has been found dead in a men's restroom during an inter-island football match. The Police reported no sign of violence.

Vanuatu hosted Papua New Guinea in a late afternoon match on the day of his death. A local fan discovered a total of six bodies in the men's restroom. The cause of death remains unclear. When found, all the guard's weapons remained holstered.

Officials canceled the remainder of the tournament pending investigation.

Vanuatu has asked France for assistance in determining the cause of the deaths. As a result, the French Service d'Aide Médicale Urgente, SAMU, dispatched a team of forensic experts to the volcanic island to determine the cause of the president's death.

(AP) Update 1
Local medical experts believe the men suffered toxic poisoning but failed to identify the poison source or how administered.

(AP) Update 2

Testing by French forensic laboratories rules out poison as the cause of death. Still, it fails to offer further details or alternatives. As a result, SAMU personnel sent additional blood samples to Paris for continued investigation.

Chapter 33

Dallas, Texas
Rick

I didn't care for his Bentley, but Toby wanted us to take it to see Dr. Graves. Coming home, I rolled it under the original horse and carriage portico at the rear of his house; Maria joined. The thermometer read ninety-three degrees in the shade. I graciously opened Toby's front door, where he reclined like a corpus.

Maria helped—taking his hand. "Mister Toby, you look so weak. Let me help with you."

I told her, "He's gaming you, Maria. There's nothing wrong with him."

"You're so full of it, Richard." My best friend pushed me away. "I'm sick. She's helping me. Leave the woman alone."

"You're not sick. It's only cancer."

Maria held Toby's arm and led him into a spotless kitchen. "Mister Toby, Maria takes care of you. You not worry."

What a spud. She parked him at the kitchen table he'd bought her. She warmed a bowl of Mayan Wedding Soup she'd brewed, ringing his plate with crackers. "You eat now. Soup good for you."

Toby glanced at me. "You see? She's better than a

wife. I pay her, and she takes care of me. No questions. It's best this way."

"Sounds like a common-law marriage." I let forth a chuckle.

"So, what treatment would you pick?" Dazed and confused at the pamphlets Graves gave him, Toby pushed them toward me.

"I'm not picking for you, pal. You're not delegating that to me. The doctor said you must decide. So, you pick one."

Toby grumbled loud enough for Maria to hear, "I should have let the Soviets shoot you under the bridge. They wanted to; you know. And I bet they would have paid good money to hand you over."

"I'm sure they would have," I answered. "I'm the best. People pay for the best. But you're the one that's going to decide on your treatment."

Toby grumbled, "Now you're trying to kill me off."

"He not kill you off. Maria, take care of Mr. Toby." She slid a spoon into his hand.

"Toby," I said, "I can't keep making decisions for you."

"You need to eat, Mr. Toby." She tried to correct my disrespect with her eyes.

Toby said to me, "I used to be able to depend on you."

Dr. Graves' tri-fold pamphlets were in front of him on the table. "These are your treatment options. Pick one. You're not going to die before I retire."

****

Esmee arrived at Medinas after I did. Her tricks have not changed. "It's not so hot we can't have dinner outside." Esmee wore Daisey Dukes over Gigi sandals and an off-shoulder floral crop top. She stood five-foot-six, desert tan, covering a slender-framed.

"You're not suckering me in," I corrected her. "That's how you got me to buy you the outfit you've got on."

What income she earns—beyond my monthly stipend—comes from the Texas Rangers baseball team for laying out their uniforms before games. She eyed Sam's dark Moroccan décor in the tiny dining room. "We've come here before. I like the owner Sam, that's right. So, play it again, Sam." Hers was the only laugh in the place.

"To celebrate fiancé number three and four. We know what happened then. Are you telling me there's a number five in the wings?"

"Nah. That's stupid."

No matter how promising her men were, she could never stand one in front of a preacher. So, my advice, and one that went way back, was to quit bragging so much about herself; let the boyfriend get a word in. Men liked to talk about themselves as much as women, maybe more.

She said, walking in front of me through the door, "I know you don't like to talk about your work."

"That's right."

Seeing us, Sam hurried, arms open for a long hug, bringing his charming Moorish smile. "Good evening." Only a slight Turkish twang remained in his American voice. "It's good to see you, and is this Mr. Rick's beautiful sister I see once again?"

Esmee sheepishly gave him an eye flutter, avoiding the hug.

I responded, to cover her rudeness, "Good memory

for a fat old man, Sam. She's buying the town tonight using my credit card, so I need you to take care of her."

Sam avoided her rejection. "Your most beautiful lady enjoys my fig martini if I remember correctly."

"She does, and I still like my Woodford Old Fashioned."

Sam led us to his favorite booth and bowed away backward to get our drinks.

So, Esmee returned. "I know you're a spy of some kind…"

I reminded her in my soft tone, "Let's not advertise to the rest of the city. If this is business, you need to hush down your voice. People have ears."

"Okay-okay." At which point she went to a near whisper. "I know you work for Laura's dad, and somewhere in there is a Brit with a last name of Gower."

"Laura's been talking with you?"

Then my sister became uncharacteristically severe, "I bet you don't know this Gower man was a British spy and a double-dipper at that."

"Double agent, not dipper, and yes, he was."

Then for no apparent reason, she paused to inspect her nails. She spotted a chip in the polish of her index finger. Not much more would transpire before that got fixed. She almost went to a whisper again. "So, did you know while he was spying in Ireland, he was bumping uglies with the wife of the Irish man you and Toby were doing business with? He got her preggers?"

"It's Northern Ireland. How do you know about what I was doing?"

Sam returned to the table with his best hummus and two drinks on a serving tray. "For my favorite friends. The hummus and pita are on me." He sat the clay bowl of hummus swimming in olive oil between us.

I acknowledged his gracious gesture. "You're always so good to me."

Sam bent himself into a slow Moroccan bow and left us to talk.

"How did you get this information?" My sister sat and picked over the pita chips and, god forbid, finally touched one with hummus. "Gross. I've puked better stuff than this. Sheeze."

"Sam's listening. Quieten it."

"I'm sorry, big brother, but I can't eat this stuff. I've tried it before. The Irish information came from this new job I have. I got a job I know how to do, which pays better. I learned about you from one of my clients." She tensed her mouth and pulled her lips tight to her teeth, anticipating my reaction. "I'm branching out into men, money, and how to separate the two."

"You've started entertaining men?"

"Do you hate me?"

"I don't hate you. I'm totally into saving money every month by not sending it to you. Are you making enough? I can stop your monthly checks?"

She ripped off a spotless piece of pita. "It pays well, and it's pretty much what you guessed. But I didn't come to tell you that. I came to tell you there's this guy from Dallas. He constantly talks, trying to impress me." She softened her voice even more. "At first, I was sure he was a bullshit artist, but then he starts going into detail about what he does. He starts telling me about your Gower guy. He says he's been here in Dallas to do his work."

"And did he say what the job was?"

"I didn't understand it, but it sounded important. It was some sort of science-sounding thing. I don't know."

"Did he have a name?"

"Do you think these guys give their real names?"

I flipped through the photographs on my phone until I came to the story about the Colorado pile-up. I showed my phone to her. It was Kelly Lake's photo.

She studied it only for the quickest moment. "Lake was his name, but that's not a picture of him."

"Then, let's not talk about this anymore. I'll cover your cost for bringing this to me. But be careful."

"Sweat not."

****

On my return drive to the house, I admitted that I enjoyed the idea of Laura and Brian getting together. Thinking about her riding him so much excites me—yes, and imagining what they are doing is the thing I needed to refresh my world. *But, exactly, what does he do? What does she do? How does he push her over the top?*

Would I be crazy for asking her to give me the details first-hand? Would she be okay telling me, maybe when we're snuggled? My argument would be to trade her kink for mine. Turnabout is fair play. That's what she tells me." I smiled, turning into the garage. *"I do. I have a kink. And that's what I'll say to her. When you get home, I want you to tell me what he did to turn you on. How does he feel?*

I settled in for a few minutes, getting myself ready to watch the recording of the day's Ranger game. I positioned my overstuffed chair to the front and center of the TV and on-axis between a pair of KLM sports speakers. That's when I realized the garage door was rising. She was early returning from Brian's. I righted myself, wanting to appear calm and collected when she came in, not the wreck inside that I was.

But she opened the door to the townhouse, and my coolness faded away. Something was wrong. Her dress hung proper, not wrinkled as I hoped. She dropped her purse on the floor.

"You're early," I said. "Didn't you see Brian? How did it go?"

"It didn't."

"What happened?"

"When I got there, my lab called. Would you be a sweetheart and pour a Woodford Reserve neat for me? El Grande." She sat disoriented in a new reality. "I might be getting fired. Something atrocious has happened on my project."

"You mean Tinker Bell?"

"Tinker Bell? No, nothing to do with her. It's something else—so horrible. I can't picture anything worse. The god-pod wants to sandwich me under the guillotine."

Her bourbon disappeared before her neck was stretched across the guillotine. I refilled her crystal glass.

She added before I could think of a way to respond, "I've been out at Boy Scout Hill on White Rock Lake," she said. "Watching the moon glistening on the water made things better—I don't know if there's anything I can do at this point but wait and see where the blade falls."

"I would ask, but…"

She drained her glass for the second time; I filled it again. Three would be her limit.

She took a deep breath and nudged me to fill the crystal glass to the top. "Your sister, how is she?"

"Being herself. Esmee's picked whoring as her next big career path. It sounds like she has what it takes. So, if she can make enough money to pay her expenses, she's got my endorsement."

My petite wife tried to shake it off. "All I can say is she better be careful. Girls like her usually end up in the hospital."

Chapter 34

*Dallas, Texas
Rick*

It was time for a break, a good steak, with one of my Old Fashioneds, so I set a course for a one-man meal at a new joint in Uptown, *East Bombers*, on Travis Ave. Je reported the box was not on *Lucy Q*. That was not much of a surprise. I helped myself to a bar seat in a gap where I found a string of empties.

Is there any possible chance this chip thing is real? Some elements look like it is. Others do not. Someone worked hard if this is a hoax: people, places, hacks, ships, killings. And if you eliminate the European Union and Moscow, how many people can hack US military networks? Kelly Lake got up on the Army net, then they took him down in weeks. If nothing more, based on the network hack, the theft looks real, at least to some extent.

But perhaps not. The Army could have done this themselves to hide something and drag McDonnells along for credibility.

I fished the orange peel from my drink and squeezed its citrus oil across the burning bar candle. A series of micro-explosions broke quietly.

Or how about a foreign government? The EU? Russia? Or maybe China?

My finger rose, signaling I needed another Old

Fashioned.

Maybe the KGB stole the formula, but their agent got killed or defected or realized the money he was carrying and got greedy. The Kremlin knows how we operate and is not above using what they know. Did the KGB formulate some bullshit story to get my team to run down their formula so they could steal it from us later?

Are we aiding and abetting Russian behavior?

And who the fuck is this Kelly Lake guy? For sure, not a park ranger. When anything happens, he turns out to be at the center. Isn't it a bit too obvious? Whoever he is, make sure everyone knows his name. But his face? Why is it that nobody knows it? Brown hair; no, black hair. He's got green eyes; no, he's got evil eyes.

Is Lake two people? OR more? Is he Gower himself? Or is he one of Gower's people from earlier years? But why the hell would Gower give a damn? He's probably dead by now anyway, feeding the crabs.

"Damn. These highball glasses don't seem to hold their liquor."

Then there's General Legg. This bastard poses a whole different batch of problems. But at least I met him face to face.

I held up another finger for round three.

Rory's reflection in the bar mirror walked my way. "What's up?"

"I need a Negroni," he answered, "Then two things you're going to find interesting."

The bartender was finishing mine, so he started on Rory's Negroni.

"Launch your butt." I pointed to the stool next to mine.

Rory had endless enthusiasm. "I did an extensive

search across the Watson network to find anything I could about General Legg. You're not going to believe this."

"Gimme."

"Legg is a stage actor in a Broadway play. It closed last month."

He was right. He sat me up on my stool. "Shit. For honest? I was just—"

"The actor's name is Buddy Pierpoint."

Rory kept on, "Pierpoint resides in New York City. He came out of acting school. He's done local TV commercials, modeled, and came from a military family. Now listen, he graduated Honor Guard from Yuma High School in Arizona. Bingo? I can send you his headshot if you'd like. We're getting somewhere."

"I suppose."

"You suppose? You're supposed to be jumping and telling me I deserve a huge raise."

The corners of my lips stayed aiming down. "I should. You're right; I should be."

"But you're not."

"I should be. You did well. My problem is I can't figure out why this case is so lame. Every time I come up with a possible solution, it seems like I've forced facts to meet the circumstance. It used to not be that way. You know what I mean?"

"Uh."

"Everybody'll tell you someone stole a formula from the Army. Why? Because a general who turns out to be a Broadway actor said so. The wind I'm breathing is starting to stink."

"Are you serious? You think this never happened?"

"I'm not saying that…exactly. Something

happened. A red bus drove by with a woman on the top, like it was supposed to. But that's the only thing. All the other facts are there to make us conclude what somebody wants. Is there a box? Probably. Does it have anything in it? Maybe. Is it a formula? No. So, what's in the box the woman was carrying? And why do we chase it?"

Rory responded, "Before you get yourself in too much of a funk, listen to this next thing. In the seventies and eighties, the US launched a string of microwave listening satellites positioned to peek over Soviet horizons from space. As the Soviets transmitted secret communications from one microwave tower to the next, some signals blew past the receiving towers and into space. The NSA satellites lined up so they could grab the blow-by data. Everything the commies transmitted shot straight into our satellite antennas; Langley recorded them and is still studying them. The program yielded a treasure trove—and at the time, the Soviets were oblivious to it."

"Aquacade," I said to him. "I remember."

"Okay, officially, there were four tin cans launched, all in the seventies, but we know of at least eight going up from Cape Canaveral into the eighties and one in the nineties."

"Emphasis on 'we know.'"

Rory smacked at the interruption. "So, here's what you need to know: last night, we downloaded a feed from NSA with a link from one of the satellites they sent up in the eighties. Guess what? It held a Russian conversation about the new metal alloy the United States plans to use for its ground armor. We don't know who it came from, but it went to Moscow's Russian Ground Forces Headquarters. It seems they are expecting to have the formula soon."

"I didn't know any of Aquacade is still orbiting."

"Me either, but since then, we've been able to find a couple of other 'dead' satellites still dumping data to Langley."

"Shame on us," I scolded the good old US of A. "And to think we told Moscow, they all burned on reentry. Where's our integrity?" My third Old-Fashioned arrived. "Until we know better, let's be careful that evidence like this isn't being sent to direct us where they want us to go. I don't know what's going on or with who, but whatever this case is, it will be bigger than any of us believe. Someone is spending too much money on controlling our conclusions. Someone wants to distract us from discovering the right answer. Which path is real?"

"This looks real to me, Rick."

"I think I'm starting to believe somebody is shipping us to Alaska when the real action is in Brazil. Is this the first message you've received related to the alloy?"

"Yup."

"Okay. Can you receive the satellite feed directly without tapping into Langley?"

"Nope. The technology is too old."

"Then I want you to put somebody monitoring NSA full time, listening to what the Russians are saying. Until we know otherwise, let's assume any Russian message coming over Aquacade contains data worth knowing. We need to rule out the possibility the Russians developed this alloy, and our Army stole it. Farfetched, but it's a possibility."

"That's interesting."

"Either way," I said, "We still need to find the box.

Stay on it. It persists; it contains something important. I'll go to New York and talk with our actor stud and determine who hired him. Dollars over diamonds, it's Kelly Lake."

****

I first talked with Dylan Cobb when the CIA assigned Toby and me to Army Command Boudreaux. We were twenty years younger—with full heads of dark brown hair. Dylan Cobb's Army career was starting, specializing in peace strategy. We three worked on developing European counteroffensive theories, more so him than us. When the counteroffensive budget ran out, Toby and I returned to Dallas. Cobb stayed on, making a career with the Army. That's when Toby and I split from the CIA and started billing the Army direct for our services.

I found Cobb's number in an old Rolodex and rang him up. As we exchanged small talk about Virginia weather, my eyes followed the raindrops falling past my building's window to the street below. "This project I'm working on," I told him, "is about an armor plating with a new magic alloy. From what you know, is this something the Army at Yuma would create?"

He grunted, and I could hear some sort of bottle open with a fizz. "Yuma? No, Yuma proves products once someone else has produced them. They don't develop anything."

"Any chance there's more than one sort of facility there?"

"Yeah, but none of them do research. Not at Yuma."

I nodded. That's what I understood about the place. "So, if a client tells me he leads Research at Yuma, he would be lying?"

"He would be lying," Cobb said.

"Hmm, one more thing. Do you know anything about the Russians owning a new alloy to wrap around their heavy armor? It's a rumor floating around the machining world."

He answered, "No."

"You might want to talk to NSA. We picked up a message going to Moscow High Command. NSA has some Russian communications you'll be interested in."

****

Hybrid buses and electric light rail make up Dallas's public transit network. The yellow commuter train dips below ground as it leaves downtown, traveling under neighborhood trees and homes for several miles before emerging at Mockingbird Station. While underground, it travels beneath McDonnell Tower, making a scheduled stop one floor below the building's main lobby. Toby's deal with the Government was to rent two deeper basement floors for computers during civil emergencies and nuclear warfare. That gave us a steady income and a private stop on the rail system.

I exited the train behind Rory, and we took the escalator to the first-floor bar. Over an Old Fashioned and a Lite beer, we talked.

I sat my drink on the table napkin. "You told Toby there's been a sudden increase in Air Force launches out of New Mexico. This might be impossible, but can you dig into what's causing them? Why's the government so hell-bent on getting new gear topside?"

Rory said, "All I can say is they're using light-launch vehicles meaning multiple satellites in low orbit. So, we assume they're replacing GPS satellites."

"Could be, but what if it's not GPS? Could they be

rebuilding the old Aquacade communications network…some secret deal like that?"

"I doubt it. Not with the amount of lift being used. Aquacade is in the Clarke Belt, twenty thousand miles straight up. What they're using right now can't put anything more than a couple of hundred miles overhead."

"Then why the secrecy of the desert? They launch GPS every day from Florida and California."

"I'll get my shovel, see what I can dig up. I can tell you this—whatever it is, the Air Force is launching them regularly. Sometimes daily." He finished his beer. "One other thing, then I need to get upstairs. The Colorado Springs Times article on the apartment fire I sent you? Your girl, Carissa, and her mother died."

"Well, damn. I was sure Carissa was the keystone to the box. Let me ask you one more thing, and I'm sure it's going to take a while to find out, if at all."

"What is it?"

"See if you can locate Mark Gower. If he's not feeding the crabs, I want to talk to him about his part in this. I suspect it's a big part."

Chapter 35

New York City, NY
Rick

After a few minutes of persistent bell ringing and severe door knocking, Pierpoint cracked the door enough for one eye to see out and his nose to fit in, "Mr. Haade. I'm surprised."

I pushed the door two eyes wide. "You can imagine my surprise," I returned with grit, Pierpoint's eyes staring through the crack. "I come to New York City and find my General Legg living in an actor's flop on Houston Street. Am I at a loss as to what to think?"

Pierpoint tried to hold the door open one eye's worth.

I continued, "What should I think when my office assistant notices my very own General on a theatrical placard using Internet Street View? Pardon my intrusion, but I had to come to see for myself."

Pierpoint resisted as I pushed the overly painted black wood door. "Okay, so what's it you want? I've done nothing wrong. Acting is what I do for a living."

"On Broadway, you're welcome to do anything you want. But, for the rest of the world, you're breaking the law when you impersonate a military officer. It's a federal offense. Oh my god, the Army? What are they going to do?"

"I don't know what you're talking about?"

"Guilty people never seem to. I took DNA saliva and handprints off your beer glass at Toby's house. Can I come in?"

"No." Pierpoint continued to push against the door, but my shoe was now wedged between the door and frame.

I bent to peek through the crack to see whatever else was going on in there. "I'm not here to arrest you. I'm not a cop."

He said, "Then I'll come out there."

I uncoiled the thrust of my legs against the door as he spoke. The new opening was enough to expose two more gentlemen in his apartment. "Well, two more…I suppose…artists. And who are these interesting lily-flower friends of yours?"

"None of your fucking business, you prick." He attempted to re-slam the door in my face. It didn't.

I kicked the door open wider, knocking Pierpoint from his feet down to his rump. "You have to understand; I decide what's my business and what's not," I said. "You and your apartment here are my business."

Pierpoint glared up from the floor, hand to his face catching blood from his nose. "I don't have to talk with you."

"That's right, but you're going to. So, it might as well be here in your place."

The other two men backed into Pierpoint's open kitchen.

"You'll talk all right," I assured. "I have this wonderful way of making people want to talk. I'm sure you don't want your Teddy Bear buddies here to watch you cry."

Pierpoint spat blood at me and wiggled his upper front tooth.

"All I want to know is who hired you for the Dallas job."

Buddy Pierpoint's guests shuffled around until I said to them, "You two need to keep your feet still while me and Buddy have a chat. Can you do that?" Once they calmed, I returned to Pierpoint. "Who hired you?"

He held a hand out for me to help him get up. His crooked nose was in his other.

I helped him to his feet and passed him a hand full of napkins from the table.

He smeared blood across his face. "A man with big money booked me for the act through my agent. He said he came to my show and liked my General."

"What's his name, the big money guy who booked you?"

"Kelly Lake."

Why did that not surprise me? "Did you meet him? Can I get a description from you?"

"No. Lake sent my payment to my agent. He paid twice Union scale. At that rate, I didn't need to meet him. When you're in an apartment like this, cash speaks."

I surveyed the room and slowly nodded. "How did you know what Lake wanted?"

"He gave my agent a storyline and talking points, but mostly it was ad-lib."

"He must have told you something. What did he tell you?"

"Can I get some ice?"

I called to the kitchen, "One of you two bring him some ice in a towel."

"He said the story was a girl on a bus was going to be part of the story. She was supposed to deliver a box to one of your people but didn't. So, I was supposed to get you to sign a contract for you to recover the box she was carrying."

"Did Lake say anything about the box? What was in it?"

"As I said, I didn't talk to him. Morris said it was something electronic—something like that."

"And you and me in Yuma?" I asked.

"In the second storyline, I was to live on the Fort. I was raised in Yuma. So I'm familiar with the area. Lake said to tell you it was him that stole the formula from the Army and give you the phony address."

I gave Pierpoint a bit more breathing room. "The guy you're working with, Kelly Lake, is a class one psychopath. Now that I've outed you, he'll most certainly come after you. And he's famous for the pain he inflicts before his victims die. If I were you, I'd gather all my nickels and head somewhere in the Canadian Rockies as far as I could go."

Returning to the Four Seasons Hotel, I kicked off my shoes and booked my flight home in the morning. Then, downing two Old Fashioneds for nerves, I examined Laura's phone tap icon. It felt like a magnet pulling my finger.

But a call from Rory interrupted my debate. "I found the information you wanted about Mark Gower. You were right. They never arrested him. He's nowhere in England. At least, I haven't found him yet—but I did find the parcel shipments out of San Juan you wanted. It took a while, but the team found four of them."

"Let's hear."

"Three carriers service the island," he started. "One showed nothing in your size or weight range. One overnighter reported a shipment exactly in your weight and size range. But it had notes that said to keep frozen, listing its content as tissue going to MD Anderson Cancer Hospital in Houston.'

"And there's the last one that we track. They received four shipments. All of them came from the same consignor. One went to a pharmacy in Londonderry, one to a residence in City Cork, one to a farmer outside Dublin, and the last one went to a freight forwarder in Boston. All were slightly over a pound each."

"You're perfect, my man."

"Remember that at review time." He snickered.

"So." I paused to think. "The original box has been divided into four smaller shipments. Carissa said the box was heavy. Four pounds might be right for her. So, they've been split. There must have been four somethings in her box, and now they are broken into one in four individual boxes. For a crime that's not real, this keeps getting more real. Send me the addresses and have somebody keep track of those four boxes, specifically when they're about to get delivered."

"Can do. By the way, Laura's phone is recharged and back online. She'd let it die."

A defensive urge against Rory flowed up my back. What did that mean? "Tell me you're not listening to my wife. Well, you better not be listening." I huffed through my nose. "Have you been listening?"

Rory answered, "Listening to what? You have such a naughty mind, Ricky."

****

Her phone GPS indicated Laura was in Pittsburgh,

at the Hotel Monaco. I relaxed back, propped up on a stack of bed pillows, wearing my boxers and black socks. I tapped the icon on my phone to open background access to her device.

Her voice came over clear. "Let's order a couple of bottles of Scotch from room service and get blasted. I got this little naughty urge going on, and I want to get so sore I can't work tomorrow."

If she drank like that at home, she'd be up all night, puking. And now she's begging him to rock her through the night.

Brian asked her, "What's wrong with you?"

"Nothing. Why do you think—?"

"You never talk like that. And I, for one, have never been able to go all night."

"Then you drink one, and I'll have the rest. We're all happy."

Brian didn't give up. "Is it work? You weren't like this last night. What happened?"

"I can't tell you…at least sober…" Their voices broke up for a moment. "…Which I don't intend to be for much longer."

This is going to be fun. I need to get a bottle of Woodford too. I might as well keep up with her. So, I pressed the room service button on the desk phone and ordered a fifth.

Over the line, Laura said, "Room Service? Could you bring up a bottle of Macallan 18 Scotch to our room?"

Then the squeaks sounded like Brian picked her up and dropped her on the bed. Kisses followed, then more kisses. "Why do you never tell me about your work?"

An obscene slurp preceded her reply. "You get me

drunk enough and fuck me hard enough, and I'll tell you anything. I want this right here as hard as a bone."

The sound of a zipper followed the clicking sounds of blouse snaps, then more kisses and slurps.

Laura responded with light moans.

Do I want to hear what's coming? I paused. *No. But what if Rory is still listening?* I sent an instant message to Rory, "Are you listening?"

Rory responded, "And if I denied it?"

"Well, I'm not ready to listen to my wife going at it with another man. I'm logging off. Tell me if she tells him what she does for a living."

****

Before today, it never occurred to me to ask Toby, "Why did you have air conditioning installed on an open backyard porch? It does nothing but blows cold air into your blazing hot Texas yard."

Toby answered me, "So I can sit out here, drink my coffee, and read."

"Ah…"

Toby gave me his once-over. "Why? Anything wrong with that?"

"Nope, Tobe, most people aren't willing to pay to cool the hot summer sun in Texas."

"I'm not paying to cool the summer sun. I'm paying to cool me."

On the side table laid the literature Dr. Grave gave him, now tattered from being read many times. "Looks like you've become a cancer treatment expert."

"I'm picking the Cyberknife Therapy. I like what this says, and I think it does the best job."

"Why?"

"Well, if Graves does blade surgery, he goes in and

cuts everything out. You get left peeing all over yourself, and most likely, you can't function as a man. I mean, no good."

"Then we'll skip it."

"With radiation, they're using x-rays to burn the cancer cells, but any slight miscalculation and you end up with holes in your guts and a bunch of skin burned to a cinder. It makes you puke, and you can end up getting your butt sewed shut because they burned it off. No, sir, not interested in my butt getting sewed shut."

"I understand. That's out."

Toby raised two fingers. He unfurled a third, fourth, and his thumb too as he described the options, "Chemo? Intentional poisoning. Freezing—that's aggressive and uncontrolled. Pellets? They're okay as long as they get them in the tumor and not something else."

"Skip, Skip, Skip."

"Now, Cyberknife. This says they can hit a small tumor inside the prostate directly, protecting the rest of my gland and my nerve. That's important. I keep the good part of my prostate, bladder, and colon. Everything stays intact. It's outpatient at Medical City. All I need to do is give Dr. Grave the okay."

Chapter 36

Dallas, Texas
Rick

In Toby's garage is a GT-S Bentley. I opened the passenger side. At the same time, he lowered the convertible roof and brought the machine through its power-on sequence. The Black Sapphire rolled out into the sunshine. The almost black sapphire paint glistened and stopped on the gravel drive. Then he accelerated, and we went off to the Stein and Swine Bar and Grill on Lower Greenville Ave.

"A Berry's Guadeloupe and my friend will take an Old Fashioned," he told the barkeep. He led our waitress and me to his favorite table, distant from the bar. "I've known you since you came out of the cocoon. It's not much you can hide from me. So, tell all. You're about to give up on this Army case, aren't you," he said.

"It could be. There's a box out there holding something we can't seem to catch. Was it stolen from Yuma? I don't think so; I don't believe a theft ever occurred. This whole case is some sort of game. It is something we don't understand."

"So, tell me."

I flipped a few spiced pumpkin seeds in my mouth and chewed. "First…I've seen enough to believe there is a government box. Four of them, now. Somebody is using this Army ruse to get our attention."

"Who?"

"No idea. But the way it's playing out tells me they don't want the box traced back to them. Whatever is going on will be devastating to them if their name gets associated with it. But the boxes don't contain a memory chip. It's too heavy."

"So, are we chasing one person, Kelly Lake, or an organization?"

I shook my head. "Probably both. Whatever's in the box must be bigger than anything on a personal level. It's being run by individuals, but it's more like something nuclear, or a new form of energy, or, God forbid, biologics."

"But the military, American?"

"I wouldn't rule out some country's government. Maybe American. People don't spend this much money on private projects. Here's something else. And I don't like it. Rory intercepted some satellite information, telling us the Russians had developed a new lightweight armor material. Everything the fake general told us could be true, except the Russians came up with the formula, not the US. Those four boxes may contain information the Army stole from the Russians and then lost. The Army is using us in case something goes wrong. They are shielded."

Severely short on Guadeloupe, Toby signaled for another round. "You're saying the boxes are Russian, and we're running around trying to recover them for our Army?"

"Yes. Or even we're trying to catch it for the Russians. When we get it, they knock us off. It's a possibility. It's out there, and I'm just saying it's a theory. I'll tell you why. Two things. If our Army got robbed, they wouldn't hesitate to ask us for help through normal channels, and we would have helped. But the actual Army doesn't seem to know anything about a stolen formula or box. And second, when I talked to Dylan Cobb…."

"… Who's Dylan Cobb? I don't know him."

"Yeah, you do, when we worked in France. He was the Army guy doing the peace strategy gig."

"I don't recall him."

"Give it a minute; he'll come to you." I signaled for a fresh drink, too. "Anyhow, Cobb now directs the Army's tech development. So, my thinking…

"… oh, him. A bit of an ass, as I recall."

"Things change, Toby. You'd be better off thinking of him as an expert in war technology who's willing to help us."

Toby thinned his lips, unimpressed. "Whatever."

"Anyway, I figure, if anybody is going to know about the U.S. having a new metal armor, it will be him. That's what he does. So, I called him. Nothing."

A touchy-feely young couple joined the near-empty establishment and took a seat by the bar. The bartender switched the overhead music from Stones to some Celtic New Age trill.

Toby asked, "So, you think Russia owns the boxes? What do you think about Mark Gower's role?"

"I think you know what I think."

Toby said, "I never considered Gower would go counterintelligence. But the old Toby-nose caught a whiff that says Gower is during the middle of this. You'll agree, when the good Lord issued smarts, Gower mistook it for farts, and ran."

Toby took a pull off his Rum. "How's Laura?"

Did Toby ask about Laura? As in his daughter, Laura—my wife? I blinked away the surprise on my face. "Fine, I guess. Laura has lots of work these days."

"I figured she must. What does she do, I mean in her work?"

I took the time to answer. "Laura works for a division of Beyer Industry. They make chemicals and health products. Her work is secret, like mine and yours."

"Does she do well? Does she get lots of promotions?" Toby leaned in closer.

"She has. She's the Master Chemist of Product Quality."

Why did Toby suddenly want to chit-chat about Laura after, what, how many years? Cancer, I guess, is making him feel mortal.

Toby nodded. "Her job sounds impressive, mighty responsible."

"Right now, she's leading a development project. It's a new something or other, I think, something no one has ever attempted, but she can't talk about it outright."

"Like us, huh? Is she popular? I mean, does she have lots of friends?"

"A few here in Dallas. But most are co-workers. She's been with Beyer for a long time, since graduating from Oxford, so she knows a lot of people."

Toby's grin let a little spark of pride leak out. "Oxford University. That's impressive."

"She got her Ph.D. in chemistry shortly before we got married. I'm sure you know that."

"I do. I like to hear it again. I don't hear much about my girl anymore. You don't have to answer this if you don't want to, but did she ever want kids? I've always been curious if she ever wanted to be a mother."

I chuckled. "So you can be a grandpa? Yeah. She wanted kids. I doubt you ever knew, but right after I met her, she got raped. Violently. The guy beat her so bad it messed up her insides."

His lips tightened. "No. I didn't know. Of course, the police arrested the thug. He's still serving time, is he?"

"He didn't live long enough to get arrested."

"Good. You're my boy. I'm proud of you for handling it the right way. Proper."

Like daughter, like the father. "The police found the guy dead outside a hotel."

Toby raised his hand above his head and ordered us another round. When the barkeeper came, Toby gave him instructions to get the caterwauling off the sound system. "Put on some Doors and begin it with People Are Strange."

The barkeep snapped back, "We've played grandpa music the whole time you two have been in here. The couple at the bar asked for something recorded this century; do you mind?"

"Come here, tiny fellow," Toby instructed the young man. "I own this bar. Shall we lock the doors and turn on the CLOSED sign because there's no bartender working today?"

The bartender straightened and stepped back. "Ah, no, sir. Sorry. I didn't know."

I waited until the bartender returned to his workstation. "You don't own this bar."

"He doesn't know it and never will. Now, Laura. Thanks for telling me. I didn't always know those things. They're important to me now."

For a moment, I nodded absently, my mind shifting to the other side of Laura. "So, are you interested in getting to know your daughter better after these years?"

Toby paused and wrinkled his nose. "I don't think so. She hates me. I don't blame her. I abandoned her. I ignored her all her life. It's too late to change that."

"She hates you for sure. But you never know what might happen if you reach out."

"Maybe. Let me change subjects," Toby said. "For a short while, I need Harley Je to chase those boxes. Let's give him a chance to dance the dance on his own and see how much gut he has." My partner swirled the last drops in his glass. "I need you to do something else."

"Intriguing." In truth, a break from the box paradox would be good. I responded, "I'll let him know. It's his field certification. If he can't handle it, I need to know."

Toby swept his eyes from one side of the barroom to the other, stopping at the winey couple, disgustingly ignoring us. They didn't appear to be commies, just innocent citizens.

"The Air Force needs to discuss a quiet project with us a-sap."

"Any idea what?"

"A guy, Colonel Wright, called. He says orders came down to him directly from the Secretary of Defense."

I checked the TV over the bar. Top of the ninth inning, the Texas Rangers were ahead of the Colorado Rockies, 7-1.

****

A few hours later, at Love Field's Commercial Terminal, an eight-passenger Air Force Lear Jet taxied in for us.

"Compliments of Colonel Wright," the pilot said.

We passed over a plethora of West Texas cotton clouds. Toby said, "Somehow, I have a feeling Gower is going to end up being key to the Army box ruse. I do."

I let myself relax into the seat. "You already said that."

"Ah. I did?"

"What I think happened is Gower learned about us through Carissa Scaffe's mother during the Londonderry days. She told him about her husband and the guns we were selling him. I always figured it odd how she would step out at night, leaving Scaffe at home with their little girl. But I figured it was none of my business."

"Ms. Scaffe going out wouldn't have been uncommon."

I sipped the raspberry-flavored sparkling water the loadmaster gave me. "Dominos, bingo, church, those sorts of things could have drawn her out."

"Right. Or a man."

With a nod, I went on, "Thinking back, Gower always had more information about us than we did him. We were his ticket to safety. During our interviews, he told us several times that he had already left the space command and could start immediately. I had Rory trace his money. He sent most of what he stole to the States before we made him a job offer."

The young Air Force Loadmaster leaned in the aisle to one knee. "We have some desert turbulence coming up. So, you guys make sure you're buckled in tight."

Toby asked the enlisted man, "Any rum in this tube?"

"No, sir. Not on an active flight."

"Then coffee, but make sure it's burned black."

With the Airman still listening, Toby told me, "We worked with a CIA partner outside Budapest who would leave the percolator on for so long the coffee would reduce to a syrup."

The Air Force Loadmaster leaned back, a bit slack at the jaw. "Percolator?"

Toby said, "You're too young."

"Another club soda will be fine for me," I told the young man, breaking the loadmaster's stupor with the coffee story. Then, when the young man was out of earshot, in the cabin rear, I continued, "One other thing, the pickup order for the Grassy Knoll came in without return message routing. I can count the number of people who know how to do that on four fingers. And you and I are two of them."

"I know nothing about return routing whatsoever. Rory takes care of that. I could never understand that stuff."

"Three people then: me, Rory, and Gower."

My soda came in an eight-ounce can. Toby's coffee came seriously black. He examined it.

I told him, "You should have kept your mouth shut. Budapest? You have never been to Budapest."

Toby snickered as the plane shuddered in the turbulence. "Well, he doesn't know that. Rory told me a lot of stuff about the theft on the Army network."

"And as soon as I brought it up with the Fort Commander in Yuma," I said, "the Army network got scrubbed spotless. Do you think Gower would have known how to penetrate a military network?"

Toby gazed into his mug as if he were reading his future in tea leaves. "Didn't we already agree Gower is behind this?"

"We did. And to boot, Mark is missing."

"Je can tackle that." Then, he asked me, "Do you believe Gower and Kelly Lake are the same person?"

"Not for a second. Kelly Lake is too nimble and quick. And Gower, with that fat belly, everyone would have remembered him."

"Then do you have any idea who Kelly Lake is?"

I sipped my club soda and, for some reason, started wondering if bubbles in the can are bigger at high altitudes than when on the ground. They could be.

"I think," I answered, "somewhere along the way, Gower enrolled a person whose looks put him perfectly in the center of the bell curve. Whoever Lake is, he's invisible. No one notices him, and more importantly, no one can describe him. He comes on stage and goes off like a piece of clear plastic wrap."

"That'll make him hard to figure out. Let's talk about our Broadway actor guy."

"Pierpoint? I believe what he's telling us is true. He believed he was a hero, and now he's afraid of Lake. I suggested he leave the country immediately and hope he did."

The Air Force pilot came across the speakers that the plane would be parking at Kirtland AFB in five minutes.

Toby said, "I hate that your little girl, Carissa, got killed. I know you liked her. No telling what she could have told us if we brought her in for protection."

"Then there's news you don't know. It turns out forensics found only one set of bones in the fire. They believe they were from the old lady."

"You know where Carissa is?"

"Not yet."

The conversation ended as the desert landscape grew closer to the plane's wheels.

I leaned across the aisle. "What did you hear from Dr. Grave?"

Toby's eyes closed, and in a gravelly voice, he said, "My treatments start next week. He has me scheduled first thing Monday at Medical City. I'd like you to be there if you can. But don't bring your banana car. You have to be a damn Gymnast to get in it."

"Then we'll take one of them hay-wagons in your garage."

"Don't call them hay-wagons. Use respect. They're refined saloons. An automobile you have no appreciation of and no skills driving. And, by the way, don't tell Laura about me asking of her."

"I won't."

"Good." Toby leaned toward the tiny window, watching the cactus racing by. "So, do you agree with me, the security police arresting Gower were on his personal payroll?"

"Totally."

Chapter 37

Albuquerque, NM
Rick

Staff Sargent H. Francis greeted us as we were disembarking the small jet.

"This way, gentlemen." Francis was a sun freckled man with blond wavy hair and a petite Air Force frame. He guided us to a sky-blue sedan parked in the front of the hanger. "If you will, gentlemen, please join me."

All the roads on the base traveled the same—two blacktop lanes made of crushed-stone-and-tar parted in the middle by endless white stripes. It was a matrix of black lines bisecting a sea of red desert sand. Our destination Francis said was the Administration Building, and that's where he parked.

Opening the door for Toby and me, Francis directed, "Colonel Wright will see you immediately. Follow me to security."

"Place your right hand on the scanner, sir," a voice spoke from the wall box. "Now, insert your ID card in the red slot."

Colonel Wright, an ex-Vietnam F-4 fighter pilot trimmed with silver hair coming from his ears, met us in the hallway following the Security Door locking behind us with a bang. He was shorter than me by a couple of inches and about the same height as Toby. The Air Force doesn't favor tall people. He shook my hand with a fighting man's grip. Behind him, posted on the wall, was a man-size photo of a cruise missile atop a low-orbit rocket engine. The picture showed them lifting skyward above a white-gold fiery tail.

Toby and I moved into Wright's office and took seats at the conference table. Wright sat to my left. Colonel Wright headed the six-person oak table.

Toby said, "You were vague in your phone call. Is there anything you would like to know about McDonnells?"

Wright signaled for the SSgt to bring him a stack of folders. "Nothing. The Secretary of Defense issued the contract with your firm during this last hour. You are here for a briefing on this important job."

I corrected him, "Assuming we're interested in your contract. One of us here has to sign it."

Wright glanced up as if caught off guard. "Right." He opened the top folder, and it contained a wallet-size photo of Toby and me stapled to its cover. "I trust you know the Air Force is not allowed to do business with the Chinese Government due to Congressional regulations."

Toby nodded. I had no idea.

Wright then said, "For the past few years, China has been working on improving their space reentry guidance systems. Our intelligence indicates they have developed circuitry, which may rival ours in accuracy. We need to know if it's true."

He flipped through folder pages one after another. "We want your company to help us obtain one of their reentry control boards."

Toby interrupted, "Are you recording us with that

camera in the drapery rod?"

Wright twisted to the window rod and answered, "Yes. Do you mind?"

"It's your building. The band plays your tune."

I added less cryptically, "No, we don't mind. So, what does this reentry thing look like? What are we after?"

Wright found the page he was searching for, unclamping a laminated photograph, and pointed to the object that contained a small computer-looking circuit board. It had several little square blocks on it and many colorful barrel-shaped components. He pushed it in my direction.

"This is the Liu Yang 12 Reentry Guidance Control System. The Chinese are systematically and quickly switching over to these devices. All Liu Yang-grade circuit boards are manufactured at an electronics shop in Hong Kong. The company's name is Dandong Win."

I took the laminate page from his hand to put my readers on to scrutinize the image. "How big is this thing?"

"The first models were the size of a Macintosh computer. This one will fit in your shirt pocket."

I told Toby, "This sounds easy enough."

"You think?" His wry grin reminded me nothing in this business is easy.

"I do." Spinning back in Wright's direction, I said, "Do you have a person over there I can work with?"

Colonel Wright nodded. "There's a woman who's worked at the Dandong Win factory for six years. She's taken one of the guidance units out in pieces, one component at a time. We want you to go get those pieces from her. Our lab will assemble them when you get back."

Toby tightened his forehead. "I'm sorry, Colonel, but I find it hard to believe the Defense Secretary sent Rick and me out here to fetch a circuit board you clearly can get yourself. You already have assets over there. You have the device. You have a runner."

I said to the colonel, "If you don't mind, Toby and I need a private moment."

Toby added, "And turn off the camera and microphone in that statue on your desk. It's too obvious."

I firmly addressed Toby, "This sounds like easy money even if the secretary didn't request it. Hong Kong lets people in with British Passports even without a Visa. I still have mine. I can fly over there tomorrow, pick up his parts, and flip back Sunday. No more than a weekend deal."

"He's not telling us what he really wants, Rick. There's something other than a Chinese circuit board."

"Does it matter? If this proves out, we can do more business with him later. So, let's give it time and see where he takes it. At least it's not me chasing four boxes."

"Those boxes are Je's certification. Not yours."

Colonel Wright rejoined us, and Toby told him, "We will help in your situation. But we doubt your story."

I immediately started listing the things I needed. "I need you to get me to LAX right now, then a first-class aisle seat on the earliest flight to Hong Kong—include a return ticket for Sunday going to Dallas. Use Cat-Pac Airlines. The hotel needs to be the Peninsula Hong Kong, a room on the top floor, south side of the building. And have ten thousand Hong Kong dollars ready for me at LAX. Of course, our regular fees apply."

Colonel Wright's brows went up, and he straightened himself in his chair at my mention of the pocket change. "Of course. My staff sergeant will take care of your arrangements. Your contact over there will be a woman named Ping Lee. She has a British father, so she's taller than the average Chinese woman. Ms. Lee lives in the Kowloon but keeps a room rented on the island. That's where she keeps the components."

"You have a picture?"

Wright flashed a photo of the woman from his folder. "She's good. She knows her way around Hong Kong in case things go wrong."

"It won't. But I absolutely have to be back Sunday, even if it means I come home empty-handed."

The colonel gave no protest. "You should easily be back then. When you're ready to meet Ping Lee, her bio is on this memory card." He handed me an unmarked MicroSD memory card. "Destroy this before the plane touches down on Chinese soil."

Chapter 38

Hong Kong, China
Rick

A soul would be hard-pressed to find better accommodations along the Asian rim than the Peninsula Hong Kong Hotel dating back in 1928. It has a fleet of Rolls Royce Phantoms picking guests up and dropping them off for shopping and business, and there are the gold-clad lobby fixtures. Oolong tea, scones, and live jazz made up high-tea, overlooking Victoria Harbor.

Today was my first day back in almost twenty years when I operated out of the hotel during the Uk-China transition. I glanced around, and sure enough, the elevator operator, a Chinese man, wore the same style black tux as back then. Mr. Hai first took care of me on his birthday some twentyish years ago.

Surprised and expressing it, Mr. Hai greeted me using his British accent, "Welcome home, Mr. Haade."

"Hai, it's been a while."

"Long enough for children to go off to college. What floor would you like? Your old one?"

I joined him in the lift. "Twenty-one."

****

Mr. Hai opened the twenty-first-floor door. Still, there was a floor concierge stationed outside the elevator. He came from his desk and greeted me, "Mr.

Haade, good to see you again." He swept his arm in the direction of my old room. "Your room is ready. Would you care for a decanter of your Woodford bourbon?"

The following morning, I taxied to a place I'd not been on the island—a new hotel, The Butterfly Hotel. Still not fully open, the Butterfly would be accessible to Ping Lee when her shift ends at the factory.

Chinese police mulled around its lobby. Following the information received on the microSD, I took the elevator to the eleventh floor. There too, police congregated. I stepped back into the elevator car, pressed the twenty-second floor, held the door open for a half minute, and then directed the elevator to express down to the lobby.

I returned to the Peninsula, switched my phone to satellite communications, then stood behind quilted drapes and sent Ping Lee a text: "Victoria Park Boat Pool 11."

At precisely eleven a.m. in Victoria Park, I made a stroll around the shallow kiddy-boat pool. I searched for Wright's woman. On the concrete pool's edge, I found two parallel chalk marks, a message from Ping Lee. She arrived before me.

A Boston Celtic woman with Asian facial features approached from the side. I asked, "Lee?"

The lady nodded while motioning for me to join in a walk. "Let's go over here. Down to the trees." We strolled, aware of the man following us dressed in a white tennis outfit. "There's been a complication," she said. "Housekeeping at the Butterfly found your friend's gift. The country has taken a considerable interest in my room."

"That's no good."

She barked a light laugh. "The room is registered under a fake ID. It's taken some time for them to identify me as an interesting person. I took a gamble at work today and brought out a whole finished circuit board. Once they discover it's gone, they'll be all over me."

I said in a low voice, "The man in a tennis outfit following us…."

"He's the police. The company may have already discovered the board missing."

"Do you have it with you?"

"No." Ping Lee leaned closer, then slapped me across the cheek.

"How long will it take you to get it?"

"It's at another location."

"Okay. Get it and follow my instructions. We'll be out of here this afternoon. I have a plane coming to meet us."

She grabbed my hand and stopped me. "I'm going to spit on you now. We need to go in different directions. I'll text you."

Watching the white guy, I told her, "Delay is our enemy. Do what you have to faster than a flash."

So, instead of her, the tennis guy followed me, strolling along a winding grassy path through the trees and pink azaleas in bloom. I stopped at a local food vendor's cart and ordered shrimpy rice soup.

Mr. Tennis nudged behind me and commanded, "Let me see your passport."

Using my British accent, I responded, "Why would a tennis player want to see my passport? I don't think so."

Mr. Tennis flashed his badge.

I handed him my British Passport.

The man in white shoes, white socks, and a white belt examined its photo page. "You're from Manchester, I see. A good football team, *The United*."

I worked to display total disinterest. "I'm a cricket man, myself."

"Cricket? People here know nothing about cricket. It's embarrassing. Everyone watches football. Manchester Cricket Club. They played at the Kowloon a few years back. They're good."

I regained my passport. "The club's name is the Lancashire Cricket Club, and they're awful. Is there something you want from me?"

The cop fixed an eye on me with a scathing glare. "I could arrest you for no more than being seen with that woman. What's your association?"

"Association? Her? The beggar bitch? None." I returned his glare. "I'm a British citizen. She wanted money. I sent her away."

"I don't believe you, Mr. Merrill. China doesn't tolerate British criminals lurking with locals in our parks. Even you who came from LAX." The policeman gave me a finger punch to my scarred shoulder and added, "You walk a straight line, Mr. Merrill. We're watching you."

****

At the Peninsula, I put the phone back into satellite mode, leaning it toward the outside southern sky. I keyed in Toby's location code and sent out a text message: "Moscow Rule needed."

He immediately responded: "1.5 hours, props spinning."

I converted back to international calling and keyed in Ping Lee's text line: "need to leave. ASAP."

She responded: "when—where."

I sent: "here @ 2:30"

I switched back to Toby's line: "can they be here by three?"

Toby texted: "3 OK. corporate terminal."

The McDonnell plane would find us at the Hong Kong Corporate Jet Terminal at three o'clock, assuming all stayed on plan.

I went to Artiberia Fine Men's Clothing store in the Peninsula lobby, where several police officers collected outside. I purchased a Berluti calf-skin briefcase, random magazines from the newsstand, a leather writing tablet with two pens. I crumpled, sorted, folded, and wrinkled the items to make them appear used. Unfortunately, the clothes I brought with me would have to stay upstairs. I didn't want it to appear I was leaving.

A black and white taxi entered the Peninsula's portico. In a light-green work jacket and green jeans, Ping Lee got out.

As quickly as she got out, I ushered her into the back of a black Rolls limo. "The driver works for us. Get in. Let me have the circuit board."

"It's safe."

"It's not safe until I have it in my fist." I slid the tiny board into a slot in the calfskin case under the magazines.

A white and orange police car with blue flashing lights broke out of the traffic line and chased us from the rear. He practically climbed our back bumper. The driver finally asked, "What do you want me to do?"

"Drive normal."

We remained steady and, once on airport property, exited in the direction of the Corporate Terminal. But, lucky, the police car continued straight toward the

Passenger Terminal.

One customs inspection officer stood in the military rest position behind a stainless-steel table opposite the metal security railing. I opened my case while he fingered through its contents. Once satisfied, he stamped my passport.

"Was your business acceptable, Mr. Merrill?"

"It was."

He buzzed me through the electric gate.

"Have a safe flight."

The inspector now focused on Ping Lee's passport and studied her face, shining a flashlight in her eyes and pressing a buzzer. His assistant entered the room from a side door and handcuffed Ping Lee immediately.

"You'll have to come with me," he told her.

Chapter 39

Taipei, Taiwan
Rick

Our Mardi Gras-colored 757 aligned on Taipei runway 23R, making its final approach for landing. Here I'll switch to a more comfortable commercial flight for the jump across the Pacific. Unfortunately, it appeared I was the only person getting off.

A black van waited on the tarmac for me to transfer to Cat-Pac Airways without going through the passenger terminal. Los Angles was fourteen hours away. Colonel Wright would be fifteen hours away waiting on the international concourse.

****

"Do you want a beer?" Wright, spotting me coming through Customs, asked.

"I'll wait while you have one."

"Then let's go to the, uh, Welcome Home Surf Pub over there."

The Surf Pub waitresses wore yellow polka-dotted bathing suit tops with red surfer shorts. The Surf Pub was little more than an open-front venue with stools lined up along the front.

"Whatcha fellas need?" she addressed Colonel Wright.

Wright grinned and gave the small plates menu a

once-over. "Just a Michelob in a bottle."

She smacked a wad of pink bubble gum between her back teeth. I half expected her to be wearing roller skates based on the place's decor. But, instead, she waited for me to say something. "And you?"

"Ask if your man over there can make an Old Fashioned. Otherwise, get me a freshly brewed cup of coffee."

Wright commented, "I understand you encountered a bit of trouble."

"Not as bad as sometimes. The Chinese figured out our woman and started setting the stage for our arrest."

"What happened?"

"The hotel maids found Ping's dingus and notified the Chinese police. The cops were watching for someone to pick them up. When I showed, they made a link from her to me. Another hour and they would have sent both of us up the Yangtze. But I'm guessing you know all of that."

"You got the board, though, right?"

"What do you think? Of course."

"Let me see." Colonel Wright examined the board's top and bottom, nodded to himself, and with pleasure on his face. Then, into his pocket, the board went. "That's the right one. What did you think about Ping Lee?"

"She was astute and quick—calm under pressure. I hope you're going to tell me it was your folks who picked her up."

Wright, pleased with the outcome, said. "Your boss somehow figured out she had been compromised. He pulled her out before she got on the plane. We have her."

"That's Toby."

Wright emptied his beer, stood, and turned. As he

walked away, he said, "Thank him for me. She's good."

****

I finally made it to the townhouse, a smoke-free townhouse, I might add. I dropped my keys and wallet on the table by my Rangers chair, slipped off my shoes, and basked in the pleasure of being back home.

Two messages were waiting. One from Je said, "Found Londonderry box at the chemist shop. Nothing in it." The second message was from Laura, "Got called out to Pitt unexpected. Home next week. Call me."

As much as I needed the bathroom, I dialed Laura if for no other reason than to hear her fresh voice. "I wanted to let you know I'm bushed and back in Dallas."

She said, "I'm glad. Where did you go, or can I ask?"

"I went to Hong Kong on a government gig. It's over. How about you?"

"Nothing good. We've been in project meetings since yesterday. It's brutal. We've broken for dinner."

Given that, it should be safe to ask, so I asked cautiously, "I take it you're not getting fired?"

"Not yet. The big boss said my team has to figure out a solution or we march to the sea. So here we are with wadding boots."

On the way to the bathroom, I checked the carpet around the bed for fresh footprints. It looked like it had been vacuumed after Laura left. Finally, I laid my phone in the nightstand Qi charger and fell facedown, drifting comatose.

****

I caught up with Je in Londonderry early my time, late his. "Your GPS tells me you've discovered Maiden O'Clery's Pub," I said.

"I hate those damn tattletales," he said. "Can we take them off our phones?"

"You'll love them as soon as we have to come to fish you out of a swamp somewhere. So, what's this about the pharmacy?"

The noise on the phone improved as if he went outside for privacy. "I wanted to tell you the content of the box shipped to the pharmacist was ground-up conch shell powder. The pharmacist uses the smelly shit to make in-house calcium capsules he sells."

"Nothing even remotely like a memory device?"

Je said honestly, "Hell, I don't even know what a memory device is. But I do know it doesn't look like tan powder. I talked with the chemist, and there's something not right about him at all. So, I'm still not ruling out him or his shop. My gut tells me something could have been buried in the powder when it arrived. It was half full when I opened it."

I worked to shovel in my breakfast biscuits and gravy. "You're right. For now, we should assume the device is somewhere there in the shop. Let's assume the pharmacist got it because he was the intended target. What do we know about the other three boxes?"

"I've called in Kaelyn from the London office to help."

"Who's Kaelyn?" Sad to admit, I didn't have enough time to manage the London office and still be the company sleuth. Je will get London after his certification.

"Kaelyn is London's closest thing to a cat burglar. I've got her going in the pharmacy tonight after it closes while the chemist is here at O'Clery's drinking."

"Make damn sure I don't get a call from the

constabulary chief about her getting caught."

Je chuckled. "Got it," he said. "Let's call his box number one. Box two went to Dublin. I've been down there myself to check it out. It's a complete bust. The station manager said they returned the box to San Juan because it was sent to a non-existing address."

"Okay. What about the box in City Cork?"

"Innocent as well. It went to a private residence. Jurgen Peters came over with Kaelyn, from London, and talked with the guy. The man said the hotel in San Juan returned his Apple phone to him. He'd left it there when he checked out."

"I don't buy it, Harley. Do you? You don't have four boxes, all the same size, and weight, coming from one consignor with a cell phone in one and shell powder in another. We know they all started with the same thing in them, or they wouldn't have weighed the same. So, get your people back to take a deeper look until they come up with something. Get the carrier's driver to give you proof of delivery the box was returned to San Juan."

"I'll do it. This is my project. I've been curious," Je said, "if the driver could be part of the scheme and opened the box to take the chip out. Then he monkeyed with the paperwork to make it look like the box was addressed to an unknown location."

"Good thought. Call Dallas and have someone go down to San Juan to see if anyone opened the box and then reclosed it. Have them tell us what the hell is in it. Probably more important, verify the thing ever came back. I bet it never did."

"Good idea."

"So how about Boston? Have you said anything to them? They may not even know what's going on."

****

I waited for Toby in his private room at the Medical City of Dallas. A nurse rolled in his gurney from recovery to let him brush off the anesthesia before going home.

Dr. Grave followed shortly and checked Toby's breathing and heart sounds. The doctor told me, "The scan shows the cyberknife can easily access his tumors."

Toby, awakening, still in a fog, asked Graves, "Tumors? Is there more than one?"

Grave accessed this mobile tablet so Toby could see and brought up an image. "There's two, Mr. McDonnell, almost right next to one another. When we treat one, we'll treat both. The cyberknife views them separately."

I stood bedside to Toby, watching the screen, when he asked me, "Does what the doctor said make sense to you? I'm confused."

I let my hand rest lightly on my buddy's shoulder. "Dr. Graves is on top of what he's doing."

Grave closed his tablet and spoke to me, "His treatments will be outpatient and take about an hour, plus or minus. We'll do seven treatments at weekly intervals. Toby will do well as long as you make sure he's here."

Chapter 40

Dallas, Texas
Rick

According to him, Toby said he was well enough for work. So Maria helped him get ready and drove his Bentley to our building at City Place. Security helped get him into the elevator and brought him up to the forty-fourth floor. Then, like a decrepit old man, he made his way to my office, shirt not tucked in.

I hit him with what was foremost on my mind. "Have you decided on Gower's replacement? Or are you staying?"

"Close your door."

I did.

"I don't know. It's good having someone keep field operations off my desk. I don't like managing others."

State the obvious. "Maybe this time, we can find someone who has experience in what we do and how we do it."

"Gower understood what we do."

"Not so much. Not as much as you think."

Toby was too proud to use a cane to maneuver himself. "I disagree."

"What Gower was good at was embezzling money, schmoozing with the rich, and sending agents around the world like idiots. I pulled us out of the pits more than you realize."

Toby cleared his throat like he was ready for his morning's first rum. "I'm going to wait and see what happens with my cancer treatments. Then, if cancer beats me, you can recruit whoever you want."

"Me? I doubt it."

"It's you. You're the only one who knows everyone on every floor. So, of course, it's you."

"I'm wearing out, just like you," I said. "We have been doing this for a long time. I'm about down to minimum tire threads, myself."

"Shit. Retire? Retirement means you can't handle your job anymore, and you don't want others to find that out. That's not my Ricky. You'll handle it."

"That's not it." I, all of a sudden, felt defensive. "When I've done this for fifty years, I'm giving it to Je. Laura and I will be moving to the islands."

"Then this works out nicely. You take over. You keep the guys out of the ruts without thinking about it. You'll have time to sell the place and take my daughter to a life of luxury."

I settled beside Toby on my sofa. "We already live a life of luxury. I don't want to talk about this anymore."

"Okay." Toby figured as much. "The real reason I came to the office today is Colonel Wright." He patted me on the thigh. "What I told you was going to happen did. He called me last night. The Air Force wants more."

"What do you mean?"

Proud of still being able to call things right, Toby pushed himself up straighter. "He wants for you to go back to Kirtland. He says he has a rather serious piece of business he needs you to take care of personally."

"What sort of business?"

"Rory has been picking up a lot of seismic activity coming from Southern New Mexico."

"He mentioned it."

"My best guess is those are Wright's missiles, and something has gone wrong. He wouldn't say, but he did say the way you handled the circuit board assignment makes you perfect for what he needs."

"And, what does he need?"

"Rory's analysis think the Air Force has started building a cloud of space-based weapons for use in wartime. But that's a guess. You'll have to go find out."

I was slow in responding. "Space-based military weapons; that'll void more than a few peace treaties."

Toby raised his brows. "I don't think they much care. My money is on the fact something about them has gone wrong. He wants you to put it right. He said Monday works for him."

"You and I are at Medical City for your treatment on Mondays. Have Andi tell him I'm busy. I'll be there Wednesday."

****

I dictated a text message to display on Je's phone, "Priorities changed. Keep in the lead on the memory boxes. Toby needs me for something. Stay focused on the deliveries in Ireland. I'll contact Dee in Washington about the Boston shipment. I'll touch bases again in a couple of days."

Dee has always been a mess to deal with, today more than ever. I instructed her, "Get your team to Boston a-sap. There's a freight forwarder you need to sweep their operations for a small box coming from San Juan."

She came back playing the pitiful overworked-me card. "I can't. We're backed up to the hilt here in DC."

"That wasn't a request, Dee. I need you to get a crew up there by eight tomorrow morning. They need to go over this company's operations. You need to stop the company from forwarding a box to anywhere."

She snapped at me, "Sorry, Rick, I need to stay on what I'm doing. You'll have to talk with Toby."

I lowered my voice down to a primal growl. "I ain't playing this fucking game with you again. You get a crew, including yourself, to Boston as soon as we hang up. Either you do this, or I'll find someone else who will."

"Let me talk to Toby first."

"Let me clarify any question in your mind. If you're not on the next train to Boston, you won't need to talk to Toby because you'll be finding another job. I've posted a picture of what we think the box looks like on your blackboard. Every shipment coming into the freight forwarder gets inspected. If anyone sees what I've posted, get it out and lock it up in a safe place where it can't be disturbed."

Dee grumbled. "You know, Haade, you're a real asshole. You know that, right?"

"Actually, Dee, I've been told that."

With the Dee call behind me, I called Laura. "Can you talk?"

"Yeah. What do you need?" She sounded harried but no worse so than usual.

"Are you planning to be in town this weekend? There's something we need to talk about."

"I can be. Give me a clue."

"Your dad assumes I am going to take over the company when he leaves. I'm not sure."

"Well now—that's a shock."

I arrived at Love Field on Wednesday to find the same flight crew from before, except this time, the pilot informed me, "My orders are to make this plane available to you at all times."

I checked at the small jet parked in front of me and grinned to myself. "That works."

Chapter 41

Scottsdale, AZ
Kelly Lake

Gower hooked me up with her once before but neglected to tell me she was Rick Haade's sister. I dialed her downtown Phoenix area code. *Don't kill her.* Mark gave me this number in case I wanted another swell time rocking on Esmee Street. When we came out the first time, he never once mentioned who she was. I dialed the next three digits. *I'll tie her up and get some pokey-poke fun first.* I don't remember what either of us said other than telling her what a good deal she was for the money. I took a deep breath and pushed the final four digits. *Be careful. Don't push it too far.* When she answered, I said, "I'm glad I found you. You might not remember me, but we've been together before in Phoenix. You said I was your first."

A middle-aged voice that I recognized responded excitedly. "I remember you. Kelly? Right?"

"That's right. I'm at the Four Seasons in Scottsdale. Can you come out this far tonight?"

Esmee didn't hesitate with an answer. "For my Kelly, Scottsdale's not too far."

Just hurt her.

I told her, "I'm lonely. I need somebody willing to talk with me. Maybe, in the end, you take care of me."

"I'd enjoy it. It's no bother. I'll come now if you want."

Am I ready? She would be naked. I held a cotton rope coiled in my hand. "Can you stay all night?"

"If you want. My rates have gone up. All night will be a thousand, but I can get you for a little cheaper."

"Do come. I'm in room 1419."

Soon she tapped on the door. I opened it. The vision of a thousand dollars' worth of a woman stared back at me from the hall. My ropes and gags were on the bed. I tingled down below.

"Come in. You're as beautiful as ever. Even more so. You've cut your hair. It makes you look like a girl from the university."

Esmee touched my cheek with her fingertips. "Thanks. I do remember you. You were my first."

I quietly eased the door closed so I didn't cause a memory imprint on anyone staying on my floor.

She slipped out of her sandals, and I opened an envelope, showing her the bills inside. It went on the floor next to her sandals.

She strolled the suite and pulled the drapes closed for privacy. "It seems like we had a bit of extra fun getting that big Indian of yours in the canoe last time. I enjoyed that. This is going to be fun."

I handed her a flute of champagne. "How have you been doing?"

"Great. I'm glad you called. After our last visit, I wanted to share how nice you were to me with my brother. I've never seen my brother so impressed. I finally found something I could do instead of tapping him each month. He used to think there was nothing I could do to take care of myself."

Esmee's nipples were like little fingers pointing at me. *Let's go. I want to see ropes tight around them, swelling them like purple grapes.* I asked, "You told your brother about me? All good, I hope. What did you tell him?"

"I told him you live in Dallas. That's where he lives. And you were my first and so far the best. You were super nice. He travels a lot, like you…those sorts of things."

"I want to do ropes tonight if you're willing." I took a few hanks of woven white cotton rope from the foot of the bed. "Do you like doing ropes? I want to tie you up tonight and explode in you."

"I've never done it but I've seen it. Yeah. Let's tie me up."

"My only rule is I get to tie you up so you can't move. Then I'll throw you on the bed and do to you what I want."

It seemed to strike her adventurous side. She touched herself. "You want me to tie you up, too?"

"No. You can't imagine what this is going to do to you."

But careful. Don't kill her.

She put her wrists together. "Let's do it." She tried to restrain a giggle. "I'm a little bit scared." Her arms were stiff and reaching toward me.

"Behind your back." I collected a pair of pink fur-covered handcuffs and tickled her cheek with the fluff.

"This is hot."

I pulled her arms behind her and clipped the cuffs closed. *I didn't think she'd let me.* I sliced off her tee-shirt with a pair of pink scissors, exposing her white shelf bra. I cut it between her breasts, and it tumbled away.

Her pert C-cup breasts stared at me. Inviting me.

"Okay, let's have some fun," I said. "Are the cuffs tight enough? Do they hurt?"

"It's kinky, sort of fun."

I looped a piece of cotton rope and wrapped it around the cuffs, and fed an end over each shoulder. Then I passed them under her armpits and back up over her shoulders. I made several loops around her breasts, tightening the rope each time. They began to swell, engorging, standing out even farther—swollen grapefruits. I passed the rope around her neck again, firm but not tight enough to hurt her. Back down to her breasts, I ran the white line. During this pass, I pulled especially hard, forcing her Cs to double Ds. They started becoming a dark blue color. I wanted that. I wanted them to become dark purple. That's when they hurt. That's what I want. Hurt. Both hurting. With every pass of the rope, I tightened more. Finally, her nipples were dark purple grapes. I started thumping each.

She let out, "That hurts. Not so hard."

That was my cue. I reached to unzip my jeans.

Chapter 42

Albuquerque, New Mexico
Rick

I could taste the tension in the air when I arrived at Colonel Wright's office. Three other high-ranking military men had sat at the table before I arrived. The weight of the air smelled misty and bore an uneasiness—that sense you get when things are on the brink of destruction.

Colonel Wright took his place at the head of the table while I landed in the chair to his left. Opposite me were the three officers. Wright had pre-facilitated the table. One official black DoD ballpoint pen per person (keep it if you please), a legal-size tablet of yellow paper, and a blue water bottle were at each seat.

"Gentlemen," Wright stated, "may I introduce Mr. Richard Haade of McDonnell and Associates in Dallas."

He began introducing me to each of the strangers. To his right and directly across from me, Major Jefferson was from Space Flight Operations stationed here at Kirtland AFB. This gentleman sported a Field Marshal Montgomery-style bushy mustachio, and round wire-rim glasses decorated his melon size face.

Next to him and to my left sat Major Carson from the Weapons Guidance Center, stationed here at Kirtland. Major Carson, a wrinkled desert fox, stood to shake my hand and welcome me.

Wright introduced the final officer, "And from Nellis Airfield in Las Vegas, is Major Jimmy Butts. He directs Strategic and Tactical Targeting." His was the sour face of the bunch. He neither stood nor tried to shake my hand, choosing to remain seated and show his scowl.

"Okay." Wright connected his laptop with the projector and shared an image on the wall. It was an Air Force logo. "Let's get the game started."

He clicked his mouse, and the image changed to one of a satellite with its solar panels unfolded. The satellite appeared to have a bomb door open on its belly like a jet bomber.

Wright cleared his throat. "The battlefield—as the gentlemen around the table know—has disappeared. The distance between a war winner and a war loser has grown massively." He pointed his index finger toward his window. "A mile from here is a building Kirtland uses to control any battlefield in the world and can do it in a few short minutes. Fifteen minutes from the time we receive an order to disable a battlefield, we can declare victory worldwide.

"What we have historically spent on defense and combat will soon be budgeted for social improvements—making our country stronger. In next year's State of the Union address, the president will announce an economic paradigm change. Our Defense budget will go nearly to zero. What we spend on tanks will be available for Alzheimer's research. Money spent on aircraft carriers is shifting to heart research. Fighter jet research is converting to free health care. As a result, you have a healthier, more powerful America."

Major Jefferson, across from me, came from space operations. He interjected, "Imagine the United States being able to tell other world leaders, 'If you don't treat your citizens with respect and dignity, we will eliminate you and your sergeants in one swift attack.'"

Wright continued, "A year from now, soldiers with weapons and missiles will be old news. National peace and human rights will have become priority one in their place. China, Russia, the Middle East…the world has changed."

He clicked to change the wall image. It was now an unnamed control room with Air Force personnel at the controls—a space of monitors and buttons.

Wright said, "From now on, war consists of small groups of airmen in comfortable control rooms stateside. With a few buttons, they can send a targeted weapon down on enemy soldiers, eliminating them anywhere in the world. Global bad people need to know they are going to be killed on the spot—from boot-grunts to battalion leaders—if they insist on disrupting the peace."

He changed the image on the wall to a matte black egg-shaped thing with guidance fins placed on the back. "We've nicknamed this an egg. It does all the work for us. This is where I turn the discussion over to Major Jefferson."

He passed the presentation clicker to Jefferson from Operations.

Jefferson started, "Kirtland is in the process of filling empty satellite slots above the earth. We're creating a low-earth cloud of first-strike weapons. Yes, we're leaving treaties to the Senators. Our view is China, Russia, and the Middle East pose a real threat to the safety of our nation, and as such, we must prepare for an attack on all fronts. To date, we have enough slotted satellites to counter most enemy threats worldwide. In a few months, we will have complete coverage."

He clicked the image to an animation showing a dense layer of low orbiting satellites swarming over and under one over another.

Major Carlson of Weapons Guidance added, "The advantage of a cloud is we can deploy any or all of our devices to Earth with exact individual targeting." His graphic changed to a technical illustration of a string of these 'eggs' equipped with fins being deployed back to earth. Carlson said, "Each egg can be individually assigned a specific target location. Then, after re-entry, it will land within eighteen inches of where we instruct it, from here at Kirtland."

Carlson caught me studying the wall. He said, "The kill ratio is 100 percent. All living, breathing organisms will die immediately."

I echoed back his words, "Organisms?"

"If it breathes or blinks, its life is over."

"Such as," I asked for clarification, "insects, people, donkeys, pigs, everything?"

"Bluebirds, snakes, and little fuzzy kittens. Everything. If it uses air to breathe and pumps blood, it's dead. But there is a good thing—after thirty minutes, the weapon neutralizes and becomes totally harmless, so our guys aren't in harm's way."

Major Butts, the grouch from their Nevada Targeting facility, finally perked up—knowing me to be inferior. "You're not grasping what we're saying. Let's say we have a terrorist organization that decides to take over a small Middle East group of Bedouins. The Bedouins scatter into the desert and flee for their lives.

The insurgents take the possessions left behind and set up a headquarters. We find out about it. Kirtland maps the village location through orbital reconnaissance and directs one of the satellites to drop an egg to retake the village. The weapon reenters the atmosphere. And within a few minutes, it overtakes the enemy, one-hundred percent dead. But the infrastructure the Bedouins left behind remains intact. The only difference is this time, the camp is sterile."

"Sterile?"

"Close enough," Butts replied.

Colonial Wright turned to me. "It really is that simple." He clicked and projected a photo of a broken-in-half egg lying in the center of a dirt road. "Once the weapon comes back to Earth, it releases its payload of liquid which quickly evaporates to gas. Anything breathing the vapors dies with the first breath. No pain, no suffering. They are lifeless within an instant. It's the most humane death we know of."

In the image background, combatants were scattered across the ground and their equipment.

I didn't know how to process what they were telling me. "Is this photo real or staged?"

Wright answered, "This was an actual weapon used during a live test."

"Using real people?"

Wright said, "It was actual combatant at a tactical location in Libya. Move on?"

I took my time and said, "Am I right in believing you are gassing people under a jazzy new name?"

"You're talking about banned gasses?" The display on the wall rotated through several images, then stopped showing a damaged human lung. "Banded gasses work by chemically burning the lining of the lungs. It's a profoundly painful death, and the individual dies slowly, stretched out over time, finally from asphyxiation. And some suffer the rest of their lives, wishing they had been killed. Their skin simply melts away from their body. That's not what our compound is. It works at a sub-cellular level."

Major Jefferson spoke again. "Rather than harming the person's lungs, Klearance, our compound, is absorbed directly into the blood and carried to the brainstem. There it shuts off the body by creating a total sodium ion barrier. The body's electrical system shuts down instantly—no heartbeat, no breathing, no anything. The entire process happens in the time it takes to get our molecules from the lung to the brainstem through the blood. Unlike bullets and explosives, the targeted individual has no awareness he was injured. He stops being and falls."

"Through the lungs?"

"Or eyes or sinuses. Any mucus membrane that will pass Klearance into the bloodstream. It's quickest through the eyes." Jefferson gave a small smile. "It's fast and painless. At most, if the combatant is in a group, he'll see a domino effect of people falling in front of him as the wall of gas approaches. But it moves so fast he has almost no time to understand what's going on."

Then it occurred to me. "What saves our soldiers?"

That fell directly into Wright's next pitch – me being his straight man. "That's what's the best—our boys aren't even there. If a clean-up is needed, Klearance vapors are volatile and revert to a safe state in thirty minutes. That's one of the safeguards. All that's left is the smell of cinnamon."

Carlson smiled. "We can drop an egg for breakfast, and our boys are there by lunch to bring home the bacon."

"I think you said you did a live test on real people?"

Carlson answered, "Those pictures you saw were from Libya. Al Qaida got into a desert battle following the Benghazi American Embassy attack. Intelligence told us, so we took them out."

Impressive. "I'd say you've got a winner. But here's the place where you stop and tell me 'Except'… How wrong have things already gotten?"

"You're astute." Wright clicked to the image of a white eighteen-wheeler whose trailer's nose had been cut open. The remaining metal hanging out like a tin door. "You're right. This is the place where I tell you something has gone very, very, very wrong." He clicked the slides through to one showing a bevy of armed airmen in sky-blue uniforms guarding the damaged rig with M-16 rifles locked and loaded. "We consigned this vehicle to deliver a sample of Klearance to Patterson Field outside Dayton, Ohio. As you can see, it didn't make it." He switched his laptop to slideshow mode, which flashed images of the damaged vehicle from different angles.

Somebody cut a man-sized hole in the front of the trailer to gain access to its cargo. I asked, "How deep did your investigation go?"

"I'll send it to you, but deep." Colonel Wright pointed to the banker boxes stacked next to his desk. "I presume you'll be staying here on the airfield. I've arranged accommodations."

Not sure, I said, "If this is interesting enough."

"I assure you, it's interesting enough. Two drivers

went out on this trip; one died, and the other disappeared. The dead man happened to be my freight wing leader."

"And the co-driver vanished?"

"Expert guess. We haven't seen his co-driver since the load went through our gate."

"Tell me about the co-driver."

"She's over here on a development assignment. She's with the Irish Army, documenting how we process highly sensitive freight."

I said, "I doubt she's around any longer. She's done skedaddled back to Ireland by now. Is there a cab video showing what happened?"

Wright nodded. "There is. The codriver killed him with an injection in the neck—that part's clear."

I had a mental triage going about the possibilities. But, before I could decide, I needed to see the colonel's documents. "I'd also like a tour of the rig and to see the forensics from the attack site. But, first, let's look at the cab video."

Wright brought a different angle picture of the trailer's nose up, showing its damage. A three-sided rectangle hole stood up about a man's height. It appeared someone cut it with a portable jigsaw rather than an acetylene torch. That was wise. Not knowing cardboard boxes were just on the inside, he could have started a trailer fire that would have taken everything.

Wright shuffled several glossy photos across the table. I fingered through them until I came to one showing the inside of the trailer, looking through the hole. "Is the only thing in here men's slippers?"

"Right."

"The cylinders you talk about, will they fit in one of those boxes?"

"The missing box held four."

"How did it get decided where the box would get packed?"

Wright answered as if I should know. "We commissioned a security study two years. The answer came back for us to mix them in men's slippers far away from the rear doors, preferably in the trailer nose, which is where this one was packed."

"Yet somebody had knowledge of exactly where to cut into the trailer?"

"Obviously."

Wright sat an example box on the table. I instantly noticed the word slipper was spelled wrong. "So what size are these cylinders?"

"Just shy of four inches long and two inches in diameter. They have triple safety valves on the top, bringing them up to about six inches, but they make them safe to handle."

"You mentioned a study. By whom?"

Wright leaned back in his chair as if bee-stung. "You don't know?"

"Why would I?" I slid the tan box back across the table toward him.

"It was your company who conducted the study," he said.

"McDonnell?"

"Since two years ago. We've used your plan at least a dozen times."

"Hold that..." I ripped my phone from my pant pocket. I messaged Toby: *"Who at McDonnell designed a hazmat plan for a surface trip between Kirtland AFB and Patterson Field? It was two years ago. That's why they called me back."* Then, to the Air Force bobbleheads, I asked, "Just how did we tell you to conceal the cylinders?"

"As you see, buried in a stack of slippers in the nose of the trailer. Cleverly, our box has the word slipper spelled wrong. It's got only one *p*."

With greater urgency, I thumbed through the rest of the photos on the table. "Do you have any reason to believe the hijackers know what Klearance is?"

The colonel disconnected the slide show and configured his laptop to be a video. "I doubt it seriously. Klearance is as hush as a can of hush-hush can hold. It only travels while being deployed. This trip was special. Patterson is doing research and needed a sample."

"Let me see the video."

My phone started doing its vibration dance as Toby returned my message. "*No such work was contracted by McDonnell.*"

At the start, the video showed people milling around and getting the truck ready for the trip. I asked Wright, "Who was aware of the cylinders in this load? I suppose you run dummy loads to confuse people. And who knows about the trick of spelling slipper wrong?"

"Every day. There's an eighteen-wheeler leaving for somewhere. They all look like this one."

"And the misspelling?"

"The loadmaster, I suppose."

"On this load?"

"The dead driver."

"Figures. How about the missing codriver?"

"Not unless Begaye told her, which I doubt. He was a by-the-rules airman. The cab audio breaks up on the video, so we're unsure what he told her. But you'll see, they talk for a while, and she kills him in cold blood."

I focused on the image. The video projecting onto the wall had three cameras; one aimed left, one toward the driver, and the other to the right on the codriver. The last one showed the dashboard controls, meters, and dials. Watching when the video showed the codriver, my heart skipped. I slapped the table with a loud pop. "Go back."

Wright jumped and reversed the image, single-stepping backward. "To where?"

"The woman's face. Get a clear shot of her face."

The image scrolled back a few more clicks. "That's about the best."

I told the men in the room, "This is too easy. This woman's name is Carissa Scaffe. She was born in Londonderry, Northern Ireland. I've known her since she was a baby. I'm after her for another case."

Excusing myself and stepping into the hall, I immediately notified my crew, Rory, Je, and Dee, with an instant message: *"STAND DOWN. Stop all work on Army boxes immediately. The content of boxes is extremely hazardous. If found, protect the boxes but do not open them."*

Chapter 43

Dallas, Texas
Rick

Toby let out an old man's chuckle leading me into the Stein and Swine Bar. "All right, smartass," he said. "I did buy this pub this morning, so no more wisecracks." With a Berry's Guadeloupe Rum waiting for him at the bar when we walked in, he took it, and we settled by the front window.

I jabbed, "You want people to see you owning the place now?"

"No. I want to hear what you think about Colonel Wright's dilemma. I've been thinking on it too."

I sipped my Old Fashioned. Toby found the barkeep skilled in Bourbon. "At least you hire good barkeeps. This is the best. So, here's what I think. I think you should have your kitchen cook us a double plate of potato skins with no sour cream."

Toby gave the order to his barkeeper, and we talked about the pub's layout, what weekend music he would play, and the crowd he would allow in. Then, when the potato skins came, we dove in.

"There is a radical group called Brahms," he said. "They date back to Old English Boudica and her tribe of marauders. They came before the Knights Templar, the Freemasons—most importantly, they ran the Romans out of London. Here's a fact. Other than the Catholic Church, Brahms is the only group to survive medieval times. These days people know almost nothing about their organization other than they're active worldwide."

Toby fingered bits and crumbles from the bottom of my potato skin. "I know you don't read the newspaper," he said, "so you probably missed the spate of strange deaths going on around the world. The President of Vanuatu was assassinated. Brahms claimed responsibility for his killing. There's a slew of others, and they all happened the same way. Given what Wright told you, I understand why their coroners couldn't find how they died."

"Brahms? I was thinking you were going to say Gower is behind…."

"…exactly. Brahms and Mark Gower are the same." He snorted a soft laugh. "I'll show you proof later at my house."

I paused and took a bite. "These killings you've read about, you think they're being killed with the Air Force gas? One whiff and lights out?" I took another bite. The skins were excellent, crisp on the outside, soft, and gooey on the inside. Bacon, cheddar, and green onions were sprinkled over them, all swimming in a buttery pool at the bottom. "I don't like having two killers using this stuff."

"I think you about got the puzzle pieces. Now you have to put them together. A lone singleton is out killing high-level leaders, and Kelly Lake is headed to Europe."

I licked the butter from my fingers. "It sounds like you think Lake is wanting Russia to pick a fight with the U.S."

"What better way is there than wiping Moscow off

the map?"

I frowned. "I wonder if the lone wolf has a connection to Kirkland? How else could he be getting his supply? Is there someone at Kirkland supplying his stuff?"

"Or, on the other hand," Toby said, "someone at Patterson Field could be ripping off samples and selling them. They've been shipped three samples so far this year. What do they do with the leftovers?"

I took the last potato skin. "And we could be talking about the space support team at Kirtland stealing an egg or two for homework. I need Colonel Wright to give me a list of people on his end who have access to the gas."

Toby sipped his rum. "And don't rule out Colonel Wright himself. I wouldn't."

Chapter 44

Dallas, Texas
Rick

As soon as I got home, I called Harley Je in Londonderry to redirect his effort. I took a glass of Pino Gris to the balcony and waited for the call to go through. When Harley Je answered, there was no time for gossip. "Your game has changed."

"For the worse, from the sound of your voice."

"Those boxes you're chasing don't contain anything from the Army; they're filled with poison gas from the Air Force. So, forget the memory chips."

"Poison gas?" There was a breathless quality in Je's voice telling me he understood the seriousness of how the game changed.

I said, "It's bad stuff. One cylinder can clear a city. Walk light."

He said. "I'm not sure I like this."

Je sounded serious. *Would he consider leaving at this point? I guess, in real life, I can't blame him. This... so he can get certified?* I asked, "Have the newspapers over there printed any stories about unexplained deaths recently?"

Je hummed, remembering. "Yesterday's paper had an article about a sheep farmer outside Dublin killed, his family and all that were with them. It happened last

Saturday. It didn't say how or why, but it did say their sheep were killed along with them."

That lined up with the box shipped to Dublin. "The box in Dublin—you said it went to some farm, right?"

"I think that's right, but the station manager told us it was a dead address, so it got sent back to San Juan."

"I'll spot you a drink; that's not how it happened. Did you get anyone in Dallas to go down and verify it? The Irish police, do they know anything?"

"I doubt it. The paper said autopsies on the people showed nothing. The paper said the medical examiner is necropsying the animals now."

The summer heat and hot batteries caused me to switch ears with my phone. "They're not going to find anything. The gas goes inert after thirty minutes. Okay. So, if you haven't figured this out, the stuff has a zero margin for error. Getting exposed to it will kill you through your eyes. You don't even have to breathe it. Call for more backup from the London Office. Don't try to do this by yourself."

"If you were me, would you do Dublin first?"

"It's your project, but if it were me, I'd talk up the delivery driver who carried the box into the countryside. My money is he delivered the box to the wrong address and left to cover his mistake. Instead, he monkeyed with the paperwork. The dead shepherd found the box, opened it, and the minute he opened the valves, his place became ground zero—season one, episode one."

"Man," Je came back.

"In the newspaper," I asked, "did it say if police recovered the cylinder?"

"It didn't."

"Then, if I were you, I'd have some from the

London office search the shepherd's place for the empty cylinder. I'll send you a picture of one. It's on your message board now."

"Got it."

"Don't jack with the valves," I told him. "I need to help Toby with something, but when I get done, I'll be over there to work this with you. You got a pretty crappy field certification project, my friend."

****

I immediately called Rory. No chit-chat this time. I instructed him, "New priority one. I need you to do a worldwide scan for any organization mentioning poison gasses. And, look for single loonies. You never know. Also, see if you can find anyone planning an attack on a large body of people. Those boxes you found out about in San Juan have a psychopath bum-rushing them to Europe. It turns out they are dangerous Air Force weapons."

"Perfect timing. The Watson Network is in a relatively quiet period. I should be able to crank out some big results really quickly. I'll call."

"And," I stopped him. "While you're at it, do a scan on the word Klearance spelled with a K and let me know what turns up."

****

When I entered the front of Toby's house, Maria greeted me with another Old Fashioned. Toby perched proudly behind her, wearing his 1960s road-touring outfit. Apparently, just before I got there, he came back from a cruise to Tyler, Texas, blazing his mind out on Interstate 20.

We walked to Toby's air-conditioned back porch while he filled me in on the thrill parts of the trip—and the college girl he picked up on her way to school at LSU.

His stupid behavior didn't sit well with me. "You're never going to grow up, are you? Did the doctor change any of your prescriptions?"

Toby shrugged. "I don't think so."

We parked ourselves outside at Toby's outdoor porch table. Toby pulled up his favorite chair, and I instructed him, "Empty your pockets. Let me see your bottles."

Though Toby hesitated for a moment, he complied, and two bottles rolled onto the walnut table surface.

I spun the bottles and read the labels. "What is this? You're not supposed to be taking oxycodone. You got two bottles of this stuff."

"They make me feel good."

"Were you taking these while you were driving?"

Toby snapped back at me, "How do you think I got the nerve to make the trip."

"Damn it, Toby. I come here to talk with you about something important, and you're here drinking rum and slamming oxy. Crap man. This shit will kill you."

"And cancer won't?"

"Well…" I returned his bottles. "Tell me, what have we been talking about?"

Toby answered in a direct way that I didn't expect, "You came to me because you lack the confidence to solve this toxic gas problem on your own. And you want me to justify your backing out of the project. Close enough? You need to make the correct decision on your own if you're going to run this company."

"I never said I would run the company."

Toby took my arm. "I want to show you something inside."

Chapter 45

Dallas, Texas
Rick

He handed me a small, deeply-patinaed brass paperweight. "I got this from Gower's desk," he said. "At times, I feel like a dead uncle. First, I think something exists, then, instantly, it doesn't."

I pursed my lips. "What is it about this company that makes people ramble nonsense when they talk? Were you nuked when you were a baby?"

Toby sniggered. "I'm funning ya. Look at it. What do you think this is?"

I studied the paperweight. "A paperweight? Or something I should throw at you?"

"You've seen this a thousand times on Gower's desk, and I bet it never meant a single thing to you."

Should it?

"Now I've got you curious." Toby grinned like the bear.

It must be something. I wanted to figure out what before Toby told me. I held it to the light. The round puck-shaped thing had raised markings, looking like Celtic writing. *Something religious? An icon? It was heavy for its size, maybe old brass.*

I guessed, "Some sort of medieval logo? Maybe identifying a tribe or such, a long way back."

"Not bad. Close. It's a replica of the Fighting Serpent brooch Queen Boudicca wore in battle, a real kick-ass fighting Englishman, er, woman. In the end, they say, she wore it when she poisoned herself."

"Well, an admirable way of becoming famous. Who knew? What happened? And why aren't you offering me Old Fashioneds tonight?"

Toby put on his stern face, the one he wears when he wants to dominate. "Only people who listen to my fascinating stories get Old Fashioneds."

"Here's my ears."

He rang Maria for my drink and then started on what he wanted to tell me. "This is well-known English history, so pay attention. Boudicca led a hundred thousand untrained warriors against Rome's legionaries who had held her beloved England. In AD 60, her army prevailed and returned England to independence quickly. Her warriors laid complete waste to the Romans during a march to London. Think General Sherman and Georgia. If it was flammable, she torched it."

He said as I laid the weight back on his display shelf, "Her problem was Roman reinforcements were moving into the city. She brought in too many soldiers for the space London had, and they couldn't maneuver around to defend themselves against the reinforcements. So the Romans slaughtered them—outnumbering her forces eight to one. As a result, Boudicca's army fell in Biblical proportions."

"Thanks, Maria." I took my drink off her silver tray.

Toby kept talking. "A minority of experts say Boudicca died from battle wounds. Other experts say it was from illness, but the majority agree she poisoned herself rather than face being a woman in the hands of filthy Roman soldiers."

"So, I'm missing the part about why this is important to me."

"Sometimes you piss me right off, Ricky. Think about it. Because Boudicca gave up doesn't mean her men gave up too. As a matter of fact, a large percentage of her army escaped, continuing to fight another day. So, two thousand years ago, they picked the word for 'free men' as their name. That name was Brahms, and they adopted the image of Boudicca's serpent as their divine driving image. So, the brass puck you sluffed off to the shelf is the symbol of Brahms."

I took the swizzle from the Old Fashioned and nodded, licking the last drop from its end. "Two thousand years ago, that's a long back."

"I'm not telling you this because I can. These are facts, son, true facts. Actual history. That's how things were, and it's still how things are today." Toby placed an examining eye on me. "Here are public facts you can find on your Google or whatever you use to verify things."

"During the Battle of Hastings in 1066, the Brahms clan captured Harold II and sold him over to the Vikings for execution. He was disemboweled and burned alive. Not good if you're Harold. In 1071, Hugues de Payens of Champaign was a Brahms pureblood. His power grew until he became the Grand Master of the Knights Templar. His was the first crusade to Jerusalem.

"In America, Fredrick Douglas was President Lincoln's advisor on human rights before the Civil War. But before that, his father, Thomas Auld, a white man, inherited his Brahms title by birthright. He passed it on to his son Fredrick. Douglas's support proved vital to the

North winning the war against slavery."

I let him finish, letting his idea settle in my mind. "I'm still missing it. What do million-year-old fighters have to do with a doomsday gas?"

"Maybe you're right. Maybe you're not ready to run the company. Brahms is who masterminded this whole scheme, right down to the Army diversion Je was after."

"How could modern-day Brahms people even know about Klearance?"

"Gower told them, boy. Look at what you were holding in your hands. Why would Gower own that?" He called Maria for a Rum. "The reason is, your Colonel Wright told him what was in the cylinders when he was working the haz-mat transportation plan. Gower is Brahms through and through, and always has been, even in Ireland. It's in his bloodline. That's why he kept the brooch on his desk."

The implications of what Toby said finally warmed me. "So, Brahms raided Gower's house and staged his arrest?"

"That way, he could be 'free' to work."

"Brahms hired Kelly Lake, then, to keep Gower from sticking out like a lit blowtorch."

Answering, he nodded. "Brahms is like the Freemasons—every class and rank of men are welcome. Lake is no more than another of Gower's fellow Freemen."

I took the orange curl out of my glass. "Mark was clever enough to hide the bucks he took from the British space program and smart enough to get himself in the States without too many questions. I can't believe his brain is big enough to coordinate that stuff."

"Quit underestimating Mark Gower. Owning this

gas puts him front and center on the six o'clock news when the story leaks. Whoever has the gas commands the world."

Maria rejoined to check on us. I asked her, "Do you want to command the world, Maria?"

"Of course." She brought in a tray of scones and French press coffee.

Before returning to the story, Toby bit the top of his cinnamon scone and waited for Maria to leave. "Rumor has it Brahms was temporarily headquartered in New England and remotely controlled those two American Airline planes flying into the twin towers of New York...."

"... well, that's a bit of a stretch, don't you think?"

"Not for a second. Put those Al Qaeda rookies in a pilot seat, and they couldn't taxi the plane much less hit something on the ground going six-hundred miles an hour."

I dunked my scone in the coffee, content with listening to Toby's idea. Toby could be the mother of all criminal minds.

Toby resumed, "The slickest modern-day job attribute to Brahms was the aircraft carrier, Forrestal. They stole 120 quarter-ton bombs from a drydocked ship in Newport—in plain sight and broad daylight. They sold the bombs to Saudi Arabia, who used them to put out oil-well fires."

I struggled with how to apply this. "So, you think Brahms recruited Gower, then recruited Kelly Lake?"

"Nope. Gower got his information about the gas and then went to them. They assigned Lake to help him."

"So, in your theory, they got Kelly Lake to steal the cylinders? I have to say, you make it sound like a James

Bond conspiracy, taking over the world."

"I'm simply telling you what I know." Toby wiped the scone sugar off his fingers. "If I'm right, we have a real three-act tragedy here."

Chapter 46

Albuquerque, New Mexico
Rick

I descended two short steps from the C-21 with my pocket phone to my ear. "Yeah?"

The man starting his daily update was Rory. "We've finished scanning the Watson Network. There's no mention of Klearance out there, except for a punk band using the name and a coin-operated laundry in Holland."

Focusing on what he said, I walked straight to the Air Force car waiting outside. It comforted me knowing the world has yet to hear of Klearance. I told him, "That's good. How about anyone who could use it?"

"Nothing so far. We've built a word search we repeat every eight hours. We'll keep monitoring."

"Why eight hours?"

"It takes a long time to scan everything in the world," he answered. "That's what you wanted."

I uttered, "Hmph. Not hitting anything is going to make the job of tracking this stuff much harder. I don't like the idea of having a nasty gas is out there, no idea of where or who has it." The rear door closed, sealing me in and the desert heat out.

Rory's voice changed from serious to playful. "How about we lighten the load for a minute?"

"What load?"

"Yours. I think Laura found your phone bug."

"How do you know that? Are you still listening to her?" In my opinion, intruding on my wife's private moments ought to be off-limits.

"What can I say? You don't mind, do you?" I could almost hear his shoulder shrug. "She's started leaving her phone tilted up, with the video camera aimed at her bed. I think she wants you to see what they're doing."

"So now you've expanded to watching my wife with another man? Yeah, my load is lightened a lot, for sure."

"Hey, you never said stop. You might like someone watching for you in case Laura says something about her job or something she's not supposed to."

It was her choice, and with me being an 'old-fashioned husband,' I capitulated. "I guess if she puts it out there, she's doing it because she wants people to see. She knows what she's doing. I've married a porn queen. Have you told anybody? I'll crack your face if you have."

He answered, "Of course not. Laura deserves her privacy. What do you think I am?"

****

Two requests for new investigations came in before I reached Kirtland. I settled into my room in the officer quarters. *Now what?* I read the requests and returned both to Operations for reassignment to one of the up comings, and then I called Colonel Wright.

"Personnel records for the two truck drivers aren't here in the file. Can you send them over?"

The senior driver's tribal name, Kele, translated from Hopi to English as 'Sparrow.' He was born in the village on Sacred Mountain. The church assigned to raise him when the village failed changed his name at an early age to a new Christian name, Tommy Begaye. The file indicated he joined the Air Force at age eighteen, but a bit of quick math said he was more like seventeen. His term in Bootcamp and his first six months went by eventless. Following the basics, he was transferred to the motor pool as an airman, then promoted to Airman First Class. By the age of twenty-one, he had come to know alcohol, and he liked it so much that when he celebrated his twenty-first birthday, he also got to know the guardhouse.

Begaye was married twice. The longest lasted two years. A baby boy came from his first marriage, and a restraining order against his wife came from the second. Since number two, he'd lived on the base maintaining a clean record.

That evening, I called Rory's home. "Can you find another address for Carissa Scaffe after her apartment in the Springs burned down? Kelly Lake burned her out, getting rid of the old lady."

"Give me a sec." Rory hung up. In five minutes, enough time for him to gain access to the company servers, he called back. "I have the system running. Let's see…after being kicked out of the burned place, we'll probably find her in a close-by motel. Let me check the motel registries in the area. Colorado Springs, nope. Denver, nothing. Woodland Park, no. Pueblo, no. What's next? Trinity, no. Ah, here she is in Raton, New Mexico—registered as Morgan Flatly at the Summit Inn…on Interstate 25."

I told him, "Message me the particulars. It's time for the little lady to come visit us in Dallas."

After Rory, I called a back-straight, chin-up librarian named Connie in Records. "Con, would you dig into something for me? Would you look to see if McDonnell has taken any business in the last two years that only Mark Gower saw? I only want the ones no one beside him was involved. It would be a contract with the Air Force. Check bids, proposals, or contracts, anything Gower alone handled. I'm guessing it will have something to do with Kirtland AFB."

"Let me look. I'll call you," Connie assured, already clicking through on her keyboard. "How's Toby? We hear he's bad sick."

"He's sick enough, but he'll get through it. You know Toby. He doesn't stay down long."

Connie slowed her keystrokes. "We're praying for him."

I remembered what I forgot to ask Rory. "On top of what I've already given you, can you find Mark Gower? Toby and I are sure he's not under arrest. When you find him, put a tracker on him in case he gets a hint of what we're doing and decides to run."

Finally, I called Anderson Weeks and stretched on the bed. "I promised I would take Toby to get his treatment tomorrow. Then here I am, stuck at Kirtland. Is there any way you could take him to Medical City for me?"

Andi answered, the weight of worry in her voice, "I'd love to, sweetie, but they've moved my grandson into Intensive Care up in Oklahoma City. So I'm about to leave."

"What happened?"

"He got himself hit in the head playing soccer. They think his skull's fractured, and infection might be setting in his brain. It's swelling and getting worse. Can you get Toby to Uber for his treatment?"

"Wrong generation, girl. I'll fly back in the morning and drive him myself."

Chapter 47

Dallas, Texas
Rick

Exiting our building and heading down exactly fourteen steps to ground level, I walked past the fountain, all the way to the waterfall in the pond. Toby followed me to the water-splashed ivy courtyard. That's where our best solutions come. Toby says it's the oxygen coming from the falling water. I pulled one of Laura's cigarettes and mounted it on my lower lip.

"How do you keep from getting hooked on those things?" Toby asked.

"I never light them."

"You look stupid sitting around with an unlit cigarette sticking out of your face. Buy a cigar. You'll look more like a man."

I grunted at him and raised a brow. "I didn't invite you out here to critique my facial fashion. I believe I've figured out how Brahms assassinated all those leaders."

"Enlighten."

I flipped the unlit cigarette into the pond. "What could a person do with a syringe full of Klearance...not a cylinder, but a syringe? There's not much gas, but it gets used in confined spaces. You don't need much."

"Okay."

"Fill the syringe with the gas in a safe place, then

close it with an airtight cap. Then penetrate the seal around a door or window with the syringe. Or maybe shoot it under a door bottom. It drifts on the currents of the room until it comes to its victim. Boom, he's DOA."

"Okay." Toby's brow rose skeptically.

"A little while later, the gas neutralizes, and there's no trace."

"You're still thinking Brahms. Where did they get it? And Vanuatu wasn't a closed room. It was an open restroom."

"The killer waited inside for the president to come to take a whiz. When he does, the killer walks out into the fresh air. Vent fans are sucking the outside air in. The killer empties the syringe into the air current; the killer is upwind, safe, and casually walks away. When the guards hear the president splat on the deck, they rush in and get gassed themselves."

Toby shook his head. "That's too simple."

"That's what's nice about it."

"Where'd they get the gas?"

"Isn't that still the question? If this is Brahms, then either they have a second source, or their man Lake has somehow figured out how to divide one of the cylinders without killing himself."

Toby stood by the waterfall where a family of little green frogs sat on a wet rock under a leaf. "I think it's more complex than we think. If Brahms has someone else spraying this stuff—and at the same time Kelly Lake is trying to push the bulk gas to the Russians, Earth is in trouble."

It was a possibility. "And it's safe to assume Mark Gower is calling the shots. He's the only one who knows McDonnell's inner workings."

Toby tightened his lips. "I should hire more boots for the streets. Could you handle them?"

"Before we do, let's think about a strategy on how to solve this. We're way outnumbered. Let's give it a couple of days."

Chapter 48

Kirtland AFB, New Mexico
Rick

An early out and doing Toby's treatment at Medical City left me beyond bushed after the flight back to Kirtland. Sorry to say, Toby's doctor visit didn't reduce the banker boxes for me to go through. In the Officer's Quarters, my junior officer room contained the same stale air I left in it yesterday. The window air conditioner failed to catch up with today's heat, which means sleeping in here will be nearly impossible. As I worked through the boxes, my thoughts switched to going back to Dallas, where air conditioning is valuable and the environment fresh.

A quick inventory of the papers on the bed and the unopened boxes on the floor said this would be a long night. I called the Staff Sergeant to bring me a dinner tray and another tray of Old Fashioneds. And for the rest of the evening, I sweated and parsed the files in the box. One of Tommy's best friends served time after being caught taking Air Force property and selling it on the black market in town.

Food gone, Old Fashioneds gone; I would read one more folder before calling it a night. The last one came from the box marked black and red. Unlike the others, this one showed an orange band across the top with a red diagonal stripe crossing it. It came from the Weapons Division in Las Vegas.

Inside, it contained details of the Libyan gas test Wright talked about. Even with me not being a hawk, I would have classified what happened as an act of war, but that's me. At least most of the villagers got out safely and returned to their homes.

The cover page said the attack took place in the Libyan desert, some miles southwest of Tripoli, in a Berber area called Wefat. Wright boasted Kirtland landed one egg in the middle of Main Street. All enemy combatants died instantly, and there was no damage to the village or its infrastructure. No Americans were killed and none injured.

Pictures were plenty, taken by a Marine group who arrived an hour following the attack. One of the handwritten accounts said, "What happened? There's nothing left alive, only mud buildings and herbs; no damage to the village other than where trucks crashed into buildings following their driver's death. But nothing survives this shit."

Nothing. The folder included color pictures of men fallen dead in the dirt streets—laying dead in their boots. People were slumped over tables still holding spoons, warriors fallen across desks inside the buildings. Vehicle drivers lay killed, resting on their steering wheels. People in chairs and beds died where they were. Wefat was like a death in Pompei.

Later pictures showed a recovered village of Wefat, ready for re-occupancy. The insurgent bodies, dead birds, and animals are all gone.

I was so tired. I moved the papers from my bed before sliding between the sheets. My phone continued to stare at me. As tired as I was, I couldn't resist. My instinct to get sleep wasn't as strong as my wanting to see Laura with her lover. I touched the wire-tap icon. My screen lit and showed two users were online—that other user had to be Rory, damn him.

I took a deep breath and touched the camera icon. As Rory said, Laura's phone lay propped and tilted toward her bed, showing Brian lying undressed atop the sheets semi-erect. Laura entered the picture bare on top and with a towel wrapped around her waist. After all these years, she remained an angel of beauty. Her firm breasts moved free as she crawled across the bed, and her towel dropped.

This is my Laura.

Then my screen went to black, and an urgent instant message box flashed red. The phone attempted to dance in my hand. "Damn it."

It was an emergency text from my sister: *"NEED HELP."*

"Damn," I said. *When is it that you don't need help, tell me that?*

I typed, *"What trouble?"*

"A man beat me. In the hospital."

"You okay?"

"I'm in the hospital. No."

This was not the time for texting. I called Esmee's number, but she didn't answer.

Her following text read, "Can't answer phone both arms broken."

"Buzz, your nurse. Have her call me and put your phone on speaker."

A few minutes later, Esmee's voice came on the line. "Rick, are you here?"

"I'm here. What happened?"

Her voice was weak. She said, "A man tied me up and then threw me out of his car on the highway."

I rose at the sense of urgency. "Nurse?"

"Yes, sir?" a man's voice joined on the line.

"Esmee's my little sister; what's going on?"

He answered, "Well, she has lots of bruising and lacerations. Both of her forearms are in casts—she has multiple stitch locations, and her nose may need correcting at some point."

"That's not sounding good."

"She's not in good shape, no sir. We spent ninety minutes removing cholla thorns from her arms and legs. The doctors think there's internal damage. Whoever did this dragged her for some distance in the cactus and scrub brush."

"Esmee," I asked, "do you have someone there in Phoenix who can care for you temporarily until I can get out there?"

The nurse corrected me, "Mr. Haade, this is the Flagstaff Trauma Unit. We're a good distance from Phoenix."

"Flagstaff." I sat up, surprised. "Let me think. I assume you have admitted my sister. Is she going to need to stay there long?"

"More than likely. The doctors are waiting on results to tell how much damage her spleen and pancreas have. The results will determine how long she needs to stay so we can monitor her."

"How much time are you talking? Days? Weeks?"

He sounded certain, "At least two weeks to heal enough so we can release her, maybe more."

"And, once she's well enough to be discharged, is

there a rehab unit there for trauma patients, at least until I can catch up with you?"

"We have one, yes. But your sister has a problem with her insurance. She doesn't appear to have any."

"I'm not surprised. I'll guarantee whatever bills there are."

"Good. I'll have Admitting call you. Is there anything else?"

I paused to code my question right. "I have a question for my sister. Is this related to your new customer service business?"

"Yes."

"Did you know the customer?"

"It was the man I told you about from Dallas."

"Okay, I'll be out there soon to bring you back. You're due for a career change. There's this old man here named Toby. He needs a personal concierge."

Chapter 49

Kirtland AFB, New Mexico
Rick

A late-night call woke me. "Yeah?"

Dee replied, "We're temporarily in Boston. Sorry for calling so early. I want you to know all of our field agents are heading to the docks."

I lay on my side. *How do they expect to protect the country when they make our soldiers sleep on these boards?*

"Good," I said. "I sent a photo of a little black egg shape gadget. It's known as the egg of death. One of them got shipped your way to Boston. Make sure everyone knows. Never touch any of the valves on it. The valves gotta stay closed, period, all the time, all three."

Dee made a groggy, muffled huff. "Je told me it's a poisonous gas. Like how poisonous?"

"Like total annihilation of Boston. If it gets open, it will kill your team so fast they won't even know they left a family behind."

Following her call, I couldn't go back to sleep. I flipped on the national news, hoping the networks failed to pick up on the family that got killed in Ireland for no cause. After thirty minutes of listening, there was no mention of it. Maybe killing a family along with their animals wasn't as newsworthy as Washington's dribble-drabble.

I considered calling Je after I checked outside my door for breakfast. As accurate as the Air Force claims to be, sure enough, a tray was waiting. It held a Thermos of coffee and two Egg-Muffins.

I brought the tray to the table, touched Je's face on the screen, and kicked the door closed behind me.

Je began his update uncharacteristically by asking, "You want the good news or the bad?"

"I just got off a call with Dee," I said, "so let's try the good."

"Good, it is. Our team in City Cork found an unopened cylinder of the gas this morning."

"Where?"

"In the guy's house who said he left his cell phone in San Juan. Our London dozen did a blitzkrieg on his place and took him and his wife back to London for questions."

"How'd they find it?"

"They brought a wall-penetrating radar with them. The man hid his cylinder in a cubby behind a stone fireplace. One of the valves was open, but the others were closed."

"They're shut now, right?"

"Tell you the truth; no one wanted to touch the thing. So, the team got in a bomb robot to get it."

"Did you talk with the couple?" Then I stopped. I happen to have a C-21 jet at my disposal. "I tell you what; I can be in Londonderry in twelve hours. Meet me at the corporate terminal at the airport. I'll be using an Air Force jet."

Within the hour, I boarded the plane, and the pilot entered a course in the navigation system. He would be flying me from Kirtland to Goose Bay to Reykjavik to Eglinton Airport in Londonderry. If there was more room for fuel, we could have made the jump in one hop, but that wasn't the case.

Harley Je met the C-21 on the airport apron. He and I climbed into his rented red Jaguar to drive to the Maldron hotel.

As we drove, he explained, "The guys from London interrogated the couple. The man insists the cylinder isn't his. He doesn't know anything about it or the cubby in his fireplace. So, of course, he didn't know anything about the sender."

"How about the woman?"

"That one's a wife I'd never admit having. She thinks it's a bomb on its way to the new resistance fighters."

"She was aware of it?"

"She was."

I said, "I don't remember; who's the New Resistance Fighters?"

"The ones who aren't the Old Resistance Fighters." He shrugged his shoulder at me. "I don't know; everybody over here is a new resistance fighter of some kind. You've been here. These fuckers are constantly fighting somebody."

"The wife; she's a talker?" I asked.

"Chatty Cathy personified. She's terrified we're going to deport her. She flipped on her husband so fast I'm not so sure they're married. But, then again, he's the one with the skin in the game."

"Or…" I shut up for a moment to think it through. "It could be the other way around. She could be in the resistance, and he's playing the dummy to protect her.

Tell London to amp up the pressure and find out."

"The wife, I think, could be an educated, English-Russian agent. She told Peter a man came to their house and talked with her husband. The man makes her leave the house before they talk, but she hears him talk in Russian about getting a bomb for an agent in Moscow."

"Moscow?"

"That's what she said. But, of course, the husband denies everything. Now, he even denies knowing her."

I switched to secure messaging on my phone as the text arrived. "*Boom. I don't think you have what it takes to catch me, little boy—Kelly Lake.*"

It caused me to forward the message immediately to Rory with a note: *This came from outside. Could Gower have sent it?*

Then, I returned my attention to Je. "Did the woman tell 'em who the visitor was or give them a description?"

Je brought his caldera red Jag to a stop in the hotel's car park and released the trunk. "A big guy in his late thirties or early forties. Dark hair. Rough-like skin. It could be anybody. She also maintains she knows nothing about the dead farmer family."

"Has anyone gone out to the sheep ranch yet?"

"That's the other bit of good news. The Dublin team found an opened cylinder in the barn of the family that got killed. It looks like the farmer broke the valve stem off. I guess the cops missed it."

I cautioned, "Then don't tell 'em. You need to get both cylinders back to Kirtland. Pack the shit out of the unopened one. Use my jet to take them to Kirtland. I'll let Colonel Wright know they're coming."

Having no more to say, Je changed subjects. "Now for Londonderry, at the chemist shop, it's bad news."

"The cylinder wasn't there, right?"

"The cylinder wasn't there. Kaelyn went in two nights ago after the shop closed and found nada. So, the rest of the UK team came in yesterday. They spent all day and most of the night probing every wall, floor, and ceiling, including the chemist's overhead apartment. Nothing. Anywhere."

"Then it's already been forwarded."

Chapter 50

Londonderry, Northern Ireland
Rick

Odd, he hadn't contacted me yet. That was unlike Rory. A digital phone, in his mind, is infinitely more secure and difficult to hack than a digital message, so his email surprised me, but then maybe not. Attached, he placed a voice file. My phone rang. It was him. He told me to listen to the voice file.

As I played it, I recognized the first voice to be that fat old Mark Gower, and it sounded like Mr. Gower was pissed.

"Two targets, and you blew both. You let both get away. How is it you give your plans away? These people should know nothing about you or what you're doing."

The other man answered Mark. *"They don't. People change plans, mate."* The other man's voice sounded younger and woodier...outback-ish. *"I did nothing wrong. I followed protocol, same as every other gank I've done for you."*

"Don't give me that. Why didn't you know that their plans changed beforehand?"

The Aussie lad could be sucking lemons from the sound in his voice, him wanting to say something he couldn't. *"I did know their plans. That's why I didn't expose myself."*

"I don't believe you. So, who's your next target? I think it's time we pick someone prominent in the United States, someone more Morning TV News material."

"I'm thinking the President of Haiti. He'll be hard to get to, but with some planning, I think I can pull it off."

"Haiti is not the United States."

"You're off balance, mate. You need a good brain-frying."

I listened to the file once again and a third time. That was Gower's voice, all right, and if Toby's newspaper killings were real, the Aussie voice was the assassin. If Rory can keep up this quality of information, maybe we could handle fights on two fronts.

I hit reply to Rory: *"This is GOLD, my man. Is it something you can continue getting?"*

Chapter 51

Londonderry, Northern Ireland
Rick

At the Maldron Hotel, I got comfortable readying myself for the last Air Force folder I had with me. In front of my crossed legs laid Tommy Begaye's toxicology report. Postmortem blood work showed a numbingly high level of Seconal and Propofol in his system, the official cause of death. With as much the report said, he wouldn't have lasted more than a few seconds.

The next section of the report left me hanging. Oxytocin is not usually in a man's blood except after having sex. *Did they? Were there any time gaps in the video?* I hadn't noticed one. The amount he had must have come from somewhere else, his co-driver, his nose spray, both. It's possible she bought a bottle of Oxy over the internet and spiked his nose spray, knowing his addiction. At these levels, her *love drug* would have him trusting anybody.

A note on the third page mentioned he was addicted to nose spray. *Ah, there you have it.* He routinely inhaled four times the maximum upper limit allowed.

A detailed look at the crime scene inventory did not list a nose spray bottle. So if Carissa spiked his spray, and she could have, he would have been dosing himself the whole trip, not knowing it. By the time they arrived in Raton, Tommy would have been so chilled that he would have trusted her no matter what strange thing she did.

I inserted the video chip of the cab into my tablet for another look-see. A few minutes before the traffic stopped on I-25, Begaye fished some nose spray from his ditty bag, but the dose didn't visibly affect him. But then, it wouldn't have.

The audio was unintelligible, coming from a cracked microphone or something else had gone wrong.

I reran the video a third time, trying to figure out what they said. Note to self: *have Andi find a lip reader to transcribe this friggin thing.*

There was the point where Carissa pawed at the door handle with a deep frown on her face. Clearly, what she said then was, "You asshole."

Begaye said something back, then pressed a switch on the ceiling. It illuminated red light. The airfield communications log said he was reporting a traffic stoppage on the Interstate. The forward-looking camera confirmed the stop, and the speedometer recorded five miles per hour, then zero.

I focused on Carissa. She rambled through her purse for a moment, exposing a golden lipstick holder. Then leaving the top on it, she unscrewed the bottom where a syringe needle was hidden. Then, as Begaye turned toward her, she stabbed him in the neck with some sort of fluid. *Clever. I've never seen that one.*

Counting the seconds—1…2…3…4…10—and Tommy Begaye went down like a bull, his head stopping in the steering wheel bowl.

The recording finally showed Carissa pulling

Tommy's limp body from the cab. She came back in the picture, working a spray plastic bottle, wiping her fingerprints from the cab interior with napkins soaked in a sudsy-muddy solution. Once done, she followed her lines with another spray of a clear watery solution. Listed on the Chemical Analysis report were three components, bleach, Palmolive detergent, and a bacteria-laden mixture of mud from around the cab. The DNA from the mud bacteria rendered human DNA samples taken in the cab meaningless.

I lifted a photograph labeled with the time and name of an Air Force drone from the folder. I went over it closely with my magnification glass. It didn't take much imagination to make out a pattern where the grass had been laid over near the truck. It was as if it had been pushed into parallel lines by rotor wash from a heavy helicopter—one hovering in position but not touching the ground. I checked the map. Carissa had parked the truck far enough from the main road that no one could have seen it or the helicopter.

I wonder why Colonel Wright's report doesn't mention a helicopter.

I sent Rory an email to check air traffic control at the Regional Fight Center in Denver. Specifically for any rotary-wing aircraft in the Sangre de Cristo Mountains around 9:47 a.m. "If so, get its tail number, where it took off from, and where it landed. Most of all, find out its owner."

Chapter 52

Londonderry, Northern Ireland
Rick

Dee rang me up. I was about to fall asleep when the phone's chime startled me. "I think we found your box."

I stretched my eyes to clear them. It was a lousy hour to be calling, but for those words, I was glad Dee didn't wait until later. "That's angels in my ears. Just what I wanted to hear."

"Don't get all excited like you usually do. We don't have it in our hands yet…Your freight forwarder received a consignment from San Juan yesterday, repackaged it last night, and sent it out this morning. It's at Logan Airport right now. It's on its way to Moscow."

"That's good…not good."

"Fate's on our side. The package got pulled while TSA was doing one of their random checks. So it's caged in quarantine."

I could breathe. At least only Boston would get killed if the thing spewed, not Moscow. No World War Three. "How fast can you get down there and get it?"

"I'm on I-90 right now."

That was newsworthy. I switched to a secure satellite link and called Colonel Wright at Kirtland. "Colonel, I bet you'd like an update on your cylinders."

"You bet."

I paused. "Ha. Okay. The news is we've found two of the eggs. One is on its way back to you from Ireland. The other, we're getting in Boston. So you should have those tomorrow."

"You stopped. The rest is bad, I suppose."

"You could say that. The third one went off outside of Dublin, killing everybody and everything on a sheep farm, including the people. There was a husband and wife and three kids. County Kildare police haven't figured out anything yet."

"Damn. Let's go back to the Boston one. What's the story there? Boston's on American soil."

"There shouldn't be any great effort there. It's hung up in a TSA safety cage. We should have it in a few hours."

Wright didn't talk for a minute or two, then said, "Outside Dublin, you used the phrase, went off, what did you mean by that? Did it detonate? Were the two halves separated?"

"I think the valves came open. You'll see. It's on its way back to Kirtland."

"Shit. When did it happen?"

"Saturday. Last weekend. The medical examiners are still examining the bodies. They think it's a new form of African virus."

I could hear a sigh of relief in his voice. "Let's let them think that. Give me more about Boston."

I searched around the bedroom, phone on speaker, opening all likely drawers. There it is. I grabbed the neck of a Woodford pint with a pink sticky note saying 'breakfast use only.' It's close enough to breakfast, I reckon. Well, at least it's after midnight. I blew the dust out of a juice glass and filled it with my stash of liquid gold.

I answered, "Ok, Boston. Your one stolen shoebox got broken into four smaller boxes in San Juan. Three of them were forwarded to Ireland. One went to Boston. We're expecting their strategy is to scatter the gas around and hope one box gets through."

The Colonel's voice sounded, "Hmm."

"The Boston cylinder is now on an outbound manifest to Moscow. It got pulled for TSA inspection. One of my people is heading down there right now."

My Woodford had a dark thing floating in the middle. I pinched it with my thumb and forefinger, wiping it on my sheet.

I said, "There's a fourth cylinder we think still in Londonderry. More to come on that."

Wright said, "You guys move fast. The Air Force would still be in committee trying to figure out how often the committee should meet."

I changed hands as my palm was getting hot.

"My turn," I said. "Tell me, why was there no mention in your reports of a helicopter involved in the hijacking?"

There was a pause then he came back. "As far as I know, there wasn't one."

"Did you let news helicopters or sightseers in the area?"

"Negative. We classified the space until we got finished."

"Go back," I helped, "look at your video. Your drone captured prop wash from a helicopter hovering, and there are faint footprints in the grass. Someone lifted your co-driver out is why you can't find her—I bet I know who."

A phone chirp assigned to Dee came across. "Boston is on the other line. I'll call you back, hopefully with good news."

When I joined the line, Dee's voice stammered like she was running. Short of breath, she said. "We lost it; it's gone. TSA cleared the box before I got here. The plane left with the cylinder in its belly."

"What?"

"Don't yell at me. I don't control the world, Rick. What can I say?"

For a second, I couldn't believe what she said. My index finger pointed into nowhere. "Fuck. Call the FAA right now. Tell them there is a bomb on board and track where they bring it down. Get our guys out there to meet it. And good lord, don't fuck this up."

I had to think. Why does thinking happen so hard when things go wrong? Was what I instructed her the right thing? What choice do I have? I condemn the people of Maine to instant death. Or would it be better for the Russians to die? I have to tell Toby. I texted him for a heads up about my call.

"I have a mess on my hands. I need you to pull some strings with FAA & ATF. Calling in a minute."

I touched his picture on my phone.

"I need a serious quick-fix. A major airline crisis and government catastrophe are about to land in our laps."

"What happened?"

"I instructed Dee to call the FAA and report a confirmed bomb on a flight heading from Boston to Moscow. One of the Air Forces' toxic cylinders is on board the plane. That's all I could think to keep the plane in US airspace. But now I'm not sure I want it to stay here."

"You did right. What can I do?"

I took a deep breath, structuring my thoughts. "I'm pretty sure by now the FAA has notified the ATF, TSA, and FBI about the bomb. So, I need you to pluck some of your strings in Washington and hold off the Calvary. I need you to ensure Washington stays away from that plane until Dee gets to its cargo bay. No way should any government thugs be there before her."

"Where is she?"

"She's on her way. She'll be the one to go in and get the box."

Toby asked me, "What about the news networks."

"I'm working with Colonel Wright. I'll get him to declare a military security zone wrapped around the plane."

"Do you know where's it coming down?"

"Not yet, Portland, somewhere up there."

"And what about Russia?"

"I'm gonna let the State Department deal with Russia."

After a brief pause, Toby came back. "I should wake up the president. All those departments you mentioned work for him. I'm sure he wouldn't want the cylinder going off anywhere on American soil."

As soon as I disconnected, I reconnected with Wright. "There's a problem. Them Stupid Assholes, that's what TSA stands for—they put the cylinder on the plane, and it's on its way to Moscow."

"What?" An incredulous gasp of inward air followed his simple word.

"Listen," I said, "My people called the FAA and told them there is a bomb on board and they need to bring the plane down. I'm expecting it to return to in either Portland or Bangor."

Wright took a deep breath and held it for a second. "What airline is it? From Logan, right?"

"Transatlantic Airline."

In the background, I could hear him rapid slapping the keys. "Give me a second. Here it is. Let me find its return destination. The FAA has given its vectors back to Portland. I'll get a couple of F-16s up to escort it back."

"One more thing," I asked. "We need you to declare this some level of top-secret, defense emergency, or whatever you call it. I need you to keep the news media as far as you can from my people. I'm sure the major networks are setting up cameras for when the plane comes down." I added, "And tell the airplane's pilot to close the cabin window shades on both sides of the plane. I don't want internet-happy passengers streaming our operations live on social media."

"Your plane will be on the ground in Portland in eleven minutes. I've declared a Security Emergency at the airport. Of course, the ticketed passengers are going to be pissed—oh well." He stopped his own words and started reading something. "It says here Air Traffic Control is directing the pilot to hold at the far end of runway L-8. They've closed the airport to all other traffic....Damn it. You did say Transatlantic Airways, right?"

"Right."

Wright held his end of the line quiet.

"What's wrong?" I asked.

He came back, "The TransAtlantic pilot failed to acknowledge FAA instructions to return to Portland.

He's still on its flight plan to St. Petersburg."

"Well, shit. Where are your F-16s?"

"They're approaching from behind, but they can't make the pilot turn if he doesn't want to."

"Damn this whole thing. Can your guys tell if the flight crew is ignoring FCC orders, or is something wrong?"

"Just a second." Click, click, click. "The F-16 wing captain is saying…hang…the Transatlantic pilot and copilot are slumped over in their seats. He's saying the passengers look like they're all dead, too. We've got a plane full of dead people headed to St Petersburg."

"Shit."

"The escorts are saying the oxygen masks did not drop. They can see service carts stationary in the aisles."

I suggested, "The plane is on autopilot, right? I mean, it's going to fly safely for a while."

Wright's voice affirmed. "But not to St. Petersburg. We'll shoot it down before we let the Russians get their hands on one of those eggs, even if it has gone off. We'll absolutely shoot them out of the sky first."

"Understood, but if you can save the aircraft and get the broken egg back into your own hands, would you support that?"

Wright said, "I'm not sure why you would ask. Of course."

I finally connected to the McDonnell Dallas systems. I said to Wright, "My FlightAware screens show the flight is heading out over the Atlantic, on a straight course for the next few hours."

"I have the same."

I said, "If our Transportation group could bring the plane back, would you oppose us?"

"Ah, no. That'll keep me from shooting the thing down; I'll give you a Presidential Medal of Honor."

Not likely, but whatever. "Okay. I'm going to call in one of our tech wizards."

I paced as I selected Rory's number. "Sorry to rustle you up at home, but do we have someone on staff who can fly a 787-9? There's a bit of a mess over the Atlantic. I'm stuck in Londonderry with Je."

"There is. Do you want him in the flight center?"

"One of the Air Force's cylinders went off on a flight from Logan to St. Petersburg. It looks like everybody's dead, including the flight deck. We need to do something to bring the plane down in friendly territory."

"The 787 dash 9 is relatively new. We have a guy who handles newer equipment, but he's never done anything like this. How soon do you need him?"

"An hour ago. The plane is on autopilot, heading over the Atlantic to nowhere. Get to the flight center."

I told Wright, still on the line. "We have a fly-by-wire control center at our Dallas offices for situations like this."

"You guys are amazing."

"To make a nickel off you guys, we have to be ready to do about anything. You won't be the first to use it."

Chapter 53

Londonderry, Northern Ireland
Rick

We three rejoined the call two hours later—Rory at the flight control center, Wright in Kirtland, and me in Londonderry. So, I said to Rory, "Let's turn the show over to you. Just bring her down in one piece."

"You said it's TransAtlantic, right? Do you have the tail number? I need to make sure we connect to the correct plane."

Colonel Wright answered, "Ah, tail number N3103."

Rory came back, "I don't see 3103 in inventory…no…here it is. The good news is we can get into it. I mean, I can't, but Brooks Gamble here can. He'll be on the yoke. Brooks…let them hear your voice."

"Gentlemen, Brooks Gamble here." Gamble flew commercial coming to us as a Navy test pilot and on the original team for the Boeing shake-down of the 787.

Rory said to Brooks in the control center, "We need to divert a deadhead plane to Fairford Field in Gloucestershire. There's a nice long RAF runway with plenty of security should things go wrong."

"By deadhead, you mean?" asked Gamble.

I answered, "The pilot and co-pilot are dead in their seats. Everyone else on the plane is dead too."

"Dead? As in not living. That'll make it simple enough. No tickets to refund if I screw up."

Gamble snickered then asked Wright, "What's the condition of the plane?"

"We're tracking it over the Atlantic on a heading to St. Petersburg. I have a pair of F-16s with it, one on each wing. No sudden moves."

"Got it." Gamble adjusted the console screens to sit the way he wanted. "Tell the escorts I am going to slow the airspeed to make sure I have control. If you would ask 'em to tell me how the plane responds."

Across the phone, Wright said, "They said it slowed by thirty knots."

"Good," Gamble answered. "Then I'll take it from here. Tell the escorts to pull off. Now let me bring Fairford Field up on the screen."

Rory updated the group, "He has three screens running. The two left are like the ones in a cockpit. He pulled the destination charts up on the other monitor."

Colonel Wright told Gamble, "Send the plane to RAF Fairford in Gloucestershire. They've got a ten-thousand-foot runway. It ought to give you plenty of space to roll out."

"Would you have an ICAO code? The autopilot will be much more accurate if I code it to the end of a specific runway."

"Fairford," Rory said, "is…EGVA."

"Okay, make sure your F-16s are clear," Gamble instructed. "The plane's about to come starboard." Gamble paused. "Rory, how many remote channels does this console have?"

"A couple of hundred at least. Two-hundred-fifty-six. Why?"

"It looks like someone else is trying to take yolk control from somewhere on the ground. Whoever it is, it's trying to route the flight to Reykjavik."

Wright spoke up immediately. "Iceland's no good. We won't be able to get the plane back. It needs to come down in the UK."

Rory clicked on a keyboard for a minute, then said to the team, "Let me change communications channels with the ground. Maybe I can block them out."

Gamble snorted out a victors laugh. "For a while, I suspect. Transatlantic Airlines has figured out something is wrong, and they're trying to coax the plane to the nearest airport they can. But guess what…."

Rory informed Gamble, "I've put you up on channel 240. So you should be in control."

"It worked. We're stable."

The chatter quieted, and I came on, "Do these things have passwords?"

"Yup," Gamble assured the three of us, "but every commercial pilot in the world can tell you what it is."

"Then why don't we change the password so if they figure out the new channel, their password won't work," I suggested, proud that I could figure out such tech-heavy crap.

"Wow," Rory broke the silence. "I know you can change it. I'm not sure how. Let me get the book—here; I got it."

I suggested we change the password to Klearance; or something appropriate.

"Klearance with a k." A few seconds passed when Rory replied, "It's changed, and Gamble, you're in total control."

I asked the Dallas guys, "How close are we?"

Wright answered in a distant voice, "My satellite link says about four hundred miles northwest of Fairford."

"That sounds about right," Gamble agreed. "I've activated the camera to the main cabin. Everyone looks slumped over dead. Nothing is moving back there. Oxygen level is normal; cabin pressure—normal to 8,500 feet. The temperature is 70 degrees. There are no alarms. The masks aren't hanging."

We all fell quiet until Gamble spoke. "What the heck? We're turning back to Reykjavik. I checked the flight deck and can't tell who, but someone has reprogrammed the autopilot back to Iceland." Gamble grunted. "I'm turning off the autopilot. No point in having it on. I'll take her in by yoke."

Colonel Wright spoke up guilty as if he'd gotten caught. "I didn't want to say anything, but the airline manufacturer has a master password to override all the others. TransAtlantic must have used it to get back in."

Gamble added, "I changed the ground communications channel again, but it's not going to take Transatlantic long to figure out what I've done. They know about us by now."

Rory asked. "Are you in control?"

"For now," Gamble told us. "I'm going back to autopilot and Fairford. Well, what the fuck? The plane is rolling opposite to the direction I'm commanding."

I asked, "What do you mean, rolling?"

Gamble grunted a brutal sound. "The best I can tell, the plane is upside down. Let me turn on the cabin camera—the passengers who were not crotch-locked in their seatbelts are laying on the ceiling."

Rory conceded, "It looks like the shoe's on the other

foot now. They have us locked out. Let me see if I can find another way to force them out and us in."

"You better hurry it up." Gamble got urgent. "They're pulling back trying to gain altitude. It looks like they don't know we're upside down. They're nosing the plane straight down instead of pulling it up. The airspeed is picking up. We've gone supersonic. Surely they know something's wrong."

"I'm not finding anything." Rory hissed. "We are hard locked out."

Gamble let out a painful yelp. "It doesn't matter. We just hit the water at seven-hundred-ninety miles an hour."

"Well shit." Rory's curse leaked out.

Wright concurred, "Damn."

Gamble said as if talking to the 250 souls on board. "Sorry, guys."

Chapter 54

Newswire, Worldwide
(AP) Associated Press
PRESIDENT AND FIRST LADY OF HAITI FOUND DEAD
By Andrew Chides
(Havana) Haitian President Charles Hoiden and First Lady Diane Westbury died this morning. It is thought they died from carbon monoxide poisoning caused by a faulty automotive exhaust. On vacation, the President and First Lady were alone outside Havana when both succumbed. Their car, a 1951 Ford Tudor, was parked near Playa Jibacoa with its windows rolled up.

The hotel manager from where they stayed reported the President and First Lady left the hotel for Playa Jibacoa last night following a sunset dinner at the hotel. Calls to the Havana Government have not been returned. A public statement released by Port-au-Prince indicated the President and First Lady were suffering marital strain from presidential duties. They had hoped to rejuvenate their relationship on this trip.

President Hoiden took office in February 2015 as a member of the Tet Kale Party. His free-trade platform, ecotourism, and alternative energy bills will remain unrealized. Haitian Prime Minister Revel will temporarily assume President and Prime Minister's role until the general elections.

His father and mother, Deni and Belle Hoiden, preceded the President in death. He is survived by four sisters and two brothers.

The First Lady is preceded in death by her father and mother, Charles and Lucille Westbury.

The President and First Lady will lie in state at the Museum of Haitian National Pantheon until the completion of state services, starting Saturday at 5 p.m.

Chapter 55

Dallas, Texas
Rick

With twelve hours until Toby's next treatment, I had no option except to stand by my promise. So I'd use the C-21 for a quick trip to Dallas. But before meeting him at his house, I decided to stop at the office for a quick buzz-buzz with Connie in Contracts. Connie was like Toby, slowing and refusing to give up on her old ways. Most notedly, her refusal to let Rory reconfigure her department with online records. I stepped into her newsroom-style office, where she awaited me.

I asked, "What did you find about Mark Gower handling contracts that no one else signed off on."

From under a waterfall of snow-colored hair, she read from a three-by-five index card she was keeping in her pocket for my return. She said, "There were several." Three rows of pearls encircled her neck, dangling when she bent to get a folder. "The most recent was fourteen months ago. The Air Force sent us a Logistics Design Request, wanting ideas on hiding hazardous material for travel on public highways. Mark was the only one who handled it. Do you want to hear what he told them?

"That's why I'm here."

"His instructions were to transport light cargo by camouflaging the items in retail shipping boxes. Then pack them in a freight truck painted to look like a large commercial carrier. He's got drawings of where to put these boxes in the nose of the trailer. Then, he said for them to weld the trailer shut at the hinges."

I figured as much.

I said aloud, "So, during that conversation, Gower could have asked Colonel Wright what the hazardous materials were, and Wright, in some stupid way, told him about Klearance. Gower, I'm guessing, then passed that information over to Kelly Lake. And that's why we've seen what we've seen."

****

Midmorning, I rolled my banana McLaren into the driveway and around behind Toby's house. Then, I switched to Toby's Bentley to give him a more comfortable trip to Building D of Medical City.

Two hours passed before a medical tech came out of the treatment's double doors. "Your father is doing well. You can be proud of his progress."

"He's my father-in-law." The tech's name badge had Noah Wilson engraved in it.

Noah corrected himself, "Your father-in-law. Todays were especially intense treatments, so expect a few aftereffects."

Toby, in the wheelchair, gruffed, "What aftereffects. I don't do aftereffects."

The technician put his hand on Toby's shoulder with a knowing smile. "You may have a little more difficulty with urination for a few days. That's all."

"What's important," I said to my elder companion, "is you're getting well."

"That he is." Technician Noah agreed while he wheeled Toby to the Bentley outside. Lifting Toby from the wheelchair and into the passenger seat, the tech again spoke, "A few more treatments, and Dr. Graves thinks you're finished. The next ones won't be as intense."

****

The C-21 proved to be a godsend. After dropping Toby off in Maria's care, I rushed to Love Field for a flight to Raton Pass, NM, rather than directly back to Londonderry. Once at Carissa's motel, I paced under the Western Hilltop Motel's portico, trying to connect with Rory. I needed him to direct my next step.

Rory sent several complex internet instructions to the Western Hilltop computer from Dallas. "Here we go. Let me find what room Carissa is in. It says room 142. So, let me see, where do they have the door lock controls? Bingo. This is so much easier than the old days of having to kick doors in, don't you agree?" But then he said, "It says no one is in the room."

I answered casually, "I've got time. I'm just bringing her back to Dallas for a few days of cold storage in the basement."

"I'll call you when she comes back."

"Sounds good.," I don't know why it mattered, but I said under my breath. "There's a bar here. I'll be in Milligan's."

I ordered my usual Old Fashioned. The smell of potted gardenia wafted on the mountain breeze, totally inappropriate for a truck stop and motel. My sister came to mind. The scent of gardenia fired off a memory of Esmee and me on the beach in South Texas. She crept up behind me and covered me with a flower-smelling perfume. Gross. That was not the thing for me to make my mark in the hood.

After the waitress brought my drink, I realized the

gardenia I smelled was coming from her. Good God, woman.

I entered Esmee's phone number, and the nurse answered. So I said, "Can you prop her phone up so we can talk?"

She did, and I said, "Esmee, you said your attacker is the same man you told me about in Dallas. Do you know his name?"

Happily, Esmee's voice sounded more robust than before. "Kelly Lake."

"Damn." A jolt of my adrenaline drowned out the rest of what she said. I took a moment to gather myself, wondering. *How has Kelly Lake infiltrated my interfamily, and I still don't have an idea who he is?*

"When I mentioned your name," Esmee said, "he lost control. He claimed he works for your boss. He said I was a spy for you or some crazy shit like that. He had already tied me up, so he beat me senselessly, and he enjoyed it."

"He went nuts on you because of me," I said. *Does he want me to feel like this is my fault? I don't.*

"You got it," she said.

I tightened my lips, wanting to comfort my sister but not make guarantees. "If it makes you feel better, I already have this guy on my screen." Either Lake selected Esmee because she was my sister, or not realizing it, he came on to her by accident. Ultimately it was moot. Lake is coming down.

"Can you tell me anything about him? How does he look? An accent? Anything?"

"I wish I knew. The guy was normal with me at first. Everybody is shrunk to presidential portraits in this business with government buildings on their back. The denomination is all that separates the men from the boys."

I urged her, "Try."

"He had a brown fold-over wallet with lots of big bills in it." She let out a rueful snicker.

"Compare him to me," I said. "Would you say he is bigger than me? Smaller?"

"I'd say taller than you but not as wide. Kelly Lake's hair is not as gray as yours. Darker, maybe a brownish-black."

My mental image of Lake had been he was tall with a French face. I was partly right. "That's good. Another difference?"

"He's younger."

My image of crow's feet on him faded. "What else?"

"His hands were big and soft. Not particularly strong. It's like he's one of those guys who avoid manual labor. He smiled a lot but wasn't a yack-yack. Well, not until he went crazy and started beating me. Then it was all slut-shaming, and spite—a real woman-hater."

"That's good." I hated the desperation of having to send my little sister down this road, reliving it again.

"Good for you, maybe. Oh, this might help: Lake has some sort of Egyptian bug tattooed on the back of his heel. A deep, colorful beetle thing."

I repeated, "An Egyptian bug?"

"Yeah. The Egyptian bug thingy. I don't know what it's called."

"A scarab?"

"That's it." My sister didn't extrude confidence. I doubt she knows enough Egyptology to understand what a scarab is, anyway.

"Which side was it on?"

"The right."

"Did he have an accent?"

She paused, then slowly responded, "I wouldn't say so, no."

"When he opened his wallet to pay, did you see anything? Credit card, driver's license, anything else? Anything with a different name on it? Could Kelly Lake be an alias?"

She said, "He stuck cash in an envelope for me, but I did catch a glimpse at his driver's license. I didn't see his name, but it was almost exactly like yours."

I said, "Do you mean a Texas license?"

She hesitated, and her voice hitched as she replied, "No question."

"Okay, you've given me something to work with." So, I have an impression of what Lake might look like for the first time. "How about being in the hospital? Are you getting everything you need?"

"I'm in the rehab center now. They moved me here at oh-my-god-how-early-is-it this morning. This is an uptown place, Bubs."

My phone vibrated, announcing a message from Rory. His text said Carissa had come back to her room.

I told my sister, "I need to go, but do you know how long they want you to stay there?"

"Couple of weeks, the nurse said, until my pancreas gets better."

"Good. I'll come and get you when you're released. Toby needs someone to help take care of him. If you agree to give up whoring, he could use someone like you to drive him around town. Could you do that?"

"Absolutely. If Mr. Toby will have me."

I sniffled an amused snort. "Laura said this would

happen to you if you stayed in business long enough. I need to run. The person I'm waiting for has come back."

"Before you go," she squeezed in before we finished, "it's still a little foggy, but Lake talked to somebody on the phone about Moscow, like revenge or a trap for you. I don't want to be in here forever…Be careful."

"I've pissed off somebody radically. See you soon, little sis." Once she disconnected, I sent Rory a message, "Get the computer to unlock the door to her room."

I tensed, checked the hallway, found the door unlocked, and went in on Carissa in a huff. She was folded over the commode when I found her— throwing up. Her heaves were butt-lifting. Sweat streamed down her glowing red face, and the veins in her neck bulged like fire hoses.

I stepped into the bathroom, carefully avoiding her legs. "When you're through with your spew, we're going to Dallas."

From behind me came a man's deep voice. "Ain't nobody goin' nowhere, pal, 'cept maybe me throwin' you out that window."

My neck hairs riled. I first froze, then came face-first with a shiny nickel Smith & Wesson. I followed the steel barrel back up to a gigantic hand, leading to an immense arm on a gargantuan man—her bodyguard, Sampson, from the depository.

An acrid, almost nasty taste climbed in the back of my throat. The last time I got that taste, a SAS bullet tumbled into my upper left shoulder, a lingering taste. It made me want to give up whiskey. Not.

But now didn't seem the time for negotiation; I kicked the bathroom door closed hard on Samson's hand.

His blunt fingers froze in the posture of a zombie, bouncing his shiny nickel gun on the tile.

I put my weight into the effort, but Sampson was younger and more muscular, forcing the door open slowly. I grabbed his zombie's fingers. I wasn't sure I still had it in me, but I hoped I had enough to stun the giant. As the door crept open and cleared, I grabbed his hand and drove the heel of my other hand through the backside of his massive elbow. I felt the three bones inside his elbow break away from each other in a sickening pop. It echoed in the tile room. His arm took on a raspberry shape bulge where a functioning joint once was.

Sampson screamed. Even the largest do.

Had he poisoned her? I lifted my girl from the bathroom, stepping over Sampson's prone kicking legs, and poured her on the bed, leaning to her ear, "Why are you throwing up? Did he poison you?"

The smell of Carissa's breath would bring down a vulture from high flight. Her skin yellowed, and she kept the appearance of Old Faithful about to blow from her face. I grabbed the desk trashcan and shoved it into her hands.

"Did King Kong drug you?" I tried again.

My girl used her head to indicate no.

"Then what's going on? You need the ER?"

She mustered a whisper. "Sour oysters in my omelet."

I stood shaking my head. *Who eats oysters in an omelet…in the hot desert?*

Some other person would need to deal with Goliath. Ignoring him, I steadied Carissa, guiding her by her tiny waist. Together, we coaxed her wobbly legs to the car and to the waiting jet. Before boarding, she stopped on the airport apron for another butt-raising hurl.

I instructed the pilot, "Get us to Love Field as quick as you can."

Strapping an oxygen bag to her face and wrapping her seatbelt around her, I positioned a flight sickness bag in her hand and arranged her head against the window. The pilot handed me a syringe of medicine. The label said atropine. I jabbed it in her thigh and squeezed the liquid into her. *She should sleep until we get to Love Field.*

As we approached Love, I called building security with instructions for the arrival party, "She needs to know we're in charge but don't abuse her. Tiny blood is okay, but not a lot. Put her in the holding room on Basement Level Five. She's not to see the sun again until I get back."

****

Over the Atlantic, en route to Northern Ireland, I took a satellite call from Rory. "Good news," he started. "The flight radar in Denver recorded an unidentified helicopter taking off from Trinidad, Colorado, but disappeared from radar behind Raton Mountain Ridge. It happened about the right time in the morning."

That trivia perked me up. "Did Denver give you a tail number?"

"No. I wish I could say yes, but the helicopter's transponder beacon was not on, so nothing got recorded. Then after seventeen minutes, it reappeared and flew on to Raton."

"Let me guess it landed at the Western Hilltop Motel."

"You should be a game show host." Rory let out a

distorted chortle.

"And how about the helicopter itself? Any information on it at all?"

"Nothing you can't already guess. It was a Robins R66, five-seater. The Colorado Highway Patrol issued a flatbed permit to transport it to Trinidad. The truck originated in Colorado Springs. And, before you ask, yes, it was Kelly Lake."

He's certainly not keeping anything secret, is he? I stared through the cloudy haze at the Atlantic below and the occasional iceberg slipping west. *You'd think he's drawing a dotted line for me to catch him.*

Chapter 56

Londonderry, Northern Ireland
Rick

Je led me away from the hotel, taking me straight forward to the Jigger Juice Bar a couple of blocks north. Once inside, he picked a private table in the rear. When our waiter came, Je ordered a squeezed medley of plant-top garden juice for both of us, a hint, I suppose, that he expected me to start taking better care of myself.

We weren't the only folks in the room. A queue of five waited at the counter for squeezes to-go.

"This pharmacist is anti-everything, a bit of a recluse," Je started. "So, after he closed and left, I had our team search his store and the one-room apartment above it."

Je squinted one by one toward everyone in the room. Satisfied no one was paying attention, he continued, "Kaelyn nabbed the bastard yesterday as he was coming out of the hospital. She took him to an abandoned gas station south of town. What a waste of time." Je leaned closer to me. Disgust at his progress was etched on his smooth skin face. "So far, he's told us a grand total of diddly squat—unless you want to know about conch powder capsules. Kaelyn has asked for you to come to do one of your talky talks with him. Me too."

I nodded his way. "You know you're going to have

to learn to do these yourself. Someday you're going to be on your own. So, pay attention this time."

I sized up the fellow at the gas station. Kaelyn had already tied his arms and legs to a slatted chair. But honestly, the guy couldn't kick a butterfly's ass. His sunken eyes and cheeks suggested a person older than I thought.

I said to him, "I understand you're the chemist who operates a drug shop on Bond Street. Right?"

The pharmacist ignored me.

"Am I right?" I repeated.

The line of the guy's spit launched toward me, leaving a half dribble-string hanging across his chin to his shirt. He grunted. "And you must be the Yank everybody's waitin' on. Go fuck yourself."

What a spirit. Too bad. "That's original."

"You're wastin' your time, Yank. I don't talk."

"Suit yourself. I'm not going to waste your time," I said. "This won't take long. You'll tell me everything I need to know."

The chemist sneered like a yapping chihuahua angry at the world. "You're off your stones if that's what you think. I've nothing to say to any of you Yankee jackasses."

"You're going to wish you'd cooperated with us." I positioned another straight-back chair in front of him and straddled its back to let him stew for a bit. "You received a box from San Juan. It had a 4-inch cylinder inside. It's not in your shop. It's not in your apartment. Where is it?"

"Snore." The chemist again spit.

There was no reason to react to the man's churlish attempt to get under my skin. I've been spit at before. I've decided it's the only way for people strapped to a chair to revolt, so that's what they do. "That cylinder contains nothing but death. You don't want it anywhere near your family or town. Where is it?"

The spindly man rolled his eyes melodramatically. "You're boring me."

I told him, "You know where it is. You're going to tell me where it is, or I'm going to put some shit in your veins you aren't going to want inside you. So it's time for you to pick."

"Oh, big man—you're going to make me? Well, here's where you get the Queen's piss-off, and I quit talking."

"That's too bad." I nodded to Kaelyn, who had already opened the hard-black case. This waste of wind is getting us nowhere. "Hit him with a full tube of *tell-me-about-it*. I've got stuff I need to be doing. Not playing with this shit."

She cracked the seal on the pre-loaded syringe forming a neon-red liquid inside. "You are not going to like this stuff," she warned the chemist. "You'd be better off telling Mr. Rick what he wants to know and save yourself the hangover."

"What I told him applies double to you, you queeny bint. You're one of us." The man's gaunt face showed a lifetime of hatred.

"Last chance." Kaelyn rocked the syringe back and forth in his face to mix the liquid.

"Just jab him," I grunted. "I wouldn't trust a word he said now, even if he insisted."

Kaelyn jabbed the syringe into the big blue vein running inside his elbow, then depressed the plunger and sent the neon fluid to his heart. If an allergic heart attack was going to happen, it would be now. But it didn't.

I counted off ten seconds for the juice to start working, "Do you work in a car park in Paris?"

"No."

"What do you do for a living?"

"I'm a chemist." That was that hazy voice I wanted to hear.

"Do you know any of us here?" I started.

"Not them, only you."

"Me?" I perked. *Me? What?*

The chemist drooped his face toward his lap, eyes closed. "You and a man named Toby sold my brigade guns when we were fighting."

That I don't remember. "Not unless you joined the brigade when you were in your knickers." *Could he have?*

"Moms says I'm too young to go to the Loughgall shoot-out. So, she wouldn't let me go, and they didn't shoot me…but they should have."

"You got a smart mom. Forget Loughgall. Let's talk about the shipment you received from Puerto Rico. Were you there when it arrived?"

"Outback. My son signed for it."

"And what's your boy's name?"

"His mother and I called him Timon, but he's the cute one and renamed himself, Little John. Stupid comes from her."

"Did you see the name of who sent the box?"

The chemist shook his head and slurred, "That's an easy one. Kelly Lake sent it to him."

"Addressed to Timon?"

"Little John."

With the Tell Me juice working, I probed further. "Do you know this Lake guy?"

"No. Only through Timon."

I asked, "So you never met him, not even once?"

"My son met him at one of them Castilian communist meetings. The stupid boy talks about Lake day and night like he's a god."

"Do you know where Timon is now? I'd like to talk to him."

The chemist feebly tried to raise his head, but it didn't work. "He's not at home. He took the cylinder to my sister's houseboat in Paris. She's supposed to help him—Kelly Lake promised him she would."

"Where about in Paris?"

"On the City River."

"It would sure have been better if you had told us this before Kaelyn pumped you. You gonna have the mother of all hangovers when this wears off." I patted the chemist on the cheek and headed back to town.

****

The aunt's houseboat had *Montagne Noire* painted in pale chipped gold over a black hull. To the right of the entrance door, someone had hung bright yellow drapes over its porthole. At the sound of us walking up, a young blond man with frightened eyes pulled the drape back and peeked at us.

Little John, is as stupid as his mother.

I let Je take the lead. This was his certification, and I wanted to see how he handles an attempted runner.

Je led, finding the front door locked. He ruggedly put his shoulder against it, and surprisingly the lightweight door gave way with a creak of rusted hinges.

I followed his quick footsteps inside. A grunt and a coffee table came our way through the air. Following it came a glass of beer scattering in every direction. Je lifted his forearm to block the incoming table edge, and, snap, it hit him. Bad move. The rear edge of the table spun around and hit him in the mouth. Then a salty red liquid came flowing over his lips. He spat the blood into his palm.

"Damn you. Stop it; god damn you."

The smell of stale beer came down on both of us as Little John threw his aunt to the floor in front of Je. Her gray head bounced off the rug. Little John grabbed the black metal box from a kitchen bookshelf and dashed toward the backdoor. He spun two spindle-back chairs toward Je, passing the sink and reaching for the back door.

Je's right foot caught in the spindles of a chair, tweaking his ankle, the wood slapping against into his shin. "Stop, damn it!"

Little John snatched a whistling tea kettle from the stove, throwing it at us before he stepped onto the tiny kitchen balcony. Je dodged the red kettle as Little John disappeared over the top rail headfirst. A giant splash spread as the water took him in.

Je limped through the kitchen rubble to the back balcony, about to follow the man in.

I yelled, "Wait until you see where he comes up."

But no blond head bobbed to the surface.

Je let out an angry grumble. "That's the shits." He spat the second concentration of blood into the Seine. "Fuck."

We rushed to the boat's front, Je's adrenalin flowing on high. "I can't believe he didn't come up. Is he dead?"

I handed him a handkerchief. "More likely, he's swimming under the hulls of these boats, so we can't see him. That's not a stupid person."

"He did have the cylinder. I saw it."

We hurried back to the stern and examined the swirls of moving water coming from under the boat. Then, finally, I said, "A person could hide under these hulls and go down the river for the rest of the day."

"You think he's trying to get back to the produce truck on the side of the road we passed coming in?"

"Good thought."

With a quick jerk back and gears grinding, Je took us to where the truck had been but was no longer.

I said, "The driver must have been Kelly Lake, in case Little John needed him. They're leaving Paris."

****

I dialed the C-21 pilot, Charles Leora, while Je called Rory. With urgency buried deep in his voice, Je asked, "I need you to look at the commercial manifests from Paris to Moscow tonight. Tell me if someone named Little John or Timon is listed."

Je then told me. "Little John is on an Aeroflot flight from Dusseldorf tonight to Moscow. So I'll get our two guys in Moscow to grab him at the airport."

I told the C-21 pilot, Leora, "Have our plane ready. We need a rush flight to Moscow. We'll be at the airport in fifteen."

Leora immediately bounced back, "That's one place I can't take you. American military planes flying in Russian airspace never last very long."

"Damn. Our missing cylinder is on an Aeroflot tonight. Diplomatic planes can fly there, can't they?"

"For the most part. There's one on the ground here right now. I can change into civilian clothes and snag it."

"See you in fifteen."

Harley Je wound the Renault's rubber band another twist tighter.

Chapter 57

Moscow, Russia
Rick

I wedged myself in the aluminum cockpit door frame, looking through the front window and at the pilot making our flight barely above treetops. The people in Washington who should know didn't, nor did the Kremlin know we were coming. The white Diplomatic Gulfstream took a low course over the frigid Baltic waves, then headed inland following the main cow trail. The pilot had followed this same path since the cold war. He dodged mountains, hills, valleys, and strategically located buildings, all used to create specific radar shadows. The Gulfstream flew unfettered on a dash through Russian airspace. Small towns passed below us until a range of northwest hills forced us to gain altitude and expose ourselves to Moscow ATC.

"If you get caught, we all burn," I said.

He kept us on the radar only for the shortest number of seconds, but it was enough for ATC to lock on to us. The red light came on, showing they had obtained a fix. We were toast. A green radar light came on, and the red one turned off. We had passed over the hill and returned to the safety of radar shadows.

"One day," he told me, "I'm gonna cross that ridge, and a SAM missile is gonna slam into my face."

Circling the city's southeast approach, barely above the treetops, the pilot made a final wings-up turn approaching an abandoned, weed-infested world war concrete runway. Wheels down and locked, nose flared, he brought the back gears down hard against the broken buff surface, and we rolled, stuck to the cracks in the concrete. Burned rubber smoke chased us as burned Jet-A exhaust leaked into the cabin. The reverse wind from the two engines forced us to slow quickly. Finally, the pilot clenched the brakes to near combustion, and the plane shook violently.

He let off, and the aircraft quietened.

Checking Je and me, his headphones neatly tucked under his ball cap, he barked, "That black van chasing us is for you. I'm lowering the airstairs. You've got twelve seconds to get out of here. Otherwise, you'll be going back to Paris."

I was drumming my fingers on the middle of my protégé's back, saying, "You know this might not come out right for either of us. Are you sure you want to go? You don't have to."

Quick on the tail of my comment, Je caught me out of the corner of his eye. "Are you going?"

"It's my job."

"Then, I'm going."

Hardly touching the white air steps, the two of us bounced down. The pilot started raising the stairs from under our feet, retracting the mechanism into the belly of the plane.

We dashed crossed the weed-laden concrete and slid into the back seat of the stolen Russian panel van.

Rightfully, I expected a West European driver to be behind the wheel, a driver with enough time on the road to be able to drive like a Muscovite and know the roads needed to get us into town quickly.

Under a black livery cap, the man with bushy brows and round face said in a voice I had heard many times before, "I guessed it would be you making trouble, Mr. Haade. One day Russia is going to catch up with you." He chuckled and extended a hand over his shoulder for a fist bump. "Cinch them belts tight, bro. The weeds and fence are our only way out. KGB is already searching for you."

He accelerated the rattling van like a stung bee. We disappeared through last year's grove of brown weeds and sticks, scrub brush, stones, ruts, and grooves. Je and I bounced off the ceiling and vinyl seat bottom, not in Lexus form.

I peered back through the missing rear window. The white jet had circled on its axis. It grew smaller as it throttled in the opposite direction, leaving us with nothing except a roar. And as easy as it landed, it was lost in the clouds.

I checked my watch. "We're late." I ratcheted up my voice to my old mate in the front. "Get us to the Okhotny Station a-sap. We've got a runner to catch."

"Not Okhotny. There's a riot put on by professional protesters going on down there today. And…your bush pilot dropped you off in the middle of rush hour."

"Still, we got to get there."

I raised my voice to Je, higher than the banging of the van crossing the ruts. "Call your two men. See where they are."

Je braced his hand against the roof, flipped out his phone, and dialed, loudspeaker set to on. Another man's voice came on. It sounded as if he was losing a jelly-roll sprint.

I brought up the city map on my phone.

"Where are you?" Je asked.

"I'm entering Lubyanka Station. Blazing Sneakers in front of me has about caught your guy. They're getting on the train heading your way. You're at Okhotny, right?" I leaned over the seat front seat to speak into the driver's ear. "Did you hear that?"

Je responded, "We're caught in traffic. It's going to be a bit yet."

"So, what do you want us to do once we get him?"

"Make damn sure you don't let him get away. If you catch our young friend, slip him a quick seven in the ribs. Then, take the gas bomb and get the hell out of there."

"What about the body?"

"I don't care who finds his body."

"I got it."

I told Bobby at the wheel, "Get us as close to the station as you can—we'll hoof it from there. So, why the hell are you back in Moscow? Toby told me you were hiding in exile."

Our lane merged onto the M-2, and Bobby revved the Russian diesel fast enough to join the Bolshoi freeway. Then, under a black-on-white sign, we exited, and he got us to Tverskaya Street. With one front wheel bounced up on the sidewalk, Bobby yanked the van to a stop.

"How far?" I asked, pushing against Je to shove him out, all the while scanning the end-of-day crowd to find the subway entrance.

"It's past the Carlton. Get gone. You can see the Metro sign from here."

"You owe me the story. I'll buy the beer."

Tverskaya Street had traffic in single file creeping a few feet at a time toward us and the ill-timed traffic light. Drivers were honking and woven into a daily gridlock. It provided them enough time to practice any newly invented swear words related to the Russian government and down a few Vodka flasks before facing big mama.

Green and red placards moved above the wave of heads down the way, circling in front of the Metro station entrance. "*Nyet, Nyet, Nyet,*" was their single loud chant.

"Stop right here," I said as we ran under the Carlton Central portico. I used the base of a streetlamp to climb and see above the crowd. As I did, the chanting stopped.

"What happened?" I quizzically searched out. "Where did the mob go? The placards are gone."

Je pointed a block away to the subway entrance. "The people have stopped coming out of the subway." Je spun to the sound of human flesh smearing against car metal. "That asshole," he yelled. "He just smashed a woman. He's rolling her against the furniture truck."

As bodies fell, a pile of lifeless humans formed at the subway entrance. And the heap of innocent citizens grew into the street and wrecked traffic. Cars rolled out of control—what little they could. No one else emerged from the tunnel.

I pressed against the gilded lobby doors, shoving Je inside. The cylinder had gone off. I typed to Toby, "*Gas went off in Moscow Metro before we got there. No idea how many were killed, but they're in vast piles. We're heading underground for safety.*"

Chapter 58

North Atlantic
Rick

Finally returning onboard the McDonnells' Marti Gras 757, I settled into one of its ergonomic leather seats—climbing out of Geneva. Now was the time to video connect with Colonel Wright and tell him the bad news. I told him, "Cylinder number one went off in central Moscow. Local death is beyond estimate." Finally, we broke through the clouds into the baby blue smooth sky.

"When did it go off?"

"In the subway during rush hour."

Wright sounded disappointed but not devastated. "I didn't hear. Shit. I suppose that's the risk we took." He was rather cavalier.

I added, "The Russian government is keeping our secret quiet. I'm on my way back to Dallas."

"Damn. Okay. I'll let DoD know. I'm sure they've not been clued in yet."

To that, I warned, "When you do, don't do anything stupid."

"Like?"

"Like using digital phones, text messages, anything you have that's digital. Russia is monitoring your net. So, for the next little while, you need to stay low-tech. Use analog phones; that's assuming you don't want the whole world to know what you did."

"We're secure."

"Tell me you don't believe what you said," I responded. "Russia is listening to every word you say around the clock, no different than what our team does. I presume you want the United States to stay out of this."

****

My flight continued across the Atlantic, now chasing an orange crescent moon. On her next stroll past me, I stopped the stewardess. "Would you bring me a bag of Fig Newton's and my Old Fashioned?"

The Marti Gras 757 television screens were parked behind the left console door in front of me. A computer monitor was behind the right. I switched on its TV to check if network news had started reporting the Russian affair. So far, the Kremlin had succeeded in keeping the story off the air. It wasn't their practice to inform the public until Russian scientists somehow explained the deaths. And in giant cases such as this, every social media outlet was taken under government control.

I reacted to the blinking red light in my armrest and accepted the incoming video.

On the screen was Rory at his Dallas workstation. "Glad you're still awake," he led. "The good news is I found Mark Gower for you in Tortola, BVI. I can kick the can down the street if you want a boot down there keeping an eye on him."

"Tortola," I asked. It didn't surprise me that Mark had burrowed a hole to hide in under the Queen's skirt. "It's tiny, but I guess it makes sense that it's British. And they kick their own cans down there. So how'd you find him?"

"It wasn't easy," Rory answered. "But people on the run never fully wipe their records clean. In his case, it was his property taxes."

"You're simply one clever fool, my friend. Have you talked with Toby? Do you know if our internal news channel is up tonight?"

"It is. Lynda is at the desk streaming right now."

"Perfect. Would you send me a link to my favorite girl?" When I got it, I sent Lynda a text, *"Hey, girl, any reason we can't spend tonight together?"*

Lynda returned a post to my screen—a flaming orange heart with an *"XOX. I hope you mean for the news...otherwise, Mrs. Ricky won't be so happy."*

"What a trifle," I sent her. *"Then let's do it the boring way. A bomb went off in one of the Moscow subway tunnels during today's evening rush. Russia is keeping it on a hush-hush. Tons of people got killed. See what you can find."*

"Let me start digging," she texted back.

On my monitor screen came the picture of young brunette Lynda as she started reading to me, and anyone else watching, what was happening at the Kremlin. First, she launched a display of Moscow maps and general facts about the city. Then up came relevant video clips followed by a message, *"The Ministry of Multimedia, Internet, and Radio has blocked all civilian wireless communications."*

The death toll on her screen showed over twelve thousand.

I typed out, *"That's what I need to see, so unless Jesus rides in with four horsemen of the apocalypse, I want you to stay with this full time for the next few hours."*

"Will do."

Lynda displayed a route map of the Moscow Metro subway and the body count from each entrance. Smaller numbers were coming from near the subway's ventilator stacks and a low number from access tunnels where the maintenance crew came and went. Occasionally she would find a photo coming from someone's satellite phone. Invariably they showed bodies piled on the streets like so many carcasses at a meathouse.

As added info came available, the maps began to show a pattern of where the gas had flowed, killing pedestrians as air blowers pushed it along. Every automobile and delivery truck operator near the entrances fell victim as they drove through the escaping vapor, and their death followed. The Ministry of Information blocked the broadcast of the most newsworthy traffic crash ever to happen in history.

I asked Lynda, *"Zoom in on the Red Line where the train passes Lubyanka."*

An enormous pile of bodies showed at Lubyanka, a bigger one than Okhotny. Little John had released the gas closest to Lubyanka, sending vapors toward Je and me. We were the lucky ones.

Over the seatback speaker in the plane, Lynda said, "Let me scan north so you can see what I'm seeing." Death stacks continued in both directions from Lubyanka but a lesser amount to the north.

"The gas jumped over to the Green Line in Okhotny and Purple Line at Kuznetsky. More bodies are getting stacked there." I instructed Lynda. "Can you put up a split-screen, one on the subway map and the other a tally of the dead?"

The screen flickered in the dim plane cabin light as

she did.

A text box popped up. *"A message came in from our partner station in Croatia. The Russian Army got dispatched to move bodies to Kubinka Air Base in southwest Moscow. Ewwww—ice is being ordered for the hangars."*

I lost track of time until the stewardess brought my dinner, a plate of brazed ribs with roasted finger potatoes. Not bad. "An Old Fashioned would do me. Oh, and check in from time to time. Don't let it run empty."

I called Colonel Wright. "Does your Air Force network allow you to log into external nets?"

"Why?"

"There's a link I'm sending. Follow its instructions."

"Got it. What is it?" the colonel asked.

"It's from our Dallas war room. You'll see my gal; her name is Lynda. The map indicates cylinder one opened south of Lubyanka Station between there and Okhotny. That's where, I presume, our guys intercepted him. The gas traveled on ventilation currents. The numbers on the right are the body counts at each tunnel entrance."

"Fifteen thousand dead. Damn." Wright paused. "That's a lot. That's how many Japanese died on Iwo Jima. And—how are you doing this? I've seen nothing about this on the DoD network."

"We have ways; that's all you need to know. You'll probably be seeing it on your network in a few hours."

After an introduction, Lynda reported, "Beijing appears to know what happened in Moscow." She summarized, "They're directing a rapid deployment defense against a fast-multiplying airborne virus. They mentioned the Moscow Metro. Moscow," she further read, "has speculation of it being an airborne virus. So, they're taking air samples from the tunnel and sending them to their labs for analysis."

Colonel Wright crowed, "That's the response we hoped would happen. They've assumed it's biological. They'll analyze it for months, years even, trying to prove themselves right."

Is this why we pay the military?

Lynda interrupted, "The US has learned of the event. Moscow says they intercepted a message from Kirtland Air Force Base in New Mexico. The message notified Washington of the event. However, there is no explanation of how Kirtland knew."

I cleared my throat, shy of telling the colonial *I told you so*. Instead, I softly responded, "You should have used analog phones or couriers."

Chapter 59

Over Chicago
Rick

Sunrise broke in the reflection of Lake Michigan below. The 757 Marti Gras made a course correction, bypassing Chicago straight to Love Field, Dallas. I adjusted the left TV screen to avoid glare from my window. The Network News Channel had still reported nothing about the subway. Neither had any of the feeds for the other G-8 nations.

Lynda's voice was wearing down, having read copy through the night. "I don't get pieces like this often…" She trailed off. "There's a short video coming from one of our satellite stations."

A front-loading green tractor scooped bodies at one of the subway entrances tossing them limp into a dump truck. The truck driver covered the bodies with blue tarps showing no decorum for the lost souls. Rough numbers on the tally screen had the death toll settling somewhere around 25,000.

Awake from an abbreviated night, Je messaged that he was going to the London office.

I must have dozed as well because I jumped when Lynda spoke on my left speaker. "I found an audio feed. The Russian Information Ministry is putting together a news release about the Business District disruption. I'll translate. The Chief Minister is telling the committee a power station in the tunnels erupted …exploded …causing gasses and a stoppage of trains. The districtwide telephone…system…failure naturally came from the…explosion. Now he is saying the people in the tunnel aren't dead at all. They…have…volunteered for a…humanitarian mission…no…that's a crisis in Africa. The explosion and the African crisis are pure coincidence. He will provide more information this afternoon."

After a hard night of work by the Russian Army, the streets were allowed to return to normal.

A woman with black shoulder-length hair replaced Lynda on the news desk.

My Fig Newtons were Fig Has-Beens.

The new screen update showed over 30,000 Muscovites had volunteered overnight to join an esteemed crisis corps in Africa and Egypt. The Network News Channel screen crawler said they would be away for three years, and NNC would be dispatching reporters for more information.

The U.S. Air Force communications network had gone dark with no explanation, and Wright was at home asleep.

Chapter 60

Dallas, Texas
Rick

I called Laura as the McDonnell plane taxied across the airport at Love to the corporate terminal. "We haven't talked. I've been gone."

"Are you at home?"

"We're taxiing in at Love. How about you?"

Her voice, as tired as mine, said, "I'm still in Pittsburg, it looks like for a couple of more days. I can't wait to get home."

The Marti Gras 757 veered off the tarmac and rolled into our private hanger. I asked Laura, "Is Brian up there with you?"

"Not this trip."

"I haven't had a chance to watch your cam show. But I will."

Through her voice, I could tell she brightened. "Brian said you eventually would. He discovered your phone hack. So why not, I said to him. It's for fun."

"That's right, for fun."

Laura's voice jumped perkily, "I've got to go to Boston first. Something's happening up there. But let's get nasty when we're all back in Dallas."

"Can't wait. Esmee called. I've got to go out to Flagstaff and collect her tomorrow. She'll need to stay at our place for a couple of days."

Chapter 61

Dallas, Texas
Rick

Toby likely would not accept Esmee as his assistant, with her dragging those white plaster casts on her arms. So our doctor at Big Baylor Hospital agreed to cut the dinosaur casts off and replace them with lightweight carbon-fiber models for Toby's sake.

I told the good doctor, "I need you to get these medieval things off her arms and put on something more modern that allows her to drive."

He x-rayed her arms, followed by measuring and fitting carbon-fiber replacements. Yes. Toby would go for these.

Back in the McLaren and firing her up, I let Esmee know, "I want you to meet Toby first, then we can go to your new apartment. When you meet Toby, you need to act grown-up. No talking about whoring. Talk about positive things."

"Like what?"

"Your job with the Rangers. Talk about that. And don't ask if Maria speaks English. Of course, she does."

"Well, duh."

Toby greeted us with his most charming smile. "I like your casts. They look like a Veyron."

Esmee's brow furled down in question.

"A Veyron is a sports car. One of those high-dollar sports cars."

She nodded toward my car in the drive. "Like your McLaren?"

"Much pricier than the banana." I chuckled.

But Toby interrupted the chat, welcoming her inside, his hand at the small of her back. "Never mind...Richard tells me you are a highly organized person. You worked for the Texas Rangers in their equipment division. That chore must be complicated."

"I guess I am. In the spring training and summer games, I keep the right uniforms in the right lockers for when our players come to town."

Toby led her and me to his air-conditioned back porch. "I've seen baseball on TV. You wouldn't believe it, but I have. It must be a great challenge to make sure all of those little pieces get sorted correctly."

Esmee perked up; this was her game. "And the colors. There are so many colors. You wouldn't think it," she sputtered. "There's blue, red, and there's white. But if you look at them on TV, all the players wear the same colors. That's because I got it right. I'm good like that."

I told Toby, "And, she's done customer satisfaction work." Then I snorted aloud. "The important thing is she knows the importance of taking care of you properly. She'll be yours dedicated. She can get you to Medical City when you need to be there. And she can take you down Greenville Avenue for a Berry's Guadeloupe in the afternoon when you want to watch the women walking by. She's a safe driver. So far, she's never so much as scratched a Bentley, so I'm sure yours is going to be fine. I've explained to her how much you like your saloon."

Toby grinned her way. "Then there's no worry."

"And one other thing," I added. "My sister's brain is like a chunk of pineapple. She can't recall the first verse of America the Beautiful if her life depends on it. So, if we accidentally say something around her, there's nothing to worry about. Thoughts and ideas never get beyond her bleached roots."

"What's important, Rick," Toby nodded, "is I trust you. Let's get her in to meet Maria. Maria will help her get started. Do you think she should wear a uniform?"

I asked my sister. "Would you like to wear a uniform?"

Esmee's eyes lit up, and she rose to her tiptoes. "I like uniforms. I would love to wear one myself. Does it have a hat?"

Toby grinned at her happy response. "If you want one."

****

I took her to the third-floor apartment in a building with an elevator. Her unit, clean and modern to a fault, shaded Cole Avenue and Blackburn across the street from Village West shopping center. Minimalist hangings decorated the walls, a white painting with an off-center red dot hung over the sofa. A black curly-neck vase on floating shelves adorned the living room wall. Tall shelves were suspended from the ceiling, awaiting books and tchotchkes.

I comforted her, "I'll pay the first three months to make sure you get some traction. Then it's on you. Toby probably won't pay whore wages, but he'll treat you good."

Esmee marveled, scanning over her place. "I can't believe this. It looks so, not me, but in a good way."

I directed her to the cream shade sofa. "Okay. Sit

down. You need to know Toby. You absolutely must treat him the right way. He's like General Patton, President Eisenhower, Castro, and the Marshmallow Man all mixed into one." I warned. She continued to look at the things in the room. Finally, I barked, "Listen to me."

She turned.

"Toby's done everything those generals have done. He's been mean and spiteful and wicked and tough, but at the same time, he'll hold you for hours to let you cry because your baby fish passed away. Toby has a lot, and he gives a lot. Toby has succeeded in everything. All he asks is, you try. You try, Esmee, and he'll show you the way. You quit or be rude, and he won't have anything to do with you."

She asked, "What do you mean?"

I raised my brow and furrowed my forehead. "It means if Toby asks you to drive him somewhere, do it. If you don't know how to get there, ask him. Don't go getting yourself lost and fall into some pity party. Ask him before things go wrong, or at least tell him when things first go wrong, and he'll help you make it right."

"I like him." Her eyes widened. "He's sick, isn't he?"

"He is. Why'd you say that?"

She flittered her fingers toward her dining area. "Toby looks like he's dying."

"He's sick, but he isn't dying. Part of your job is to get him to Medical City for treatments every Monday so he doesn't die. They're taking care of him."

"I'm a soothsayer, my good brother. Maybe he simply looks like a man dying. Like you. You're afraid you made a mistake recommending me."

"Listen, what I need is for you to take your job seriously. I can't work while I'm chauffeuring Toby to his appointments, and I have two things I must finish. One of which you'll like. I'm going to catch the asshole who busted you up. And I'm going to get the Mark Gower guy. After that, things will settle in for us."

Chapter 62

Dallas, Texas
Rick

I dropped a dollar on the counter and picked up a Morning News, taking it to my booth and flipping through the pages. I went to the back of Section A. Happily, there was nothing related to the subway disaster. However, an article was there on Russia's humanitarian project. It said 30,000 citizens were being sent to improve agriculture methods and bring water to African farmland.

I left the paper at the White Rock Tea & Coffee bar, having an appointment awaiting in Interrogation Room Two.

Our building has forty-four stories above ground and eight in the basement. The first basement level was parking. The second held facilities to support the building. The federal government rented three floors to house their war readiness computers. The others were there for unique needs like today. Three rooms were blocked off on level 5 for special interrogation, fully soundproofed, and drains on the floor to hose down fluids coming from deep interrogations. Things sometimes accidentally happened in Interrogation Two that no one on the planet needs to know.

I quickly stepped from my downward trip on the

elevator, asking the uniformed guard standing watch, "Is she ready?"

"As instructed."

I took a deep breath, held it, then snap-opened the door. My girl was at the table in front of me.

Carissa shifted her weight disapprovingly, sitting at a dark-stained table with two wooden chairs opposite each other. One of her guards had extended her arms in metal shackles, attaching them to the table. She was in white pants and blouse, her legs open and connected to floor bolts using steel rope. Her readying team also placed a blurring mask over her eyes.

I took another deep breath and closed the steel door behind me.

I told Carissa, "I wish you had cooperated, and we didn't have to do this."

She raised her head in the direction of my voice. Through tears on her cheeks, she said, "I should have, I know. So, there's no reason to hurt me anymore, Mr. Haade. I'll tell you what you need to hear."

"That's the problem, Carissa. You've been telling me what you think I need to hear. You should have been smarter than that. Now I'll have to give you a shot of happy juice. It'll make you tell me the truth." I removed the pink protective cap from the needle.

Carissa pleaded, "Please, Mr. Haade, I don't need juice."

I found a vein at the bend in her elbow, slipped the needle in, and pushed the neon-red fluid in her bloodstream. In a couple of seconds, her eyes slid closed, and her face morphed with happiness.

I said, "Okay when you were a little girl. Where did you live?"

She willingly answered with no hesitation, "In Londonderry, Northern Ireland. In a little house. I had red shoes and a yellow shirt with green flowers."

"Your father, what do you remember of him?"

"Oh, I loved my daddy. He was a machinist on boats by the river. He fell in the water one time and got in trouble with my mom. River peoples aren't supposed to fall in the water."

I asked, "Can you tell me his name?"

"Daddy. You know, he died. My mother buried him in the church cemetery. He has a marker and all."

"Do you remember who I am from when you were a little girl?"

Her face soured, and she was slow to answer.

"Why are you frowning?"

"Because the man who came after you left hurt my mother. He made her take her clothes off, and she cried real loud after Daddy died."

I pulled Mark Gower's picture up on my phone and lifted her blur mask. "Is this the man?"

"Yes. He wanted me to call him Uncle Mark, but he wasn't my uncle. He's the man who shot my father. He pulled out a pistol he hid in his pocket."

What an asshole.

"When I visited you in Colorado Springs, the woman living with you didn't look like your real mother."

Carissa promptly agreed, "Nope. Kelly Lake got her from a temporary agency to play my mother. See— Uncle Mark kidnapped my real mother. He took her away, but he swears to me she's still alive. I do what he tells me to see her again someday, but still, he won't let me see her. Do you think she's still alive?"

"So, you still see Mark Gower?"

"Sometimes."

"Just to make sure I understand, Kelly Lake is different from Uncle Mark? They are two different people. You know for sure?"

"Yes."

"When did you see Mark Gower last?"

"On my birthday. He's as big as a cow, now." The shackles kept her from showing me how big of a cow is.

"I know the man. I used to work with him. You're right; he's large."

"God damn him. Do you know he broke our goose's neck with his bare hands because she honked in the backyard too much? Then he made us eat her."

"Jerk. Let's talk about Kelly Lake. Can you tell me what he looks like?"

She let out a funny laugh and whispered, "Pretty nice, I'd say. Kelly's like you, except handsome."

"Right. What's his height?"

"Taller than you. And more hair. Yours is thin."

"Eyes?"

"Both are brown." She giggled.

That aligns with Esmee; unfortunately, it fits half the men in America. "Okay, let's change subjects to what you did for him."

"Oh," she said after thinking, "I did lots of things. I acted like I would bring a box to someone in Dallas. I think that's when I saw you in that car, but all I did was ride around for a while on that tall red bus. I had fun. I bought new clothes and stayed in an expensive hotel. I had a bodyguard."

"Did you ever take anything from an Army base in Arizona?"

"I don't think so, do you? Kelly moved me from my apartment in Phoenix then to Colorado. She died, you know."

"How?"

Carissa squirmed to draw her restrained knees to her chest. "He pushed a knife into her tummy. She bled on the floor. She wanted me to help her, but Kelly held her down until she stopped fighting."

I pressed. "And the fire?"

"Kelly Lake, he lit it in the kitchen with a newspaper so he could burn her up. Then he carried me in his pickup truck to an apartment in Pueblo."

"Do you remember the place's name?"

"No." She shook the question off.

"Okay. Let's talk shoe boxes in an Air Force truck. How did you know where to look for them?"

"He told me where to cut the trailer open. Then, he wanted me to ride in a tractor-trailer and get some black eggs out and give them to him."

"And you did?"

"I did, perfectly. I cut open the trailer with this sawing tool in the bag he gave me. Not a single mistake. I did it right."

"Did you kill the Air Force driver, Tommy Begaye?"

Carissa hemmed at the question, squirming, "I liked him, but I might have… I got those four little eggs out of the trailer. Kelly said I did a good job."

"So, you know," I told her, "you did kill Tommy Begaye."

"That's a bad girl, isn't it?" She bowed her head.

I nodded. "Yup. How did you get away from the Air Force truck?"

"Kelly Lake picked me up in a helicopter. Oh, let me tell you, when we were way high, way above the mountains, my bodyguard, King Kong, pushed the copilot out the helicopter door. We were over a bunch of trees. He stuck himself in the treetop. He yelled while he fell."

I leaned back and crossed my arms. The New Mexico or Colorado police will have to deal with that. "So, where did the helicopter take you?"

"To the motel where you kidnapped me. The big man took care of me. You called him King Kong. No, that's not right. I called him King Kong." She snickered.

"And the traffic accident on Interstate 40? Were you part of that?"

Carissa said, "Did you know Kelly Lake made that accident happen in the mountains? He injured the truck's brakes. And emailed the pictures to you. He talks about you a lot."

"Me?" *What did that mean?* I leaned forward, elbows against the steel table. "What does he say?"

"Whatever. Kelly's planning to stuff you and hang you over his fireplace."

Chapter 63

Dallas, Texas
Rick

So, that's it. Mark Gower is in the center of this and his hate of Toby, and I probably goes back as far as our gun-running in Londonderry.

I walked across our media center. Lou Gartner of Network News was on the TV reading his morning script. "An unknown flu epidemic is reported sweeping through Moscow this week. As a result, public transportation has come to a stand-still, and the Russian Health Chairman is urging people to stay away from the Metro tunnels until the disease has subsided." Gartner changed camera angles and continued reading his report. "They are also informing people who have been in the Metro tunnels to report to their local hospital for blood sampling."

I realized that I hadn't seen Je since we got back. The bombing is still his case and will be until we close the gap Mark Gower continues to slither through. So I called his satellite number.

I said, "Unless you have something vital going on, I need you in Tortola to help put an end to the Gower case. Then, maybe you'll get the London Office. I'm sure you'll find your golden mermaid."

"When do you want to go?"

"Tomorrow is good. Rory found Mark Gower living on Tortola island. Colonel Wright signed a new contract for us to nab him and serve justice; no bother wasting court time, he says."

"That should close it," Je answered, "But, you remember Gower is still my responsibility. I'm still the agent-in-charge."

****

I arrived at Scrub Island beach, shoes and socks off, my butt on a stool at the tiki bar, still wearing my jeans from the flight.

The bartender queried me after a few drinks had disappeared down the old gullet, "Got the stomach for another Cable Car?" The forty-something, wavy hair bartender was disassembling a mai-tai umbrella and picked shit from between his teeth with the toothpick.

And the gall, anyone wondering if I could handle another drink. A pure insult. The barman amused me. "I'm guessing your folks didn't waste money on sending you to finishing school. How many have I downed so far?"

The tiki hut bar swirled in an eddy of a light Atlantic breeze.

The bartender twirled another umbrella. "This will be five."

"Then six it'll be. But first, let's take care of business." I slipped a picture of Mark Gower from my *Visit Scrub Island* shirt pocket. "This man lives on the island. Have you ever seen him around here? A heavy man."

"Are you government?" The man thumped his mouth-soaked toothpick into the sand, took my Gower picture, and studied it before answering. "I can't say so, no." He leaned the picture back toward me.

I was not sure why, but my voice started slurring. And unexpectedly, I asked, "You got a girl or wife of some sort?"

"How many sorts are there?" He put a fresh stick in his mouth, and it wiggled. "A girlfriend."

"Would you let her sleep with another man, you know, and somehow make it all right in your mind?" *Why did I even blurt that out?*

"That's what your picture guy did? So now, you're after him?"

"No. I was wondering. The picture-guy is something else."

The bartender failed to answer but took another umbrella pick and began working stuff out from under his nails.

I swirled my drink and gave the cherry back to him. He ate it.

"Man alive, what's in this concoction," I asked.

He wiped the umbrella stick clean and thumped it too into the beach sand. "Does it matter?"

"I don't suppose it does."

He said back, "Okay, what's this with wifey? Are you here on vacation, and she's getting the beach-meat throbs?"

"No...I told her she can."

"And now you're having second thoughts?" His slouchy shirt got closer, leaning into my space, resting on his elbows.

"Goodness, no." I slowly took another sip of his hell-in-a-glass mix. "I'm starting to get a kick out of it—the idea of her doing naughty girly things if you know what I mean."

"Then go for it. People do it down here all the time."
"Shush."

I held my palm forward like a crossing guard as Harley Je came round the corner from the hotel.

I said, "I rented you a jet ski. It's waiting down by the water for you. Get on it. And don't let this wicked sun-wart start you on Cable Cars. He's the devil in flip-flops. Now, I'm ready for the wheelchair to take me to my room."

Chapter 64

Tortola, British Virgin Islands
Rick

I asked the hotel concierge to find us a four-wheel-drive truck. He gave us a tan-and-green canvas top to negotiate the mountain roads of Tortola. Instinctively, I figured Gower would choose a remote location on the island—well isolated on the northern half, and his street address supported it.

I parked the Tan and Green in the volcano gravel lot by an icehouse. I spotted a BVI Postal Courier. "Do you know a man, Mark Gower?" I asked. "The hotel told me he lives around here, somewhere."

The dark-skinned man, considering the year-round sun, came over. "Donkey ears, I know deh Yank, Mark Gower. He gone Barbados for to cut dem rum grass."

"So, he's not here on the island? Could you tell me where his house is? I've read it's a cool place to see. I'd like to."

The letter carrier didn't hesitate in answering, "Certainly. Follow di tourist signs to Myall Point, den as yuh get closa you notice a turnoff to Trunk Bay. Take dat right turn, and den follow it straight to di end. Dat be his place."

So, we endured a continuous bounce over the packed lava road. Gower's place hung on the side of a low mountain ledge. Several hundred feet above a private horseshoe-shaped sand beach, we perched on a stone wall absorbing the face breeze and view. Gower's little snow white and equally innocent Trunk Bay beach lay below. I realized a human body could lay stranded down there until the sea and sun reduced it to nothing. And, of course, no one would be the wiser.

The main house was wow, a tall glass showcase, with the Atlantic Ocean framing the front and forested vines and trees from Mt. Sage providing its backdrop. An infinity pool traversed the house's front jut, providing the illusion of sea and life as one. Two floor-to-ceiling glass doors separated us from the inside.

Je, numbed in luxury, said. "Nice. I understand why he cashed out and escaped."

I twisted the front door lever. Surprise, the door opened. A wall-to-wall glass floor held us up. I cautiously stepped across the glass to the sitting area—the scent of perfume filled the air. Fish frenzied below the glass floor in a manmade bay. An auto-feeder kept the fish within view. A few pieces of mail were about the room…and there was an insider magazine from the British Space Communications Command. I quickly thumbed through it—then read his mail. It contained little more than a domestic dribble. But there was this one with his Barbados address on the envelope. That one I put in my pocket.

I realized a security light on the wall panel began blinking red. I told Harley Je, "We need to get going. The cops are coming."

****

An early dusk flight on a de Havilland Sea Otter put us at Crane's Island Resort on Barbados near dark. But, more importantly, it put me at an open-air bar, 'the 1887', with a tan hostess and my toes in the sand.

Je snickered. "Are you daring enough to compare the Cable Car here to the one last night?"

"I'll die a slow death first," I answered. "Give me one of my good Old Fashioneds. That's what I need." So, as we waited, I piddled with the doodads on our high-top table. A matchbook interested me. It had a tourist advertisement on the front promoting the SCC Sugar Plantation. I opened it and then stuffed it in my pant pocket. "That would be something interesting to do," I told Je. "There's an advertisement for a tour of a local sugar mill. Maybe if we were tourists."

Je countered by saying, "I think I'd like to stay here for a week after we've done our business. I need an unwinding. And, hey, now that I'm a new field agent, I have to be privileged."

"Den yuh need ta take yuh privileges tuh a different island." I mocked the earlier postman. "I don't want to read you got arrested here for murder."

Chapter 65

Bridgetown, Barbados
Rick

Je and I connected the following morning as he scraped egg and bacon into a breakfast taco. Then, we talked under a palm frond roof, watching the waves break.

"Well, we're here; where do you think Gower is?" I asked Harley, my bright-eyed underling, who was pouring a pineapple-shaped mug of coffee. "You're agent-in-charge. You should know already."

"Sorry?" Je blinked at my comment.

I pulled the matchbook from my pocket. "Last night, these were laying all over the place. You couldn't spit without knocking a dozen off the table."

He pinched it from my fingers and read it aloud, "'*SCC Sugar. Join us for a visit. Or bring your own cane for your first crush.*' So you read that to mean Mark Gower?"

"Who else?"

He reread the cover and said. "SCC could be sugar cane company or whatever."

"You're the field agent. You've puppied me for seven years. This should be second nature to you. What do you know about Mark Gower's beginning? MI-6 Space Communications Command. He worshipped the place; it was his only family. It's obvious. Get the internet up and find the SCC Plantation's business address, not its mill address. That's where we'll find Mark."

"You always make this look so easy."

We quickly scoffed down our breakfast and hit the road. Gower's cane plantation sat on a gradually upsloping hill leaving the Atlantic below. His business address was his home address, as predicted. Like Tortola, Mark had arranged a magnificent view of a sapphire sea. I parked in his drive at the point where it encircled a pineapple-themed fountain, then we walked to the back of his house.

We found Gower sitting on his back veranda, bending to reach a polished coral coffee table in front of him.

I approached slowly and quietly—the porch spanning the house's rear. I walked in front of Mark and Je around his back.

Surprised, Gower said, "Oh, my friends from Texas have come to visit me and, if I can forecast, want to learn how to make a great sugar crop." The dominant belly man leaned to his side to watch the morning breeze blow waves across his high stalks of cane, the air cooling as it rose from the sea. "It makes such a beautiful view, the fields, and the ocean. Don't you agree?"

I said, "What's wrong with you, Mark? You don't seem…you seem weird."

"Nothing, Ricky. I'm fine. The hotel manager called when you left, so I fixed us a special drink." Before him, perched on the coffee table, sat a French press. "Would you care for some locally grown coffee? I know you like refined coffee. It's ready if you would like a cup. I have enough for your friend here too, Mr. Je, I believe. Did you have a hard time finding my place?"

I shook my head, watching Mark watch the cane dance in the breeze. "I don't think so. We're only going to be here a little while. You left good clues."

Gower bobbed his overly round head a little drunk-like, and his jowls jiggled. "I have wonderfully splendid honey to go with my coffee. I have hives down the hill. You must have seen them when you passed. Most of my visitors are business people wanting to buy my sugarcane." He poured a demitasse for me with a heavy spoon of honey. "I never get visitors, much fewer old work buddies. I'm glad you came to see me."

"You surprise me, Mark." I again waved off the coffee.

A bit irritated at the rejection, he took another sip of his own. "I'm curious; I chose this property because it's beautiful and, more importantly, because of its total seclusion. How did you find me?"

Je had his hobble blade at the ready. I said, "You left directions on your matchbook cover. Tourists will go to the mill. But we aren't interested in the mill. We're interested in you, so we got your address off the internet. I figure you wanted me to find you. You wouldn't slip up like that."

"In a way." Erratic motions in his fingers, he started slurring his words. "Only you would have figured it out. Your little friend here was clueless; that's my guess. Am I right? Are you sure you won't drink my coffee? I fixed it special for you. Did you ever figure out Brahms? I know you never did figure out about the gas."

I nodded. "I did. And I did figure out about the gas; we were always too far behind to catch your runner."

"It's a good thing you didn't. You would have been killed. I instructed the boy to open the valves if his men got too close. He didn't know any better. I suppose you came to find out why I worked with Brahms and why I designed such a great puzzle, insisting only you try to solve it. Right? Am I right?"

I wiped the sweat from the lower part of my face. Je stood at the ready with his blade. I answered Mark, "We're here mostly because the Air Force has contracted justice for what you did in the Russian Metro tunnels using their gas. And yes, I would also like to know about Brahms. What interest do they have in the gas? What's wrong with you? You're acting like you're living in slow motion."

Gower countered with a silly grin, "Or, maybe you're going super-fast. Did you ever think of that possibility? Why do you think Brahms is interested?"

"I have some conspiracy theory ideas, but I want to know the truth."

"Well, it happened to be fun, didn't it, my little puzzle?" Mark sipped his French press coffee and added a little more honey. "I wish you would drink some of my coffee."

What's the deal with the friggin coffee? I answered him, "With thirty thousand people dead, I wouldn't call it a fun puzzle, Mark, no."

"Oh, but it was. You take things too seriously, Ricky, my boy."

I assessed his veranda. It had two doors going inside, one on each end. The couch's softness prevented Mark from jumping and running—assuming he could even run anymore. There was no place he could conceal a gun. With his size, a knife would be useless. From what I could hear, no one in the house could interfere. The only activity appeared to be the cane waving in the wind. A metal paperweight kept two well-read issues of *IN* magazine from blowing away. They were next to his French press.

Gower hummed as if he was in thought. "Let's see, what does Brahms have to do with this? It should be ever so obvious, even for you, Ricky. Peace. They want global peace. That has been their creed since Boudicca led us. Peace for the country, freedom for the world."

I scoffed. "Isn't that a nice way of saying fear of global annihilation? That's not freedom. That's a dictatorship."

"Pay attention, Ricky. You're moving too slow. Think big," Gower slurred. "You view everything in shades of black. There's more to life. There are bouncing beach balls and vibrant colors and breezes everywhere. Look at the beauty of the waves in my cane fields. Given time, people will forget about the gas. And life will once again be worth living. But here, you want to ruin it."

"Xanadu," I said, "didn't last forever. Toby tells me you're a direct descendant of Boudicca. Is there anything to what he believes, or were you promoting your own ideas?"

"That's not important. But you should listen to Toby. My blood goes back to Boudicca's loins, herself. And that's a big statement, my boy, knowing you come from such a great leader." Mark stretched to pick up his cup from the table, but his trembling fingers knocked the cup and its saucer over, splashing the dark liquid across his magazines.

I helped him, picking up the French press and smelling what was inside. "What's in this?" It had a parsley-parsnips fragrance that I recognized. "Hemlock? You're trying to kill yourself?" Then I became aware of my coffee cup. "And you're trying to take me with you?"

"It's the only true and honorable way left to celebrate great success…I call it Socrates's Honor." He pointed feebly at me; muscular paralysis was starting to set in. "In a short time, Brahms will be able to manufacture the gas themselves."

I shook my head. "I doubt it." Then I thought, *how am I supposed to kill a man who is already killing himself? Just watch? Give him the seven now?* The hemlock had begun working. I guess Je and I had the time to wait. Maybe that was the honorable thing?

"My only regret," Gower uttered, "is Kelly Lake has not already killed you and Toby. My cocktail is…I'll miss seeing you and Toby heading to the morgue slabs."

"Well, I can see how your timing faux pas is screwing things up," I said, almost sympathetically for the fat gentleman whose passing would be met by no one who cared.

Gower tried to refill his cup again, add more honey to counteract the bitterness, and then sat back. "I know you don't believe it, but I secretly did fieldwork in Londonderry, watching you and Toby selling guns to that little band of IRA soldiers. And so, you know, I reported it back to MI-6. So, yes, I did do spy work, real spy work; believe it or not. So, take that."

"Actually, I've seen enough to believe you. And I also suspect you were sharpening both sides of the ax. First, you sold golden British information to the IRA and returned river rocks for London. You got paid nicely in both directions. Then, as soon as the Brits figured out what you were doing, you dashed to Toby and me for work and an honorable way to get out of the country. No way the crown would chase you to America."

Gower involuntarily snorted, spitting up a bit, before he replied, "I brought London good stuff, well worth what they paid for it."

How long does this hemlock shit take? It's not instant, and it looks like it's starting to be painful.

Mark grimaced.

Then he glanced at Je standing to his rear. "Why is he behind me not saying anything?"

"So, he can admire your massive crop of sugar cane," I said.

Je confirmed, "He's right. It's enormous."

"Well, I don't like him standing there." Gower slumped a bit to his right side.

I returned the conversation to Ireland while I had time. "You killed a good man in Tim Scaffe, and you killed him in cold blood."

Mark gasped. "That, my friend, was entirely his fault."

"You shot him point-blank in the chest."

Gower grinned. "It was his responsibility to get out of the way. He could see that I had a revolver." Then Mark labored to light an unfiltered Barbados cigarette and blew out the wooden match. "You know the one thing that's special about today. I can smoke all I want and not have to worry about catching lung cancer. Isn't it ironic? I have always been afraid cancer was going to be my undoing. Now I don't care. A life of smoking tobacco and I survived it."

"Shooting Scaffe was sick even for you, Mark. All you wanted was Vienna."

"And I got her. She's been good to me." Gower

inhaled and blew Chinese dragon smoke from his nostrils. "Very good indeed. After you and Toby left, I took Scaffe's widow under my wing. She's here on the plantation with me, now."

"Tim Scaffe's wife?" I asked, not actually believing the words he said.

"She's my wife now. Vienna Gower. We married." Mark labored to catch his breath. "I take excellent care of her. I had her in Dallas with me. I'm surprised you never realized that."

"Here? Where?"

"Don't fret. Vienna's nicely stored. I'm not telling you anything else." The big man arched his back, gasping for another breath. "I think you don't like me. Well, I don't like you or Toby. I wish Kelly Lake had already killed both of you. He will. I paid him to do it."

I admired the emerald cane field stretching out over the horizon. "Is all of this land yours?"

Gower controlled his finger twitch enough to point to the horizon. "To the far ridge over there. Then it's government land. So, I have no neighbors to worry about. I keep my privacy."

"You picked a nice place to die, sitting here watching the breeze blowing your cane. How long before you have to cut the cane?"

"Six weeks. I pay a company to cut it. They'll haul it to the mill. I guess that's moot at this point. Ha."

"So, nobody will be here until then." I couldn't tell if the shakes were from his nerves dying or the pain taking over.

"Nope." He labored for another deep breath. "It's automatic from here. All those sugar canes…making tiny sugar crystals…dropping dollars into my bank account."

Je waited patiently with his hobbler knife pointed at the back of Gower's neck. Je asked me, "Are you finished with him yet?"

Gower acted surprised, eyes opening. "Finished with me?"

I gave him a simple affirmative.

"I figured that's the reason you had him behind me. That's so typical, Ricky. If you're going to kill me, do it now. This hemlock isn't as honorable as writers make it."

Je caught the back of Mark's collar to keep the fat fart from slumping farther into his seat.

"I never believed I would end a job by doing you a favor," I said.

Gower crossed his arms over his chest, Boudica style.

"Do it," I commanded Je.

His thin blade slipped between Gower's top cervical bones and his skull, severing the man's spinal cord. Mark jerked once. His coffee fell into his lap, and his dead weight pulled his body out of Je's grip, forward enough to extract the blade.

In a way, it pissed me off that Gower chose to kill himself and steal that privilege from me. He stole my project's ending. He could have killed himself before we got here. Or waited until I was ready for Je to kill him. The hemlock was simply rude—typical Mark Gower.

"Let's drag him out in the cane field and find Carissa's mother."

It took us under a half-hour of going over his place until we found her. She was without water and emaciated in a concealed wine cellar below the kitchen. I carried her into the sunlight. She rolled to cover her eyes with her arms, protecting them from the light. It had been a while.

"Mark Gower's dead," I told her. "He's not going to be bothering you anymore. We're here to take you home."

"I'm thirsty," is all she could say. "Can I have water?"

I aimed Je to get a jelly glass on the table. "Get her some water. How long have you been down there?"

Mrs. Scaffe spoke through parched lips. "A year." She downed the jar of water, then another. "Can I have food?"

Je scouted a can of baked beans in the cabinet. She drank the liquid from the can first, then poured the beans into her mouth and chewed them—my baby owl experiencing a new taste of flesh.

"You look familiar," she said to me. "Do I know you?"

"A long time ago," I said. "You stayed with me in Londonderry after Tim got killed. Slow down. Take your time."

She thought. "You had a friend named Toby." Her bones protruded around her elbows, and she finally smiled at me.

"That's right."

I said to Harley Je, "Carissa said Gower treated her like a chained slave five years ago."

"I can believe it, the way she looks." He brought her another jar of water.

Mrs. Scaffe weakly gazed up at me, still softly resting in my arms. "Carissa? Is she alive?"

"Alive and well, in Dallas," I assured. "And we're

going to get you back so you can be with her."

I told Harley, "When you get done, search the house for computers. We'll have Rory find out what Mark's been doing."

Chapter 66

Dallas, Texas
Rick

Having reconnected Vienna with Carissa in our office basement, I sped out of the garage in the McLaren. *Now what? What do I do with Carissa? On the one hand, she'd killed a man and done mighty evil things but, on the other hand, none were of her own volition. Any decent attorney would be able to turn a jury against Kelly Lake. He had mentally manipulated her. It's not the first time. And when all was said and done, would she walk? Probably. So why complicate matters? She needed to be around to care for her mother. I'll talk to Toby.*

Toby left the decision with me. *Thanks.*

Now for Kelly Lake. Technically, he was still mine. Je did what Toby asked of him. And honestly, Lake could take out Je without thinking. Je finding Lake during the man's manic state would end up with Je wearing a toe tag in the morgue, not this year's fashion, at least according to GQ.

I brewed a pot of my darkest coffee and took it, along with three almond biscotti fingers, to my best chair on the balcony. The younger generation of Uptown strolled below me, their long-hair dog varieties on leashes and cats in fluffy baskets. They would never understand what happened to the old man resting above them and how the world nearly ended.

I had my shortwave radio on BBC America. I found a man's voice reporting how Moscow police found the bodies of two British men in a burned-out van parked in Sokolniki Park. Unable to identify them, they buried the men in a pauper's grave.

"That sucks." I grabbed the radio knob to change stations.

As Laura came through the door, she slammed it closed behind her. This was the wrong time of day for her to be home. I twisted the radio volume off and listened to her crash her keys against the table, bang her purse on the sofa, and instantly position herself in the balcony door behind me, fists on her hips.

She announced so the world would know, "I got fired. They blamed me for the entire Moscow fuck job. Our corporate gods gave away the gas, and what happens? They shoot me. Me?"

Each word was easy enough for me to hear, as well as those on the street below us.

"What Moscow fuck job?" I returned.

"That flu crap they're spewing over every television station. There's no flu epidemic over there. Those people got gassed with a product my team developed. The Air Force, those numbnuts, lost four cylinders of it. Beyer loaded their complete incompetence on me."

I nudged her back out of the doorway and into the living room. "You shouldn't be talking like that out here. Cats in fluffy baskets have ears."

Laura outpaced me to the bar. "Who gives a damn?" she said while lighting another long cigarette even though she had one already working in the ashtray.

Astounded at her implication, I asked, "Your team

developed Klearance? So Klearance is your project?"

"Number one. I'm it. I, personally, invented Klearance. Klearance is mine." She slowed as she realized the implication of what I asked. "How do you know about Klearance? That's top-secret."

"Klearance is yours?" I repeated, stepping behind the bar and to the bourbon rack.

"Mine. I invented it. Quite a project, I'd say. I wish I had some right now."

I think our rule about not talking about work just hit the shitter. "How'd you know Klearance got released in Moscow?"

"I get a report. This company provides me information about my products."

"A company?" My question trailed off under a wrinkled brow.

"Yes, USAssure. God damn Beyer—give me the Woodford."

I pulled a personal logo from my phone's screen. "Is this the company?"

"Yeah."

"Your dad and I publish USAssure. We provided your subscription service. Trying to stop Moscow was my project."

"Yours? I don't believe it. I truly, truly don't believe this crap." Her empty glass came down.

I said, "Those dead British men BBC is reporting worked for Je. They were chasing the lunatic in the Metro tunnel. Then he set it off."

"I don't fucking believe it. This is way too much." She huffed in more smoke-loaded air.

I snickered. "You have to admit it's ironic, my team chasing your product and neither of us knowing."

She loaded Woodford up to above the cut marks in her crystal. "Yeah. A real Laurel and Hardy. The Air Force said they wanted a humane chemical weapon."

I wrapped my arm around her waist, and she relaxed. We both moved onto the balcony. "Isn't inventing a humane chemical weapon a lot like organizing an orgy for virgins?"

She paused and contemplated. "That's right." Her glass tilted, and she poured her Woodford to the street below, then kissed me.

Chapter 67

Dallas, Texas
Rick

I slid the McLaren sideways into Toby's circle driveway and gunned it, taking me around back.

Joining me outside, Toby warned, "I'm not getting in your damn car again so don't offer. Come. I want to tell you that Rory kicked up a gold rabbit for me."

"Get in anyway. I didn't know you were rabbit hunting."

He growled as I raised the passenger side gullwing for him. "Rory found the man who's been gassing those political people."

I'm impressed.

"He's an Australian name of Taylor Walker. It's a way outback story—he's a stockman who lives at Victoria Branch Station." Toby sounded a disgruntled noise as he slipped into his seat. "You didn't ask me how."

I killed the roar of the 720-hp engine. "How?"

Reluctantly, Toby tightened his white knuckles around the car's grab bar, one hand at a time. "It was ingenious how he did it. He figured Gower would use the word Klearance in an email. The email would be deeply encrypted and go through our proxy server. So, he decrypted all our company emails from last year, searching for Klearance. Bingo. There it was. He finds three, all sent either to or from Taylor Walker. Not bad, huh?"

I raised my gullwing door and got in. "Well, should I feel stupid?"

"Don't be hurt," Toby teased. "Rory also knows the next target, where the murder will take place, and when. Now that's useful spy work." He finger-jabbed the air between us.

"Are you going to tell me who?"

"The Governor of New York state, Jock Durham. Walker plans to kill him during a visit on May 15th, except we'll arrange for Jock to stay with us in the capitol building overnight."

****

At the governor's uptown office, I rolled up my white sleeves. Durham told his office aide we would be working through the night. Toby dialed in a Sherlock Holmes novel on his tablet. Durham's desk clock pointed to eleven-twenty p.m.

I went over the hit in my mind. "Where is your wife," I asked the governor.

He replied, "I bought her a pair of impossible-to-get tickets to *Nefarious* on Broadway. So, she'll be staying with her friend, Gladys, on Forty-second Street."

Forty-second street would be safer than the Governor's Mansion up the Hudson.

I connected my laptop to the internet and linked it to the mansion's security cameras. Durham peered over my shoulder. The grounds were usual, with every leaf on the hedges in place and grass manicured. I gazed there then switched to the entry camera. His two security guards were face down on the steps.

In the foyer, another guard lay sprawled on the floor. Outside the governor's bedroom, his night watchman lay motionless.

Durham muttered, "Damn. I'm going to throw up. Those men were family."

"Governor," I said, "we need access to your bedroom door before you report this to anyone."

****

Our forensic team laser-scanned his door and walls for prints as well as collecting DNA. There was plenty, as expected. Along the bottom edge of the door, they checked it for flatness. The laser showed a small indention on the hall side of the bedroom door.

Toby asked, "What do you think that is?"

The tech wearing a white contamination suit, booties, and mask replied, "It's in the shape of an asthma inhaler like the perpetrator pushed the nozzle under the door."

Toby said, "It doesn't take much. The perp must have filled an inhaler with Klearance, then shot one or two puffs into the room. Any ideas on how Taylor Walker keeps from killing himself?"

"He's on the security video. He's wearing a respirator."

Chapter 68

Dallas, Texas
Rick

I was wearing a blue pin-striped shirt, a sports jacket, and no tie as I touched Laura's warm fingertips across from me at the high-top table. We were meeting Rory after work at El Biernat Burrito to celebrate closing the case. Against a backlight from the entryway, Laura's capelet sheath dress provided a distinct silhouette of her curved midriff for Rory to enjoy as well as the lads at the bar. They appreciated her effort and the view. I half expected some applause.

I told the lady waiter, "A French 75 for my wife. A Woodford Old Fashioned for me and a Seagram and Seven for our friend."

Out of habit, I scanned the place for normalcy. "Wow, what a rough few weeks."

Rory idly examined the menu leaning against the table's candlelight. Then, finally, he acknowledged, "But things are getting better. What's easy is everybody looks up to you."

Laura leaned in over the high top. "Can we stop talking shop tonight? Everything between you two is work. Work this, work that."

"To you." I raised my Old Fashioned.

Rory raised his glass to Laura. "To Laura. No work

tonight."

Laura finally lifted her French 75. "Okay. To fair words and straight talk among good friends." She tapped her glass with a fingernail. "Well, good. The wife finally gets the floor between two men—it's weird. So, there's something I want to know, something we've never talked about."

Rory joked over his Seven and Seven, "We can fix that."

She said, "I want to know if you two enjoy watching Brian and me doing our love dance over the telephone. Can we talk about that?"

We two beside her went silent. Air left the room.

With the conversation stuck in silence, I lowered my glass. Meanwhile, Rory coughed up a piece of beef hors d'oeuvre.

Laura innocently sat, sipping her French 75. "I, for one, like doing it. How about you, Rory? You watch more than Rick; what do you like to see me do?"

Rory tongued the bite of beef out of his mouth and onto his side plate. Then, sheepish, he waited for my lead. Finally, he said, "I'm not sure what to say…? This is awkward."

"It's not awkward," she countered, pressing a toothpick into a crab and mushroom ball. "I'm doing what I want, and you're doing what you want. There's nothing wrong with that."

Rory gave her plate his full attention. "Well…I've never sat across from the woman I've been watching doing…her thing…and take a pop quiz."

Laura said, "Think about it. I want to know."

Given the awkwardness, I opted to toss Rory under the bus, "I think you know I've never watched."

"But why?"

"Why? Because..." Now, the hot seat was on me. I should have kept my mouth shut. "I don't know why. Maybe I like the fantasy of you giving satisfaction to other men more than actually watching you do it."

"I get satisfaction. Don't you like seeing me satisfied?"

This was not a conversation I wanted to have in a restaurant. "If I ever did watch, it would be for that reason. I love you. But seeing Brian shooting his stuff all over you is not part of what excites me. That's what I'm not interested in."

Laura was playing pretty. She went back to Rory. "Now you?"

Rory stammered again. "Oh, jeez, I don't want to be part of this conversation, you know. But I guess if I must be, I'm like Rick. I think Brian can be disrespectful when he forces you to let him shoot in your face. I wouldn't say I like that. But I love seeing you get all tensed up and making those little sounds in the end when it's over."

"That's a good answer." Laura rested her hand on Rory's forearm. "I'll think about you sometimes."

Rory asked, "I can't tell because the camera never gets close enough, but now that it's out in the open, Brian has something on the back of his heel. What is that? A birthmark?"

"On his right heel?"

"Yeah."

"It's a tattoo he got in Alexandria, a scarab. It's cute. I'll get him to show you a close-up."

Rory enlarged his eyes. "That'd be cool."

My mind flipped to Esmee's description of her assailant. My heartbeat raced. "Tell me again. Brian has a scarab tattooed on the back of his heel?"

"He does, and it's cool."

The truth was in her eyes. "Was Brian in Europe at the same time as the Moscow explosion?"

She answered, "He was over there a lot. Yeah, I think he was in France, I think." She wiped her palms.

I slammed the rest of the Old Fashioned down and told them both, "Your Brian is my Kelly Lake, the man who killed all those Muscovites with your gas. How long have you known he's Kelly Lake? Where is he?" It skimmed my mind; *why didn't I go ahead and watch you on the phone as you wanted?*

"I had no idea." A blank expression froze on her face. "He's at his Cole Avenue apartment."

The messenger buzzed on her phone on the table. She glanced at it, then angled the phone so I could see it. The message read:

--You shouldn't have told him.--

She hissed breathlessly, "He's been listening to us. He knows you're coming."

Chapter 69

Dallas, Texas
Rick

On McKinney Avenue, I cut the yellow McLaren northward, its engine pressed too hard and loud. People on the sidewalks became a blur in an instant. I turned at the cemetery. Then, at Oliver Street. I snapped the banana left. Then again at Cole. Immediately I recognized a black pickup pulling from a private parking lot. I caught up with him on the one-way street. Lake stuck his arm out the driver's window and gave me the finger.

I allowed the British engine to wind up to six thousand RPMs. The black truck and yellow McLaren, nuts-to-butts, rapidly approached Fitzhugh. Lake went west toward Oak Lawn. We accelerated like twins to where the bridge crossed Turtle Creek.

Ahead, night crews worked on repouring part of the concrete surface. For two blocks we shot past a stream of orange cones, workers in chartreuse vests, and night flood lamps. Suddenly, Lake jerked his black truck left into the wet concrete, blowing safety cones and men scattering. His pickup dropped in, climbing out the opposite side. He rooster-tailed a plume of gray mush high toward me.

I hit the brakes to keep the flying wet concrete off

my McLaren. Lake's truck climbed from the soup on the other side, and his taillights disappeared south.

I yelled, "Son of a bitch! I'm not putting the McLaren in that crap. Damn it to hell." I rolled to a stop and took a deep breath. I closed my eyes. *He's on his way to a place he can't get caught. What the hell is wrong with me?*

I pulled the McLaren off into an apartment parking lot, where I shut down the engine. *Laura was part of this.*

My cell buzzed. Then its blue screen lit with a message:

—*Tell your lovely bride goodbye for me. Beddy-bye was fun. Kelly.*—

Chapter 70

Dallas, Texas
Rick

She may still be at El Biernat Burrito. I called Laura. "Are you still at El Biernat?"

"Rory brought me to Skywalkers. Is Brian dead?"

"He got away. I decided to not trash the McLaren. I'll be there in a minute."

I angled out of the parking lot, revving through the gears, Skywalker is my next port of call. I avoided the valet podium and found a parking spot by the door marked VALET ONLY.

Laura was downing a French 75. I slid next to her and ordered a Cable Car. The chase was over.

I said to the waiter, "I can't take any more of these things. Gimme an Old Fashioned."

Laura held her hand up, telling the waiter. "I'm fine."

I laid Laura's phone on the table and removed its batteries, jabbing a steak knife through the front glass and pinning it to the table. Its screen was black, a spark or two coming out the bottom. "Did you know Mark Gower wanted your dad and me dead? He hired Kelly Lake to do it. I suppose Lake wanted you to lure me in through your sexcapades.."

Laura swirled her 75. "How do you know this

stuff?"

"It's what I do. How long have you known Brian was Kelly Lake?"

"Honest, only since you told me at El Biernat. Not a minute sooner. I swear."

"Then how did he know so much about Klearance if you didn't tell him?"

She lifted her impaled phone and pulled the knife out. "I never said I didn't tell Brian. I just didn't know who he was. We talked about it in bed. He sounded innocent. I didn't realize anything."

"But you did tell him? Did it ever occur to you he was the person who pushed your friend out the tenth-floor window after she caught him searching through your files?"

Laura had nothing to say.

I finished my Old Fashioned. "You could be in deep shit. Let's go home."

Chapter 71

Dallas, Texas
Rick

In the morning, I awoke in better spirits. Laura had not slept on her side of the bed. I got up and walked into the breakfast room, where I found Emilie had not made me my breakfast.

On my empty plate lay a powder-blue envelope with my name on it. I pulled the letter from inside:

My always loving Ricky,

You, of course, have figured out I'm not coming home. Of all the people on Earth, I could never have found a better person for me than you have been. When I was sick, you healed me. When I cried, you were my shoulder. You were my strength and armor. I have come to understand you are the part of me I couldn't be for myself in so many ways. There are so many souls in this world; how did yours come to know mine? I love you so completely and, as I type this, I'm crying. The possibility of a life without you is more than my heart can bear.

I hope someday you find Brian.

The moment Rory brought up the 'scarab', I was certain that Brian was your man. I've seen your look so many times, and knowing I will never see it again breaks me.

When you told me Brian had been in town the night

Elena chased her chair through the window, I nearly broke down because I realized Elena died trying to protect me.

I'm sure you've also discovered I supplied Brahms 4 with small quantities of diluted Klearance. Himbury said he represented a veterinary research facility. His story sounded legit, and he had the correct paperwork.

I'm sure the evidence will imply otherwise, but I want you to know Lake somehow had the basics of Klearance before I met him, probably from the files. He pumped me for details. Using hindsight, he was never interested in me as a lover at all. He sought access to Klearance, and he struck it rich with me. I failed the most straightforward test—the excitement of a new relationship with a man who swooned over me made me talk more than I should. I didn't follow better wisdom.

You would never have fallen for that.

I guess I look like a sucker because that's what I ended up being, a giant sucker. Lake took me; Brahms took me. I feel devastated for the victims and their families. I would give anything to undo what I've done.

I'm sorry I didn't get a chance to square things with my dad. I know you wanted me to. Believe me, I wanted to. But I couldn't help but be afraid he would know what an evil person I have become if I met him face to face. You know how he can read everyone. I don't know what I would have done had he figured it out. I don't know what he would have done.

My guess is after you read this, you will go out somewhere on McKinney Avenue and have some of your Old Fashioneds. And when you've finished, you'll come home and start to build your new life. You're so Ricky.

I'm leaving the country now. Let's let my estrangement be my punishment. I'm starting a new life in a country that doesn't have extradition treaties with the US, so I should be safe and secure there. With your computers and all, I know you can find me if you want to, but please don't. I feel sick enough for what I've done without having to die in a jail cell.

Here is one last cherry for you—thanks for so soundly dealing with the man who raped me.

Look in St. Mary's, Nova Scotia. There is a glacial lake there named Kelly Lake. There's an island in the middle with a boathouse and one home. Both are owned by a man named Brian Huff.

You knew I could never be your virgin bride when you met me because of my lifestyle. But I want you to know you were the man who took my heart's virginity. You were my first and only real love. Even with all I did with Brian, I still consider myself a one-man woman. My commitment to you happened when you claimed my heart, and I want you to know it has never left.

I remain yours until the end.

Your loving wife forever,

Laura

"Hmm." I held the powder blue page up to the sunrise, examined it, and reread it. Then, I helped myself to a jigger glass with fresh Woodford from the liquor shelf. I took in its aroma, placed it by the paper, and lit our gas cooktop. As I raked the lower half of the page over the flame, a clear ink became brown, and the words appeared. *There was an inoculant I added to your bourbon. You are immune and have always been safe.* It would have been unlike her to have developed such a heinous product without a prevention.

I let the rest of the paper combust and timed my Woodford, so they both ended together. Then I collected all the ashes, took them to the faucet, crushed them in my palms, and let the water wash them through the fully revved garbage disposal. Away they went along with her knowledge. And as they disappeared, I held the jigger glass between my thumb and forefinger, letting it drop into the whirring blades.

The glass exploded into a million shards.

A word about the author...

Lee Wilkins is an award-winning debut novelist. His manuscript, Lisbon, is a bridgework linking Casablanca to Hemingway's, To Have and Have Not won the Best Mystery award from the Greater Dallas Writers Association. Lee also authors short stories and is published in The Raven Chronicles, a literary magazine in the pacific northwest. Since retiring, the adventures of his protagonist, Rick Haade, and his boat, The Carolina Rose, fill his days.

If you liked Moscow Down, please go to your book seller's website and leave a review. That would help me a lot.

Thank you for purchasing
this publication of The Wild Rose Press, Inc.

For questions or more information
contact us at
info@thewildrosepress.com.

The Wild Rose Press, Inc.
www.thewildrosepress.com

CPSIA information can be obtained
at www.ICGtesting.com
Printed in the USA
BVHW060158151222
654221BV00020B/948